Bateman was a journalist in Irelaer.
His first novel, DIVORCING J. nd
all his novels have been criticall ys
for the feature films DIVORCIN RY
and the popular BBC TV series MURPHY'S LAW starring James
Nesbitt. Bateman lives in Ireland with his family.

Praise for Bateman's novels:

'Sometimes brutal, often blackly humorous and always terrific'
Observer

'If Roddy Doyle was as good as people say, he would probably write
novels like this' *Arena*

'Bateman has a truly unique voice . . . He is a dark and brilliant champion of words' James Nesbitt

'Fast and furious . . . Laugh-a-minute lad lit' *Daily Mirror*

'He shows a high talent for farce and a way with comic detail'
Guardian

'Jaw-achingly funny dialogue . . . there is no other literary escapism so
flawlessly-dubious, hysteria-inducing or downright chaotic' *Irish Post*

'Bateman has barged fearlessly into the previously unsuspected middle
ground between Carl Hiaasen and Irvine Welsh and claimed it for his
own' *GQ*

'Extremely funny, brilliantly dark, addictively readable' *Loaded*

'Terrific, mordant wit and a fine sense of the ridiculous . . . the writing
is great' *Evening Standard*

'A joy from start to finish . . . witty, fast-paced and throbbing with
menace' *Time Out*

'Bateman's snappy one-liners keep you turning the pages'
Belfast Telegraph

CHAPTER &VERSE

BATEMAN

headline

First published in 2003 by
HEADLINE PUBLISHING GROUP

First published in paperback in 2003 by
HEADLINE PUBLISHING GROUP

First published in this paperback edition in 2008 by
HEADLINE PUBLISHING GROUP

2

Cataloguing in Publication Data is available from the British Library

ISBN 978 0 7553 4363 8

Typeset in Times by Palimpsest Book Production Limited
Grangemouth, Stirlingshire

Printed and bound in the UK by
CPI Mackays, Chatham ME5 8TD

Headline's policy is to use papers that are natural, renewable and recyclable products and
made from wood grown in sustainable forests. The logging and manufacturing processes
are expected to conform to the environmental regulations of the country of origin.

HEADLINE PUBLISHING GROUP
An Hachette Livre UK Company
338 Euston Road
London NW1 3BH

www.headline.co.uk
www.hachettelivre.co.uk

For Andrea and Matthew

1

Julie's voice is nicotine.

'She doesn't see me comin'. I have her by the hair, pull the head straight back, then slit her throat.'

The woman who put the *dead* in *dead*pan.

'I use a knife – the knife she bought me on our first anniversary. She doesn't even make a noise, the blood just burbles out.'

'Burbles?'

Ivan glances up from his fingernails. Michelle, right at the back.

'Burbles, yeah – okay?' says Julie, her voice caught between embarrassment and threat.

'Let her finish, Michelle,' Ivan says. 'It's not easy.'

Julie nods curtly at him, then returns her attention to the page. Her fingers follow the words. 'The blood just *burbles* out . . .' She tosses a defiant look back at Michelle. Michelle tosses it back. '. . . And then she collapses in my arms. She's dead. I kiss her once—'

There's a chorus of *ooooooohs!* from the rest of the class. Julie waits for them to settle again before continuing. 'I kiss her once on the lips, then I bury her in her own garden, just where we used to sit in the summer.' She nods to herself for a moment, then adds a quiet, 'The end.'

They applaud politely. They enjoyed it, but they're nervous about being asked next.

'Ah, yes, very, um, descriptive, Julie.' Ivan gets off his desk and taps his chalk on the blackboard. 'Of course, the title of our essay assignment was actually *What I Will Do On My First Day Home From Prison*. I, ah, wouldn't show that to the Parole Board.'

They laugh. He likes to make them laugh. Julie gives him a limp-wristed bog-off wave. 'Oh Mr Connor,' she says, 'what would you know about writing fiction?'

Ivan smiles. 'Okay, who's next?' Eyes are averted. 'Come on, we're all friends here. Eileen?' A shake of the head. 'Betty?' Not even a shake, just a stare at the floor. A small, elfin-featured girl slowly raises her hand. 'Donna? Right, off you go.'

Donna licks her lips, pushes hair from her brow. 'The—'

'Stand up so we can see you, Donna.'

She gets up. Her voice is soft. 'The light of the ark surrounds me, the dark of the night astounds me . . .'

'Is that a poem, Donna?' Ivan asks.

'Yes, Mr Connor.'

'It *was* an essay I specifically . . .' He trails off. He glances at his watch and sighs. 'Okay, let's hear it.'

'Will I start again?'

'Come on, girl!' Michelle shouts. 'Spit it out!'

'All right, Michelle. Yes, Donna, from the top.'

She nods slightly. 'The—'

'Shit!'

Donna looks up sharply to see Mr Connor with his foot on a chair, and the broken end of a shoe lace held up as evidence of a legitimate excuse. 'Sorry, Donna. Please . . .'

Donna swallows, takes a deep breath. 'The—'

At that moment the bell rings and class is over. They're up out of their chairs just as if they were back at school, then they remember they're volunteers for this class, and they aren't going anywhere. They slow down. Ivan scoops up his own books and joins the exodus. He doesn't notice Donna, still standing with her poem in her hand.

Ivan is forty years old, he wears an old raincoat, his hair is long and straggled. He has been teaching this class in the women's prison twice a week for the past eight weeks. It pays reasonably well, enough to tide him over until the new contract is sorted out. He looks at his watch. He's caught in heavy traffic, not moving. Ben Elton would get a novel and a million quid out of it. Ivan's Metro is decrepit. He's listening to Dvorak on a tape. His most recent novel, *Chapter & Verse*, sits open on the passenger seat. The passages he will shortly read at Waterstones are highlighted in yellow. Beside the book there's a half-eaten packet of Starburst, although he will call them Opal Fruits until he goes to his grave.

He lifts the book and reads aloud, his voice strong, confident: 'But it was not only by playing backgammon with the Baronet, that the little governess rendered herself agreeable to her employer. She found many different

3

ways of being useful to him. She read over, with inde-fatigable patience, all those law papers . . .'

He stops because he's aware of being watched. He looks out and then up at the cab of a lorry, facing in the other direction, and the bearded driver laughing at him. Ivan closes his book, sets it back on the passenger seat, then grips his steering wheel with both hands. A moment later music booms out from the truck. Someone with at least a fingernail on the pulse of popular music would recognise it as rap, but to Ivan it is noise. And noise annoys.

Ivan scratches suddenly at his head. He thinks he may have picked up nits in the prison.

Ivan hurries across the busy road, freezing rain slicing into his face. Halfway across he steps out of the shoe with the broken lace, and before he can go back for it a car drags it along the road for a hundred yards and he has to hop after it. Look at the great author! Stepping off his lofty pedestal to pursue an Oxford brogue along the tarmac! He picks it up and hugs it against his chest.

Campbell is watching him from the Waterstones door-way. His agent gets 10 per cent of everything he earns. Ivan's coat is ancient, but at least he has one. Campbell is damp and cold. Ivan hurries up, full of apologies.

He isn't nervous until he sets a damp foot in the bookshop, but the moment he crosses the threshold, the weight of literature and competition is suddenly upon him. Thousands and thousands and thousands of books. Half of them appear to be about a young boy called Harry Potter. Ivan admires anyone who can make that much money, yet hates Her with a vengeance. He wonders if She will ever write *Harry Potter and the Provisional IRA*, or *Harry Potter and the Palestinian Question*. He loves corrupting popular titles and idles away many hours of his writing life at this very pursuit. His favourites are *Love in the Time of a Really Bad Flu*, *The Day of the Jack Russell* and *A Quarter to Three in the Garden of Good and Evil*.

As he moves through the shop Ivan becomes aware that the aisles are actually very crowded. This is a good sign. Campbell pushes ahead of him, then comes to a halt at the edge of a seated area; a hundred seats and they are *all filled*. Butterflies flap in his stomach. This is better than he could ever have hoped. At previous readings he has been lucky to scrape up a dozen hardy souls. He glows. Word of mouth. He has never quite been popular enough to be considered a cult, but perhaps this is the beginning of something. He is ready to be acclaimed. He observes the microphone, the small lectern, the table with the bottle of Evian water, the glass, the chair, the pen for signing books afterwards.

The manager of the shop steps up to the microphone and taps it once. 'Ladies and gentlemen, sorry to keep you waiting, but our author has at last emerged from the nightmare that is our traffic.' They laugh. 'Our guest tonight is quite simply a writer who needs no introduction. Universally acclaimed, a master of the English language . . .' Ivan swallows nervously, takes a first step forward . . . 'put your hands together for Francesca Brady!'

Ivan freezes. Applause erupts around him. Posters curl down suddenly from the ceiling. A mile-wide smile, expansive hair, red-red lipstick, the cover of a book, but the spitting image of the author now emerging from the audience not six feet away from him. His heart is racing. His first impulse is to dive on her, force her to the ground, and then batter her to death with a copy of *Insanity Fair*, her latest 'novel'. Ivan always makes that little quotation-marks sign with his fingers when anyone mentions *Insanity Fair*, or even Francesca Brady. She writes fat romantic books for fat romantic people. She dresses them up with smart one-liners so that she can appear hip, but she's really – *ugh!* – Mills and Boon for the e-generation, and every time he thinks of her he suffers a vowel problem. Francesca Brady takes the stage with a modest wave, pretends to look surprised at the posters.

Ivan jumps as he's tapped on the shoulder. There's a boy of about twelve, wearing acne and a Waterstones identity badge around his neck like a US Marine with a dogtag – and why not? Bookselling is war, and the enemy never stops coming.

'Mr Connor? We've been looking everywhere for you. You're in the basement. Follow me.'

BEN, it says on the dogtag. BEN turns and leads Ivan back through the crowds of people still arriving to hear Francesca Brady. She's milking the applause – 'Thank you, thank you, I keep looking behind me thinking a real author must be standing there' – and they're all bloody laughing as Ivan, Campbell and BEN hurry down the stairs into the basement.

BEN charges ahead. Ivan glances back at Campbell, who shrugs helplessly. Signs for *Astrology*, *Military History*, *School Texts*, *Gay & Lesbian*, *Erotica* flash past like inter-city

Stations of the Cross. Finally they emerge into a small circular area in which there are set about thirty chairs. Ivan quickly calculates that 77 per cent of the chairs are filled. Something salvaged, at least. There is already a small, balding, middle-aged man standing at the microphone, the literary equivalent of a warm-up guy, a no-hoper, a glorified typist who's stumbled into a book deal because he's slept with someone famous or been held hostage in an obscure country for several years. No problem.

There is a lectern. A table with a bottle of Evian water. A chair. A pen. The man is saying: 'For me, philately is not so much a passion as a way of—'

Ivan becomes aware of BEN waving urgently at him from three aisles across, under a sign that says *True Crime*. Campbell gives him a gentle push and Ivan skirts the outer ring of chairs; BEN turns and hurries away. Ivan passes through *Science Fiction*, *Science Fantasy*, *Terry Pratchett* and then finally arrives at a tiny rectangular area set out with a dozen chairs. Seven of them are filled. There is a lectern. A microphone. A table, chair, bottle of Evian water and a pen for signing copies of his books, which sit in several tremulously high columns on another table.

BEN taps the microphone. He squints at the folded piece of paper he has removed from the back pocket of his black jeans. He glances up at the giant air-conditioning system which whirrs and blows above him, then speaks into the microphone.

'Ladies and gentlemen, sorry to keep you waiting, but our author has at last emerged from the nightmare that is our traffic.' He pauses for laughter, but it is not forthcoming. 'Our guest tonight is quite simply a writer who

7

needs no introduction. Universally acclaimed, a master of the English language, put your hands together for Ian Connor!'

Campbell hisses, 'Ivan!'

'Ivan Connor!' BEN shoots back quickly, but he has already stepped away from the microphone. His voice is not drowned out by the applause, which is on the dead side of restrained, but by the air conditioning, which booms and coughs like an approaching storm.

Ivan steps forward. He sets the hardback edition of *Chapter & Verse* down on the table and pours himself a glass of Evian. His heart is racing again. There is no reason for him to be nervous, but he is. He always is. He lifts the glass and sets it down somewhat precariously on the narrow base of the lectern.

'Th-thank you all very much for coming,' Ivan says into the microphone. 'I, ah, am gonna . . . *going to* . . . read from my new novel.' He holds it up for them to admire, but the book slips out of the dust jacket and crashes down onto the glass of water, which immediately cracks. Ivan makes a desperate attempt to retrieve the situation, although it looks to the audience as if he is indulging in some kind of bizarre performance art, juggling broken glass, damp novel and handfuls of water. Meanwhile, the dust jacket floats gently away on the breeze from the air conditioner.

Ivan smiles foolishly while BEN removes the broken glass and soaks up what he can of the water with a Kleenex. Ivan tries to peel apart the damp pages of *Chapter & Verse* in order to find the section he intends to read. Campbell hides himself in *Graphic Novels*.

When they are ready to start again, Ivan decides to ignore the water incident. 'The, um, new novel . . . which is set in England in the eighteenth century, an era which I'm sure you're all . . .' He blinks at them. 'Anyway, this is from Chapter Three.' He clears his throat. 'He took Rebecca to task once or twice about the propriety of playing backgammon—'

'Speak up!'

He glances up at a gnarled, elderly man sitting at the back.

'Y-yes, of course: He took Rebecca to task once or twice—'

'Louder!'

'HE TOOK REBECCA TO TASK ONCE OR—'

'Philately!'

Another man, in the second row, is on his feet, waving a finger at him.

'I'm sorry?'

'Stamps, man! We're here for the stamps!'

BEN bounds up to the microphone. 'B2,' he says. 'The stamps lecture is in B2. Third down on the right.'

As the man shuffles along the row of seats Ivan is aghast to see five other members of his audience, including the deaf man, get to their feet and shuffle after him, leaving only an old lady in the front row.

Campbell retreats into *Occult*.

Ivan waits until some strength returns to his legs, then smiles weakly down at the old lady. 'Mother,' he says, 'I can read to you when I get home.'

'You can read to me now, Ivan. I didn't come all this way not to be read to.'

He shakes his head. He laughs. He does love her. 'Well,' he says, reaching up to move the microphone, 'at least I won't be needing this.'

Except the spilled water has soaked into the wires, and the moment he touches it there's a crack and flash and the author of *Chapter & Verse* is hurled into the air.

He is not seriously injured. His eyebrows are singed and his hair stands on end. The paramedics nevertheless insist on taking him to the hospital for a check-up. They also insist that he leaves on a stretcher. Regulations. His mother holds his hand and tells him he's going to be okay. The paramedics heave and blow as they carry him back through *Science Fiction*, *Science Fantasy*, *Terry Pratchett*, then *Astrology*, *Military History*, *School Texts*, *Gay & Lesbian*, and *Erotica*. When they reach the ground floor their exit is blocked by a crowd surrounding Francesca Brady, who has called a halt to her signing session, suffering from cramp, and has been pursued to the front door by adoring fans. She notices Ivan on his stretcher and immediately goes over to him. She places a hand on his chest and purrs, 'I'm so glad you could come.' An assistant hands her a copy of *Insanity Fair*. 'Please have this as a gift and I hope you'll be feeling better soon,' she says, handing it to Ivan, but making sure the cover is turned towards the camera which takes their picture.

As she strides out of the door, Francesca Brady scratches suddenly at her head.

The hospital wants nothing to do with him. Campbell takes him to a pub and they get very drunk and rail against the state of the world, and publishing. Then he's in a taxi, and he can't remember where Campbell went – but here he is, home again, except the key won't fit in the door. He hammers on the wood, he presses the bell. A window slides up high above him and two kids look out.

'Daddy? What are you doing here?' Michael calls down.

'I sleep, perchance to . . . Michael, open the door, there's a good chap.'

Michael is pulled away by his mother. She glares down at Ivan.

'Avril, darlin' . . .'

'Go away. You're drunk.'

'And you are ugly, but in the morning I will be sober.' He cackles. Avril slams the window down while Ivan struts around in front of the house. 'We will fight them on the beaches . . . nevuh evuh, in the field of human conflict . . . AVRIL, FOR CHRIST'S SAKE OPEN THE DOOR.'

There is no movement on the door front. Ivan is dizzy and giddy and has recently been electrocuted. He bangs on the door again. He staggers back. He sees shadows moving behind curtains. He yells through the letter box.

'I am forty years old! I have created two widely respected children and eight beautiful novels! My publisher does not care about me! I am represented by an estate agent! Nobody cares! AND I THINK I HAVE NITS IN MY HAIR!'

The door opens suddenly and a man he does not recognise punches his lights out.

He is in the kitchen he once decorated, or at least paid

a man to decorate. He sits at the table while Avril, in nightie and dressing gown, sponges the blood from his face. She is saying, 'If you apologise again, *I'll* punch you on the nose.'

'Sorry,' he says. 'He didn't have to hit me.'

'Yes, he did.'

'What sort of a name is Alfred anyway? Is he great?'

On cue, Alfred calls from outside. Avril shouts back, 'No, go to bed, I'll be fine!' but he won't do so. He'll linger in the hall, trying to hear.

Ivan's nose isn't throbbing quite as much now, but there's a small gash just above his hairline where he hit his head on the pavement. Avril leans forward to examine it. Ivan puts a hand on her breast.

'Don't,' she says, and slaps it away.

He puts his hand back on her breast.

'Stop it,' she says. She slaps it away again. 'Oh Ivan, when are you ever going to grow up?'

'We must have made love, what, a thousand times? And now you won't let me touch your tit.'

'Don't call it that. And we're divorced.'

He looks wistfully at her. 'Oh Avril, where did we go wrong?'

'*We?* I don't think so.'

'Avril, darling, I'm a writer.'

'Stop it. I don't want to hear this shit.'

'Is everything okay in there?' Alfred calls from the hall.

'Yes! Go to bed!'

'A writer has to grow, experience, live . . . inhabit the spirit, create the legend . . .'

'It's crap, Ivan. You spend half your life sitting in a little room making up little stories nobody reads, and then you spend the other half of your life fucking around making everyone else miserable and you have a perfect excuse because it's all in the name of LIT-ER-AT-URE! Well, it's all *crap*, Ivan! Then you come round here to moan at us because your publisher's no good and you expect us to be interested? Well, why don't you write something that somebody wants to read, instead of trying to bore everyone to death!'

He blinks at her for several moments, then gives a childish shrug. 'I only wanted to feel your booby.'

She rolls her eyes and opens her dressing gown. He puts his hand on her breast.

'This Alfred, do you love him?'

'He's good and he's straight and he loves me. And yes, I'm starting to love him.'

'That's good.'

'I do like your books.'

'I know.'

She smiles down at him, then frowns and leans forward to examine his hair. She pulls her dressing gown across, then hurries to the door and opens it. *'Alfred! The nit comb!'*

When the prison officer leads the girls into the classroom, they find Ivan Connor stamping his feet on a newspaper. He has seen his own photograph, smiling dumbly from a stretcher in Waterstones. *Francesca Brady Meets Disabled Fan* gushes the caption.

The world is not a just place.

13

The reading of the previous week's assignments continues. Mairaid, Ann-Marie, Bethany, some of the Albanian names he cannot pronounce. He stares out of the window and fumes. Francesca Brady. That it should come to this. He seethes.

'The light of the ark surrounds me, the dark of the night astounds me—'

He's up out of his chair. 'Christ almighty, Donna! What's your problem? I said *essay*! Why's it always poetry?'

'I like poetry.'

'Like? It's not about *like*! Poetry is an art, it's a technical wonder. What the hell could *you* possibly know about poetry?'

'I just, you know, like—'

'And I like opera, but I don't delude myself I'm Pava-*bloody*-rotti! Do you even know the first thing about poetry? Do you even *know* what a sonnet is? Well – do you? Or iambic pentameter – can you tell me about that? Come on! Anyone?' They're looking at the floor, at the ceiling, at their books.

He moves swiftly up the aisle and makes a grab for Donna's exercise book. She tries to hold on to it, but he pulls it free. 'Don't be shy now, Donna! Let me read it for you!'

She's on the verge of tears as he begins to read it, but not like a poem; he gives it the rhythm of the rap he has heard spewing out of the radio. 'The light of the ark *surrounds me*, the dark of the night *astounds me*, You make me smile like Jesus *and fight like* . . .' He closes the book, shakes his head, then slaps it back down on her desk. 'This isn't poetry, Donna. These are *lyrics*.'

Donna lowers her eyes. There are tears rolling down her cheeks.

Nicotine Julie raises her hand. 'Mr Connor?'

'Julie?'

'Can I ask a question, Mr Connor?'

'Yes, Julie.'

'When exactly did you turn into an arsehole? 'Cause we got enough arseholes in here without having to bring one in from outside.'

He looks at her, and he looks at the class, and it seems to be the consensus of opinion that he is, indeed, an arsehole.

Later he wonders if he could sell a book about lesbians in prison.

2

Ivan wakes on a small settee opposite his computer at a little after seven-thirty. The screen is still on. He's dressed, unshaven, scruffy, there's ash on his chest and a half bottle of whisky, empty, is on its side on the floor. He gets up, opens the curtains, yelps, blinded by the sun, then closes them again. He sits down at the computer screen and begins to examine what he has written. Then he uses the mouse to highlight his words, and presses *Delete*. They disappear.

A doorbell sounds in the distance. He waits for a moment, looks admiringly up at the landscape on the front of the 1985 Constable calendar, which hides the old, but much-loved *Sports Illustrated Swimwear Calendar* behind it, then he moves forward again and begins to type.

Downstairs, his mother opens the front door to find two children standing there expectantly. One is Michael, seven, wearing a blue windcheater over his school uniform, with the hood pulled down tight around his face, and the other is Anna, eleven, in a different school uniform.

Mother looks sternly at them. 'Yes?'

Anna shakes her head, then pushes past. 'Oh Granny, grow up,' she says.

Michael smiles up. 'Anna has nits in her hair.'

'I *do not*!' Anna calls back.

Michael follows Anna into the house while his granny curls her nose up in fake disgust.

Ivan appears at the top of the stairs, and the kids bound up to him and give him a hug. Mother stands at the door meanwhile, looking down the path to the gate where Avril is standing looking back at her. They don't speak. They haven't, for some time.

Ivan disengages from the kids, directs them back down to the living room, then shrugs as he passes his mother in the doorway. He walks down the path to Avril. He sticks his hands in his pockets. He stands on one side of the gate, Avril on the other, and shrugs.

'You look like shit,' Avril says. 'You've got bags under your eyes bigger than my arse.'

'Thanks,' he replies. They stand in awkward silence for several moments.

'Kind of symbolic, this gate,' he says.

'That was some performance last week,' she responds, ignoring him.

'Sorry,' he says.

'How's your head?'

'All better.'

'I need you to take Michael to school and then I need you to pick him up.'

'I can't. I'm going to see my publisher.'

'What time are you seeing your publisher?'

'Twelve.'

'He gets out at two-thirty. You can do it. You can do this one thing for me.'

'What's wrong with you? That's why you got custody, Avril, to do things like this.'

'Don't get me started, Ivan.'

'What's wrong with Alfred? Why can't *he* pick him up?'

'I said don't get me started. Are you going to pick him up or not?'

He nods.

'Good. Anna can look after herself, I just need you to look after Michael – okay? I'll pick him up at four.'

'Where are you going that's so important?'

'Never you mind. I don't ask very often, so don't make a big thing of it.'

She leaves, and takes Anna with her. Michael sits in the lounge watching cartoons while Ivan shaves and showers.

Mother says to Michael, 'You're in the house, you can take your hood down.'

Michael ignores her.

'It's like déjà vu,' Mother says.

On the drive to school Michael sits belted into the back seat, two small brown eyes blinking out of a voluminous hood. 'Dad,' he asks, 'what do you do for a living?'

'You know what I do for a living.'

'Mum says you don't have a job.'

'Of course I have a job.'

19

'She says you sit on your lazy arse all day and type. Mum says you're a glorified secretary.'

He snaps, 'Mum doesn't know what the fuck she's talking about!'

It doesn't phase his son at all. 'I'll tell her you said that,' he says.

'How old are you, Michael?'

'Seven. Why?'

'Just checking.' He sighs. 'Of course I have a job. I tell stories.'

'Alfred says you go to hell if you tell stories.'

'Yes, well, Alfred can go—'

Michael giggles suddenly.

'What?'

'Nothing,' Michael says.

'What?'

'Promise you won't tell?'

'Of course.'

'Anna says Mummy takes her clothes off in front of Alfred.'

Ivan sighs.

'What are handcuffs, Daddy?'

Ivan almost pulls the car off the road. 'They're . . . Never you mind!'

He sighs with relief as he sees the school in the distance.

Campbell sits in the passenger seat as Ivan drives them into the city. The photograph in the *Evening Standard* is open on Campbell's lap. 'I didn't think they were going to use it,' he says. 'It's over a week now.'

'I know how long it is, Campbell.'

'A week is a long time in politics,' Campbell says. Then pauses as he searches vainly for a suitable literary analogy. When nothing comes, he fills the space with a simple nod.

If Campbell says there is no such thing as bad publicity, Ivan swears to himself that he will press the ejector seat button. His agent will shoot out of the car at a hundred miles per hour, and then be flattened by a bus. Ivan is aware that this is the Mini Metro model which does not come with an ejector seat. He will therefore press an imaginary ejector seat button and fantasise. Or he will swipe the paper from Campbell's grasp and throw it out of the window. With his luck, he will then be arrested for littering.

He glances again at the photograph. It is amazing how it manages to render his features both ghostly and saggy, but shows up every beautifully defined line of Francesca Brady's sensational face. He would like to whack that face with the collected works of Louis de Bernières.

'Best-selling author Francesca Brady,' Campbell reads from the caption, 'presents a copy of her new novel, *Insanity Fair*, to disabled fan Ian Connor.'

'*Ian?*'

Campbell nods. 'They do say there's no such thing as—'

Ivan presses the button. He emits a low growl.

Campbell sucks on his lip, then continues reading. 'Miss Brady has recently signed a five million pounds contract with Random House for her next novel, the largest sum ever signed by a literary author with a British publishing house.'

'*Literary*? Fuck. Now we really are in trouble.' Ivan sighs. It is getting dark already, and it's just after lunchtime. He has spent the morning toying with a single paragraph and cultivating a sore head.

There is a green opposite his mother's house, and a small pond beyond it. It affords him a beautiful, relaxing, inspiring view from his study, with added ducks. But all morning there was a large furniture removal van parked on the other side of the street, which blocked his view of much of the green, most of the pond and all of the ducks. He was unable to write fluently due to this absence of view. It was frustrating for him, and he shouted at his mother for no good reason. He doesn't like doing that. His mother, as per usual, brought him up a brunch of boiled eggs, but he suspects that she deliberately boiled them hard to pay him back for shouting. She also failed to cut his toast into soldiers.

When they are stuck in traffic at Ealing Broadway, he sees Francesca Brady. She is all over the side of a bus.

When they are stuck in traffic at Hammersmith, he sees Francesca Brady plastered across a huge billboard. She is huge and beautiful and might as well be selling bras as books.

'Christ,' Ivan says. 'You're my agent. You've been my agent for eleven years.' He nods at the poster. 'Why am I not up there?'

'Who wants to be up there?'

'I do. Campbell, I write better books. I get better reviews. Why am I not up there?'

'You don't really want to be up there, Ivan.'

'Yes, I do.' Ivan reaches inside his jacket and removes a

somewhat battered, hard-bound spiralspined notebook.

'Please, Ivan,' says Campbell, 'concentrate on the driving.'

They are hopelessly stuck in traffic. Ivan points this out. Campbell sighs helplessly.

Ivan opens the notebook. Yellowing snippets from newspapers are Sellotaped on to page after page. 'Emotionally devastating,' Ivan reads, *'New York Times.'* He nods to himself, then flicks to the next page. 'A dynamic new voice. *Partisan Review.* Ivan Connor isn't the voice of a generation, he's the heart. *Boston Globe.'*

'This is really sad, Ivan.'

'I'm the heart of a generation! I have *respect*!' He thumbs up at the massive poster of Francesca Brady. 'What does she have?'

They look at each other, then spontaneously address the question together. 'About five million pounds.'

They smile ruefully, and the lights turn green.

'Don't worry about it, Ivan, everything's going to work out okay. *The Last December* is the best thing you've ever written. Winfrey phoned yesterday, and they say it's the best thing you've ever written.'

'Yeah.'

'It is. Ivan, all things come to he who waits.'

'I don't see Francesca Brady hanging around any bus stops.'

'Francesca Brady isn't in your league.'

'I know. She's in the premier league. I'm in the third division.'

Campbell sighs. 'Do you ever think of anti-depressants?'

'Frequently,' Ivan says.

Campbell reaches across and squeezes his leg. 'Ivan, *The Last December* is going to win the Booker Prize. I swear to God.'

'Can I have that in writing?' Ivan asks.

Campbell ignores him. 'At least that's one thing Francesca *fucking* Brady is never going to win,' he says.

Winfrey Books is an impressive building by any standards. There is much glass, and inside, a large, airy atrium is dominated by several water features and copious numbers of plants. There are few books on display. As Ivan signs in, Campbell's eyes wander to a display board behind the security guard. Plastic letters attached to it spell out: *Winfrey Books welcomes Ian Connor*. Campbell decides not to point out the error.

They are kept waiting for fifteen minutes in reception. Campbell reads a newspaper while Ivan paces. Then an attractive young lady in a short skirt escorts them upstairs and through the large, open-plan editorial department to a boardroom. Waiting for them is a small crowd of people. They are introduced to Julia Malone, the thirtysomething Chief Editor whom Ivan has never met – he deals strictly with an intense man called Geoffrey, who adores his work and never dares change a word without first taking Ivan out to lunch. Julia is petite, hair flecked with grey and tied back, glasses, mid-length skirt. Carson Winfrey, the Managing Director, is sober-suited, bland-faced but with eager, excitable eyes, and his father Nathan, the octogenarian founder of the publishing house, is looking dapper in bow tie, pink shirt and tweeds. There are four heads of department, standing chatting around a large metal flask of tea – UK Sales, Marketing, Publicity, Overseas Sales. They quickly move to their seats as Ivan and Campbell enter; conversely Julia, Carson and Nathan rise from their own seats to shake hands effusively with the author and his agent. Campbell asks Nathan about his ailing wife, Francine. Nathan says she's doing as well as can be expected. Campbell started out in publishing as a postboy at Winfrey Books, and rose to be postman before escaping.

As they take their seats at the boardroom table, Nathan looks Ivan in the eye, lovingly pats the fat manuscript sitting before him, and says, 'Young man, *The Last December* is a fantastic achievement. Haven't read a novel like it in thirty years.'

Ivan blushes slightly. He is not used to in-your-face praise. 'Why thank you, Mr Winfrey.'

'*Nathan*, please,' Nathan says.

Ivan scratches suddenly at his head. *Nits*.

Carson clears his throat, then clasps his hands in front of him. 'Ivan, before we begin, I just want to say on behalf of all of us gathered here, that we believe *The Last December* is a work of genius. It is, without doubt, your finest achievement.'

Ivan doesn't quite know where to look. Campbell winks at him. Heads nod all around the table.

'It therefore pains me personally, and the company completely, to have to tell you that we have decided against offering you a contract.'

'*What?*' Campbell is immediately on his feet.

Ivan just feels . . . nothing. He stares blankly at Carson, the smiling assassin.

'It's not the book, Campbell, it's the market.'

It's the market is repeated around the table.

'But your father—' Campbell starts to say.

'My father spoke the truth: there *hasn't* been a book like it in thirty years. It's just another way of saying it's an old-fashioned book. It's not *en vogue*. You must know, Campbell, that even literary fiction follows the market. And I'm afraid *The Last December* is *out*.' He nods across the table at a young woman in an expensive suit. 'Daphne, the figures.'

Daphne reaches forward and presses a button on the laptop computer sitting before her. Immediately, Ivan sees the front covers of his previous books projected onto the far wall of the boardroom. Daphne uses the blunt end of a pencil to tap each cover in succession on the screen of her computer, an action which is replicated and exaggerated on the wall. Ivan thinks it's little short of magic what they can do now. He is sure that weeks, possibly months of preparation have gone into this little display. He is half-expecting tiny animated figures to dance across the wall and then sing to him about his fading career.

'*Trader John*,' Daphne says, 'sold fifteen thousand in hardcover, seventy-five thousand in paper. Excellent for a first novel. But your subsequent books – well, they haven't sold that many combined. It's been a downward spiral, Mr Connor, and frankly, there hasn't even been much of a spiral.'

Heads nod in agreement around the table. Even Ivan finds himself nodding.

'Your current novel, *Chapter & Verse*, has sold just three

hundred copies in hardcover which, I'm afraid, indicates that it would not be financially judicious to issue it in paperback.'

She lets that sit gravely in the air, then suddenly scratches at her hair.

Campbell says, 'Sales might pick up towards Christmas – he has a large family.'

The remark sits in the air like a fart at a funeral.

Campbell breaks the silence of his own making by tutting. 'Carson,' he then says, 'if this is a ploy to beat the price down, well I'm too old in the tooth to fall for that one, and you know it. You pay the boy what he's worth or we take him elsewhere.'

'That's not what I'm saying, Campbell. I'm saying he's off our list.'

'But I don't . . .' He turns to the elderly man, who immediately drops his eyes to the table. 'Nathan. You've nurtured Ivan Connor since he was a boy – it's never been about sales.'

Before Nathan can respond, Carson slams his fist down on the table. 'Which is exactly why this company is teetering on the brink of destruction! Too much dead wood!'

Campbell jumps to his feet and also brings his own fist down on the table at the same time. 'My client is not dead wood!'

'Anyone who is not selling books is dead wood as far as I'm concerned!' Carson bellows, jabbing his finger at the red-faced agent.

'Is this a publishers or a lumber yard?'

'Until this company turns a profit, it's a lumber yard!'

'Is this your decision as well, Nathan?'

Nathan looks as if he's on the verge of tears, but nevertheless nods his head slowly. 'It's for the good of the company,' he says. 'I'm very sorry, Campbell. And Ivan, of course.'

Ivan is on the verge of saying, 'That's quite all right,' but stops when Campbell literally grabs his hand and pulls him to his feet.

'Ivan,' Campbell says urgently, 'don't you listen to them.' Ivan stands awkwardly while Campbell faces the boardroom again. 'This boy is the greatest writer you've ever had. *The Last December* is the first great novel of the twenty-first century, and when the history of publishing is written, Winfrey Books will be remembered only as the company that turned down the chance to publish *The Last December*.'

Ivan thinks it's rather an epic speech.

Carson, on the other hand, looks completely unmoved. 'Quite,' he says, then adds needlessly, 'that's more or less what Salman said as well.'

'It's nothing personal, Ivan,' Julia says. 'It's just business.'

Campbell again replies on his behalf. 'That says it all.' He then leads Ivan from the room.

The Publisher, the Chief Executive, the Fiction Editor and the rest of the staff sit quietly for a few respectful moments. Then Carson lights a cigar. 'Who do these guys think they are?' he asks. Heads shake around the table. 'They should try working down a coal mine. Okay, show in the next batch.'

A moment later he scratches suddenly at his hair.

*   *   *

28

Outside on the cold, damp pavement, Campbell is pacing back and forth, flexing his hands, shouting at nobody and everybody. 'Philistines! Bankers! Lumberjacks!'

'Settle down, Campbell,' Ivan says, embarrassed in front of the passers-by. 'It's not the end of the world.'

'Bastards!' He shakes his fist at Winfrey Books, then sighs. His shoulders seem to collapse down; his chest detracts. He looks suddenly ten years older. 'Ivan – I'm sorry, what can I say?'

'No – no! You were fantastic! You said exactly what was going through my head, but I couldn't say a word. I can write it, but I can't say it. Fuck them, Campbell! Fuck them!' He grabs Campbell by the shoulders, suddenly and belatedly enthused. 'Dead wood, are we? Who needs them! We'll get another publisher, one that really cares about its writers! One that doesn't put profit before art! First thing tomorrow you get on the phone, set up some meetings, we'll—'

Campbell gently removes Ivan's hands from his shoulders. 'It's no use.'

'Of course it is, we'll just—'

'I've already tried all the other publishers.'

'What?'

'I had bad vibes from Winfrey, Ivan. To tell you the truth, I don't think they even read it. So I talked to other publishers. Nobody's biting.'

'But – but – but . . .'

'It's cold outside, Ivan. Literature is dying.'

'But – but my reviews! I'm the heart of—'

'Reviews?' Campbell laughs bitterly. 'Reviews aren't worth shit, Ivan. Nobody reads them any more. It's all about looking good, giving good sound bite. If you'd tits and a smile, my friend, I'd sell you for a million. But you're just a brilliant writer, and that's not enough any more.' He holds his hands up apologetically. 'Call me tomorrow, when I've had a chance to cool off. We'll work something out.'

Campbell pulls the collar of his flimsy jacket up, then raises a hand to flag down a cab. 'Can I drop you some-where?' he asks.

'No. My car – we came . . .'

Ivan somehow doubts if Campbell even remembers coming into town in his Mini Metro. The cab comes and takes his agent away, leaving Ivan standing alone outside Winfrey Books.

3

A daymare. A complete waking daymare. The rain is hammering down as Ivan drives out of town, his world fallen apart, his very being shamed by universal rejection, his whole creative life condemned to posterity by corporate philistines. He should be in a bar, he should be getting very drunk, railing against the world, but instead he's stuck in traffic again. He has to pick his boy up from school.

He blasts his horn, he rolls down his window and shouts, he fires imaginary missiles at black cabs which fail to explode.

The best book I've read in thirty years.

Giving with one hand and ripping it back with the other, then getting you down on the ground and beating you about the head with a club, with spikes in the end.

He thinks again about the lesbians-in-prison novel. He could research that relatively easily. He's up there every week. But oh what a laughing stock he'd be. His peers, and the young novelists coming up would gloat: 'Ivan Connor, sold his soul to the devil, sold his *soul*.' No, he will never be reduced to that. But what else? Penury! Metaphorically, at least. He will have a roof over his head. He won't starve, not while Mother lives and breathes. He may have to eat hard-boiled eggs and indivisible soldiers, but he won't starve. He has a little money saved. He will write, he will always write! He *will* create a masterpiece!

But you've already written a masterpiece.

Best novel I've read in thirty years.

And nobody wants to publish it!

He blasts his horn again.

He arrives at the primary school – Christ, he doesn't even know its name; he resolves to become more involved in his son's life, he'll have the time now that his career is over – with just a couple of minutes to spare. By the time he parks the car and locates his umbrella the kids are already streaming out and the parents are massed about the gates like lesbians at feeding time.

Lesbians? Why did he think *lesbians*?

Lions. Lions at feeding time. Literary lions.

I am a literary lion! I will roar and they will listen!

He splashes up to the parents and pushes through the dangerous ranks of umbrellas, facing his own downwards at a lethal angle, and scans the playground. Most of the kids are filing out in a relatively contented fashion, but half a dozen are charging back and forth across the playground pretending to be space aliens, impervious to the pounding rain or the muted shouts of their parents. Ivan spots Michael's trademark coat, hood up, pulled strangulation tight and calls him; once, twice, three times. He is completely ignored.

This isn't the day for a small child to ignore Ivan Connor. A literary lion has *teeth*!

Ivan storms across the playground and grabs Michael by the back of his coat. Michael lets out a surprised shout and tries to speak, but Ivan cuts him dead. 'I called you *three* times, now be quiet and *start walking*.'

'I don't—'

'Be quiet!'

He takes his hand and drags him angrily through the crowd of parents and on towards the gate. Michael is crying and dragging his feet.

'Stop that nonsense *now*!'

The other parents are looking at him. He doesn't see admonishment in their eyes, he sees respect, envy. *I'd love to be able to speak like that to my kids, but I feel pressured by the moral constraints of society not to show anger or violence towards them.* Or something pithy like that.

Michael tries to make a run for it. Ivan grabs him and yanks him back. 'I don't know how you behave with your mother, but I'll tell you this, young man, I'm not having it. Now just be quiet!'

'But I—'

'God help me I'll smack you so hard!'

'*I want my Mummy!*' he screeches.

'I'll give you your mummy, you spoiled little brat!' And he slaps the back of his bare legs.

They get to the car. Ivan pulls the front passenger seat forward and herds Michael into the back. The boy is nearly hysterical.

'I won't put up with this!' Ivan shouts. He stamps round to the driver's side and opens the door. 'You'll go straight to your room when we get home and you'll stay there until your mummy comes and boy, then you'll be in even bigger trouble.'

Michael sobs loudly.

Ivan slams the door shut and starts the engine. He slaps a tape into the cassette to drown out the noise of Michael's crying and drives off to the sound of the Rolling Stones.

I can't get no Satisfaction.

He marches Michael up the drive, through the front door and up the stairs. Halfway up Mother comes out of the kitchen and says, 'Ivan, what are you doing?'

'I am father to a spoiled brat,' Ivan replies, and pushes a still crying Michael ahead of him. He prods him along the landing and into the bedroom the children use when they come to stay. It's just a bedroom. Mother hasn't allowed them to decorate it with posters or stickers and there are only a couple of small toys that they have long grown out of.

Ivan leaves Michael standing crying in the middle of the room. At the door he pauses and waves an angry finger back at him. 'You've got a lot of learning to do,' he says. 'And get that bloody coat off!'

Ivan closes the door and goes back downstairs, breathing hard, his head throbbing. Mother gives him a look and he says, by way of justification, 'I won't put up with that kind of behaviour,' as he passes her. He goes into the lounge, and pours himself a drink from the cabinet.

'What behaviour?'

Ivan glares at her. He's no longer quite sure exactly what the behaviour was that made him so angry. He sighs. 'He's just impossible.'

'He's only seven,' Mother says.

'I know what age he is. It's no excuse.'

'Ivan, are you just going to leave him up there?'

'Yes. Mother, just let him stew in it for a while, okay?'

'If you think it's right, dear.'

'I do.'

'Will I take him up a glass of milk?'

'No!'

She moves across and pours herself a small sherry. She turns to him and says, 'Did your meeting not go well?'

'That's got nothing to do with it!' He storms off upstairs to his study.

He sits and sips and stares out of the window. The removal van has gone now and he can see the pond and the ducks. Combined with the whisky, it has something of a calming influence. Perhaps he was a smidgen tough with the little man. Perhaps he overreacted to . . . what? He sighs. Still, it won't do him any harm. This is no time to appear weak and indecisive. The boy wouldn't behave, so he'll stay in his room and learn his lesson.

He'll give him twenty minutes. Then they'll make up. And have fun.

Ivan switches his computer on. He has been making some notes for his next novel, which he intends to call *Story of the Blues*. It will deal with growing up in his home town and his love for a beautiful girl, who wasn't the slightest bit interested. It will be a departure for him. It will be young and vibrant and funny and heart-breaking and he knows in his soul that he will probably never write it. Literature is dead. *The Last December* is the best novel of the last thirty years and he *can't get it published*.

What hope is there for anything he writes?

Oh, what is the point?

What is the bloody point?

He looks at his notes for *Story of the Blues* and thinks, Who is going to care? He turns his computer off and sips some more of his whisky.

In the far background, he can hear Michael sobbing.

Perhaps Avril is right. He doesn't have a job. He sits on his lardy arse all day and makes up stories. Serious stories about serious people doing serious things in serious times before Game Boys, DVDs, laptop computers or, indeed, electricity ruined the world. He is an intellectual Luddite; literature has gone the way of silent movies and Betamax video recorders. It's not about fine writing any more, it's about entertainment. To survive he must become part of the entertainment industry, but he is what he is, a literary dinosaur lost in the era of *Jurassic Park 3*.

But why can't you change, Ivan?

Adapt! Move with the times! He must write novelisations of popcorn movies! He must ghost-write the memoirs of a former soap star! He must churn out hundreds of thousands of words about shopping and fucking. There must be an explosion at the end of every chapter! This serial killer will run and run!

He buries his head in his hands.

He has been dumped by his publisher, and no others are biting.

Francesca Brady has signed a deal for five million pounds. She's laughing all the way to the bookshop.

Ivan won't cry. But with one more drink, he might.

Half an hour later the doorbell goes. Ivan is downstairs fixing himself another drink and his mother is out in the back garden unpegging clothes from the line, so he goes to answer it. He sees Avril's outline through the glass and curses silently because Michael's still upstairs and they haven't yet become chums again and he knows she'll give him a hard time about it. It's the last thing he needs. He needs sympathy and sex, and neither of them are very likely at this moment in time. The sex, in fact, will be impossible. As he approaches the door he tries to think of the last time he had sex, but fails, although it was certainly with Avril and it was definitely before they got divorced.

That was three years ago. That's a long time.

He opens the door. Before he can launch into his excuses she beats him to it with a heartfelt 'Sorry, love.'

'That's quite all right.'

They nod at each other for several moments.

'What are you sorry for?' he asks.

'I tried calling your mobile.'

'I got rid of it months ago.'

'Oh. Sorry. But I tried.'

'That's okay. Why, what's . . . ?'

'I thought I'd see you at the school, but you must have been late.'

'I was dead on time.'

'Oh God, I'm sorry. It was the rain and all the umbrellas. But I looked, I really looked.'

'I don't quite understand.'

'Please try. I did look for you. It was just so miserable and I'd no umbrella and Anna was in the car by herself and I didn't want to leave her too long. Sorry, these are really weak excuses for behaving so abominably.'

'Avril, what exactly have you done? If you crashed the car, that's your problem. It's nothing to do with me.'

'No, of course I didn't, Ivan. I got finished early, so I thought I'd nip round and pick Michael up, save you the trouble. I called your mobile . . .'

'Yes, we've established that.'

'And you know your mum won't speak to me.'

'Yes, we know that.'

'So I just thought I'd pick him up, except I didn't see you and – I'm sorry. You must have hung around for ages waiting for him.'

'Not really, no.'

'Did someone tell you, then?'

'Tell me what?'

'That I'd picked him up.'

'You didn't pick him up. I picked him up. Avril, are you feeling okay?'

'Are *you* feeling okay? Of course I picked him up. He's in the car with Anna.'

Ivan laughs. 'Yes. Very good. Well, let's go and have a word with him, shall we?'

'Ivan?'

'Come on then, Avril,' Ivan says, leading the way grandly down the drive. 'Let's see how the little monster managed *The Great Escape*, eh? I'm sure it will be a great laugh.' She hurries after him. 'You know, today of all days,' he says, 'this is exactly what I can do without.'

'Ivan – what's got into you?' He laughs dismissively. 'I said I was sorry,' she repeats.

They arrive at the car and the glass is all steamed up. Ivan raps sharply on the rear window and Anna rolls it down; a moment later Michael's face appears behind her, smiling. 'Hiya, Daddy,' he says.

Ivan stands back. How did . . . no tears, no sign of crying . . . He turns confused eyes on Avril, and then glances back at the house, at his mother standing with her arms folded, watching from the doorway, and then he looks up to the bedroom where he imprisoned his son an hour before.

Michael is looking out of the upstairs window. No, a child wearing an identical coat to Michael's, with an identical hood, is looking out of the upstairs window. His hand is against the glass, pleading silently.

'Oh Holy Christ,' Ivan says.

'What is it?' She sees that what little colour he had has drained from his face. 'Ivan?'

'I brought the wrong child home from school.'

'You . . .'

'I brought the wrong fucking child home from school!'

Before they can even think about calling the child's parents – his name is Daniel Westbrook, and he's in Michael's class and those fucking coats are all the rage – or his school or the NSPCC, a police car comes rolling up to the house.

'Oh Holy Christ,' Ivan says and dashes up the drive. 'They're going to put me away.'

Avril follows him up the drive. 'Ivan, how could you bring the wrong child home from school!'

'They all look the same!' he bellows. He pushes past his mother and dashes up the stairs.

Avril tries to follow, but Mother blocks the way. 'You're not coming into my house,' she says.

'Oh Irene, for God's sake!'

'For God's sake nothing. You think you can break my boy's heart and still expect to—'

'Madam?'

Avril turns to find two young police officers standing behind her. They have approached her with remarkable stealth and speed. 'Yes, Constable?'

'Is this where Ivan Connor lives? The writer?'

'Yes, it is.'

'Judas!' Ivan shouts from his study window.

He has bolted the door and placed a chair against it. He will hold out until his last shot of whisky. He wonders if someone will end up teaching *him* creative writing in prison. Perhaps not, but he'll definitely be taught a lesson. That's what happens to men who mess around with children. He'll have his balls cut off. He'll be nailed to a table. How will he even be able to begin writing his *Les Miserables*, *Papillon* or *Borstal Boy* if his hands have been ground to a pulp by the jackboots of an incarcerated underclass venting their spleen on a haggard *nonce*?

He's waiting for the good cop/bad cop routine. They bring

him coffee, he's allowed his cigarettes. He's shaking and tearful. He's demanding freedom and justice, although he would probably settle for a hug and somebody telling him it's going to be okay.

Once, because it seemed the decent thing to do, and also because it did wonders for his credibility amongst a small group of female students who attached themselves to him for about three weeks while he was a writer-in-residence at some cheap college for foreigners, he did some readings on behalf of Amnesty International, and he wonders now if it is too soon to put a call in to them. He suspects that they would want nothing to do with him. Child molesters are not very p.c.

There is also PEN, which speaks out and campaigns on behalf of imprisoned writers. He wonders if they could put the fear of Godot into those pious, self-loving cops trying to pin all manner of atrocious crimes on him. 'I'll have that Harold Pinter on you,' he could say, and they would quake with fear. Or more likely, respond, 'Who? Is he Legal Aid?'

They bring him a scone, already cut – so that he won't try and commit suicide with a plastic knife – and liberally spread with butter and jam, and he gobbles it hungrily while contemplating the likely success of his hunger strike. He wonders if there is a way of going on a hunger strike *between* meals.

The hunger strike you can undertake without ruining your appetite.

Alternatively, if justice is not forthcoming, he could always threaten to block the release of his new novel.

That would really cause pandemonium. Especially in the colonies. They'd be rioting on Boston Harbour when the next instalment of *The Last December* failed to arrive.

Ivan buries his head in his hands, and stares at the table. How many innocent men have sat here, awaiting torture? How many innocent men have prayed to their gods for salvation? How many poor souls have been tortured sitting in this very chair? Strobe lights, electric shocks, water torture.

By God! There's still blood on the table from the last unfortunate's beating.

He will be strong! He will tell them nothing! He will defend his right to free speech! He will fight for liberty, equality and fraternity!

Then he realises that it isn't blood, but raspberry jam from his scone.

'Mr Connor, would you like another cup of coffee?'

'Yes, please.'

'Sugar and cream?'

'That would be lovely.'

The interview room door closes again.

It will be his *J'Accuse*. His name will be up there with Dreyfus.

'My name will be up there with Dreyfus,' he tells his solicitor as he sits down.

'Richard Dreyfuss? That guy from *Jaws* and *Close Encounters*? Anyway, I've had a word, and you're free to go. Your wife is waiting upstairs.'

'Oh right.'

Instead of life and slow death in prison, they give him

a severe ticking off instead, and he looks suitably guilty and apologises profusely.

While they wait for the paperwork to be completed Avril explains that the unfortunate victim of Ivan's kidnapping, Daniel, is one of six boys in the same class who wear identical coats and who all run in the same gang. Pre-coats, it was known as the *Nosebleed Gang*. With the arrival of the fashionable new coats, with their elasticated hoods, it became known naturally as the *Hood Gang*, and its members as the *hoods*.

Daniel is a hood, Michael is a hood – they're the best of friends.

Daniel's mother was, of course, concerned by his disappearance, but it was the second time he'd been taken home by mistake in the past week, so she wasn't *overly* concerned. Besides, someone recognised Ivan; it just took a little while to track him down.

'Somebody recognised me?' Ivan asks.

'One of the mothers told Daniel's mother that she thought she'd seen her boy leaving the school with you.'

'But how did she know me? I'm never at the school.'

'She's a big fan of your books, apparently. Recognised you from the dust jacket.'

Ivan beams.

Avril looks at him.

Ivan shrugs and says, 'Nobody wants to publish my books.'

'You could have gone to prison for this, Ivan.'

'They just tossed me off like a used condom.'

'You need to live in the real world, Ivan. And realise it doesn't revolve around you.'

'Isn't it remarkable that somebody recognised me at the school? From a dust flap? They must be real fans. Carson Winfrey doesn't know what the hell he's talking about.'

She shakes her head.

'It's a good idea for a story, though, isn't it?'

'What is, Ivan?'

'Confused author brings child home by mistake.'

'*Ivan.*'

'You could take it either way – they bond and the boy doesn't want to go back to his real, cruel parents, who beat him with toilet ducks, or he goes on the run accused of a crime he didn't commit.'

'Look, you need to get a grip on things.'

'Of course, it's not the sort of thing I could write. It's more like a Hollywood movie or something they'd put on BBC 1 on a Sunday evening, starting just before the watershed but finishing with all the violence and stuff quite late on. I could write an outline, though.'

'I'm going to go now. Do you want a lift home?'

'No. I'll need time to gather my thoughts. I'll need to prepare a statement for the press. Let my fans know I'm okay.'

Avril starts to say something else, then stops, shakes her head again, then reaches up and kisses Ivan on the cheek. She walks out of the station.

He calls after her; 'I bet Alfred wouldn't have brought the wrong child home.'

She ignores him.

Let her go.

He will tell the press that they even took his shoe laces,

so that he couldn't attempt suicide. And hope that they don't look at his slip-ons.

He stands on the steps outside the station and gives his press conference. His is, indeed, a harrowing tale; the highlight is undoubtedly his bravery while his fingernails were ripped from his bloody hands. He drops to his knees in the rain and gives thanks to Almighty God for rescuing him from Devil's Island.

Of course, he is addressing nobody, and now he has wet knees. It is a cold, miserable night and he has left his wallet at home. He does what all rough, tough ex-cons do the moment they get out of prison. He phones his mum.

4

When he next returns to teach his creative-writing class
in the prison, Donna fails to attend. He knows he was
horrible to her, he would like to make amends. Praise
her lyrics, or something. But what can he do, she's
not there. He tries to concentrate on what he's telling
the rest of them, but his eyes keep coming back to
her chair. He can't help it – it's like when you're told
not to look at that horrible purple birthmark on that
poor man's face; it's the first thing you do, and you
keep coming back to it. Eventually, nonchalantly, he
asks where Donna is today. He tries to make a joke
of it. 'Has she been released? Or has she been signed
up by a record company? Should I be watching *Top of
the Pops*?'

It was meant to be funny, but they don't get it. They just
kind of shrug. Julie rasps, 'It's bleedin' up to her whether
she comes, innit?'

'Yes, I do suppose it is,' Ivan says.

When the class is over, Ivan asks the warder if there's any chance of having a quick word with Donna.

'No,' says the warder.

'I'm a little concerned about her. I wasn't very nice to her last time I was here. About her . . . poetry.'

The warder, a rotund woman in a too-tight navy-blue uniform, gives him an *are you fucking joking* look.

'Sometimes you can be too critical. Because I'm from a very literary background, I have a tendency to—'

'Mr Connor, this is a prison. I don't think Donna's gonna get upset 'cause something don't rhyme right, you understand? They all got bigger things to worry about.'

'Yes. Quite. I understand that. But still. I'd really like a word.'

'Visitin's over for today.'

'Yes, I realise that.' He clears his throat. 'But I thought perhaps . . .'

'You want to go down to her cell? You want me to take you down the wing and take you into her cell?'

'That would be great.'

'They'd tear you apart, Mr Connor. Some of them haven't had their hands on a man in twenty years.'

'Yes, well . . .'

'Some of them haven't had their hands on a man at all, of course.' She winks and starts to move him on.

He goes a few steps, then stops again and says, 'Really, just a quick word.'

She shakes her head, then sighs. 'Okay. Let me check, but it'll be no.' She turns away from him, then raises a walkie-talkie.

Ivan stands looking at the grey interior of the prison.

48

If the dice had fallen a different way, he might well have been spending the next twenty years in a place not unlike this. Except it would be men, not women, behind the bars, men intent on killing him. He would have been kept in solitary confinement. He would have a cockroach for a friend. A robin redbreast would come to the window every morning to be fed crumbs from his breakfast. And one morning the robin would keel over and die, its insides sliced by the powdered glass laced into Ivan's breakfast by the vengeful chefs.

The roll of the dice, indeed.

Ivan wonders if there is a book to be written about the roll of the dice, about chance, about making your life decisions according to what way the dice falls. One for go left, two for right, three for up, four for down etc. He has, of course, read *The Dice Man* some time previously, but he is a great one for improving what he sees as flawed texts. At other times he has contemplated writing books about a very large whale, a story about two cities, a massive fantasy novel about a Lord who has magic rings and is plagued by little creatures, all stories which have been attempted before but not, he thinks, very successfully.

The warder looks at him and shakes her head again. 'Seems you have influence,' she says.

Ivan looks surprised.

'Walk this way,' the prison officer says.

'This is how it works,' the warder says when they're standing outside Donna's cell. 'The door remains open, you keep two feet on the ground at all times; if you go within six feet of her I'll come in and beat you to a pulp.'

'I just want to talk to her.'

'That's what the priest said, and he's in hospital.'

'A priest attacked Donna?'

'Not Donna, no.'

Ivan nods.

The prison officer opens the door. Just *opens* it, doesn't unlock it. Like it's a youth hostel. Donna is lying on her bed, holding a copy of *Insanity Fair* up above her. She doesn't look up.

'Good book?' Ivan asks.

This shakes her. She drops the book and struggles up into a sitting position; she's flustered and perhaps a little frightened by the sudden intrusion. Ivan smiles warmly, he hopes. 'You were miles away,' he says.

The warder nods at him and takes up a position just outside the door.

Donna draws her knees up on the bed and looks at him, brow furrowed. 'What are you doing here?'

Ivan shrugs. He's rather disappointed, actually. He had expected to find a cold concrete floor, the wind whistling through prison bars, a dirty stinking blanket, blood on the walls, fingernail scratches depicting the passage of each day, each week, each month, each year. But it's quite warm and brightly painted and almost homely. There's a comfortable-looking bed, a reading light, a desk, lots of paperbacks, a clock radio, a private toilet cubicle, an expressionist print on the wall, paper, pens, a *Writers' & Artists' Yearbook*.

And the door wasn't even locked. Not so much *Midnight Express* as *Breakfast at Tiffany's.*

'I said, what are you doing here?'

'Sorry,' he says. 'Never been in a prison cell before. It's quite nice, isn't it?'

'Oh yes,' she says, 'it's really lovely.'

'I'm sorry,' he says again, 'I didn't mean . . .'

'What do you want?'

Now that he looks at her properly – she's not wearing make-up, but she's undeniably pretty in a starved working-class kind of a way – he can see that she's quite uncomfortable with him being there. This isn't just because he's a man in a women's prison, if you can even call it a prison, with unlocked doors, but because she's a little in awe of him. He's a successful (!) author and she's a struggling amateur. Ivan remembers what he was like before he was published. He would go to readings in Waterstones and just look at the authors, watch how they moved, how they spoke, how they fidgeted before being called to read, what they drank while they waited, if they made eye-contact, how they responded to inane questions. (The number one most popular question is: *Where do you get your ideas from?* Ivan always says, 'A small shop in Covent Garden.') There is always one cheeky young scamp who asks: 'How much do you get paid?' and the audience laughs. Ivan responds, 'If I'd half as much money as people seem to think I have, then I'd have twice as much money as I actually do have,' and the audience just looks puzzled. Actually, Ivan is not often asked questions. Usually they sit in silence and depart in silence, if they're actually there at all. Having done it once, and made the *Evening Standard*, Ivan wonders if he should actually build electrocution into his readings in future, make it an integral part of his 'act'; it would certainly make it more of a performance. People would talk about it, word would spread, readings would be crammed. In fact, he wouldn't need to read at all, he could just electrocute himself each time, steadily building up the voltage week by week. It could culminate in one massive . . .

'ARE YOU ON DRUGS OR SOMETHING?'

Ivan blinks at Donna who has now moved off the bed and is standing with her arms folded before her, and before him.

Ivan says, 'Sorry?' for the third time.

The prison officer puts her head around the door. 'Everything okay?'

'Fine, fine,' Ivan says hurriedly. The prison officer looks doubtfully at him, and then at Donna, who rolls her eyes. The prison officer hesitates for a moment and then withdraws again.

Focus.

'You weren't at class today, Donna,' he says. 'I was concerned.'

'Why?' she asks flatly.

'Because I wasn't very nice to you last time. My behaviour was inexcusable.'

She isn't quite sure how to take this. She shrugs.

'I was having a bad day,' he goes on, 'I shouldn't take it out on my students. It must be difficult enough being in here without me being—'

'An arsehole,' she says.

'Quite.'

He purses his lips. He nods. He's said it, he doesn't quite know where to go from here. He hopes to God she won't get her lyrics out and ask for advice. He turns a little to his left so that he can study the paperback books she has on her shelf. 'So,' he says, 'you seem to enjoy reading.'

'I don't get out much.'

He nods, but he isn't really listening. He's looking to see if she has any of his novels. But no. There are books by Maeve Binchy, Joyce Carol Oates, James Joyce, Agatha Christie and Nick Hornby. There are books by John Hegley, Charles Dickens, John Cheever, Martin Amis and Walter Scott. But still, none of his. 'Tell me, Donna,' he says somewhat vaguely, as if he hasn't been thinking about it from the moment he walked into the prison this afternoon, 'are there really a lot of lesbians in a women's prison?' He continues to examine the books. Jack Higgins, Salman Rushdie, Roddy Doyle.

'Mr Connor?'

'Ivan, call me Ivan.'

'Ivan.'

He doesn't turn. He doesn't realise that she has deftly moved a lot closer to him. He says, 'Hmmmm?'

'Do you think poetry can literally be a physical experience?'

Christ.

'Well, Donna,' he says, finally turning towards her, 'poetry is certainly a—'

She punches him hard in the stomach with her small but solid fist, and he collapses to the floor with a *whoof*!

In the brief moment before the prison officer scrambles through the door calling for assistance, he is aware of Donna standing over him with her fists raised. She shouts, 'Good poetry is like a punch to the stomach!'

53

He's coughing, trying to catch his breath, trying not to retch. 'I – quite – agree –' he manages to say as the warder's whistle blast fills the room.

Mother stands over Michael and Anna as they pull on their coats and lift their schoolbags. Avril is visible through the frosted glass of the front door, which will remain closed until the last possible moment. Michael pulls up the hood of his distinctive coat. Mother shakes her head and pulls it down again. She ruffles his hair. Anna kisses her on the cheek, then says – 'Granny, do you want to see me play a trick on Mummy?'

'Not really, no.'

Mother opens the door. Avril looks at the ground, Mother studies the wallpaper in the hall. Michael runs out past his mother towards the car.

Anna steps out of the house. 'Mummy . . . ?'

She indicates that she wants to whisper something in her ear. Avril bends to listen, but instead Anna reaches up and yanks at her mother's hair – and it starts to come away in her hands. It's a wig. She's bald underneath. Anna bursts into laughter, then runs away down the drive after Michael while Avril scrambles to replace her wig. She glances, mortified at Mother, then hurries away. Mother looks after her confused and shocked and then retreats inside.

There are twelve beds in the hospital wing, all empty but his. This is not a surprise to him, it being more like a hotel than a prison. The doctor has examined him and found him to be fine, although he was advised to get his cholesterol checked. They gave him a cup of tea and a low-fat bun and now he sits fully dressed on top of the starched sheets and thinks about Yossarian in *Catch 22* and the pain in his liver which stops just short of being jaundice.

He has often thought, in those grey periods when his own creative juices would not flow, of constructing a book entirely made out of sentences lifted from so-called classic texts. He could plunder at will from the entire canon of English Literature. The artistry would be in constructing the purloined sentences into a seamless, coherent whole. Or if that seemed too much like hard work he could just use them in no particular order and present it as a work of experimental fiction. Either way, the book would probably sell in its millions; it would be like a multi-dimensional crossword puzzle for literary sleuths. He could even throw in a few of his own sentences just to see if anyone could tell the difference. He imagines that they would sit quite happily with the best of Dickens, Melville or Joyce.

'Mr Connor, isn't it?'

A small, middle-aged woman with spiky hair is standing before him. She introduces herself as Barbara Cohen, the prison's new Chief Executive. Not Governor, not even Governess, but Chief Executive. Ivan silently laments the passage of Governors and locked doors. He is convinced that the removal of carpets and bedside lights from the prisoners' cells and the re-introduction of cockroaches and weekly beatings would have a much more beneficial effect on them. It would certainly deter them from punching their visitors.

'We're going to bring her up on a charge,' Barbara Cohen says.

'Who?' Ivan asks.

'Donna Carbone.'

'Oh. Right.' Ivan nods. He's confused and hurt. What was Donna thinking of? He was apologising, for Christ's sake – he doesn't do that every day.

More to the point, what is she actually inside for?

He is amazed that he hasn't even thought of it before. He had imagined a women's prison to be filled with those who had committed vaguely girly-type crimes, like shoplifting or prostitution. But what if Donna was actually in for something altogether more serious, like a grisly murder? What if she had chopped up her lover or burned down an orphanage? Had he unwittingly taken his life in his hands by venturing into her cell? She could have torn him limb from limb. She might have eaten his flesh, she might be Hannibalina Lecter (trashy novel, but RESPECT THE SALES).

But, but . . .

But what if her anger, the punch to his stomach, the defiant fists raised, was not a sign of her insanity, but an indication of her determination to prove that . . .

She'd been *framed*. For a murder she *did not commit*.

He sees it all forming now. A big, bold novel, a real page-turner. They start off as adversaries, he the young writer, turning his back on commercial success to try and inspire these young unfortunates to a passion for literature, showing them a way to be free mentally while remaining incarcerated physically; and she, the tragic innocent victim of a love affair gone wrong, or a bank robbery, the gangster's moll, bitter and twisted and want- ing nothing to do with life, let alone literature. But he sees something in her, a spark, and he perseveres and slowly, slowly, he wins her respect; she embraces life again, and poetry, and with his help she starts to write, slowly at first, but then faster and faster and in the writing it comes back to her – she has lost her memory, of course, brought on by the shock of being arrested – who really did murder the baker, the banker or the candlestick-maker, that she was set up by the real villain – a politician, or a bishop. He is able to secure the politician/bishop/celebrity chef's confession and wins her release from prison.

'Mr Connor? We'll need you to make a statement so that Donna can be brought up on the charge.'

'Of course.' He takes another sip of his tea.

'Unless, of course, it was a stomach cramp.'

'I'm sorry?'

She looks keenly at him, gives something that's half- way between a blink and a wink. 'A stomach cramp, a sudden cramp. Donna was merely trying to help you and the guard misinterpreted.'

'No, no, she definitely thumped me.'

'Mr Connor, Donna's a good girl, she hasn't long to go here. This would give her another six months, minimum.'

'And well deserved. She can't go around punching best-selling authors.'

'She didn't, Mr Connor. She punched *you*.'

His mouth drops open. 'I think that's uncalled for.'

She sits back a little and smiles. 'Mr Connor, I very much appreciate what you do here for us. I'm a great believer in using the arts to show our girls a different world, a world they've usually been denied. These girls come from difficult backgrounds, they haven't had the same opportunities that we have had, do you understand?' He nods vaguely, not quite sure where this is going. 'But it's also important that the girls have a certain faith and trust in their teacher. I mean, if they were to lose that, why would they bother turning up for the class at all?'

Ivan nods, slowly.

'If they were to lose confidence in you, then I'd have to seriously consider whether it was time to cancel the class, or perhaps look at bringing in a different writer who might more easily adapt to the peculiar conditions which go hand in hand with teaching in a confined environment like this.'

'You're threatening me,' Ivan says.

'Mr Connor, perhaps you don't realise that the Prison Service is the great unsung champion of English Literature. Up and down the country, in dozens and dozens of prisons, through programmes like this, we are providing financial support for authors who are experiencing hard times. You see, Mr Connor, I have worked in a number of different facilities, and I know that authors are a peculiar breed. They are not really equipped to survive in the real world, yet is it not their peculiar task to tell us about that very world? A conundrum indeed. So we help the authors, and in turn the authors help us. Everyone is happy. However, you will agree that a *best-selling* author would perhaps not have either the time nor the inclination to spend his time teaching creative writing in a women's prison when he has great novels he should be writing. Nor would one imagine that a *best-selling* author could find it *so* fulfilling, or indeed financially rewarding – so rewarding that only recently he enquired about the possibility of increasing the frequency of his classes.'

'I have an ex-wife and two small children to support,' Ivan says glumly. 'And I'm being held to ransom by a prison governor.'

'Chief Executive,' Barbara Cohen corrects.

'My sincere apologies,' Ivan says.

'So,' Barbara Cohen asks, folding her hands in her lap, 'how are we really feeling?'

Ivan sighs. 'The stomach cramps are diminishing by the second.'

'I'm very glad to hear that.'

Ivan shakes his head, then rolls his eyes and gives a short laugh. 'I hope you're this concerned about all of your prisoners.'

'I try to be.' She nods appreciatively, then reaches down for something in a battered leather briefcase at her feet. 'I wondered if you would mind signing this, Mr Connor?'

He thinks it's going to be some kind of release form, but when she produces it he sees that it's actually a well-thumbed copy of *Chapter & Verse*.

He's a little taken aback.

'I don't often do this,' she says as she offers him a pen. 'In fact, I usually find that authors are such a disappointment when you meet them in the flesh.'

Ivan takes the pen, then hesitates over the title page. He looks up at her. 'Is that some kind of a compliment?' he asks.

She smiles. 'I suppose it is. And I do so hate to see you fallen on hard times.'

Ivan, who wouldn't know a hard time if it came up and broke his hip, nods along, then signs his name with a flourish.

She takes the book back from him, briefly examines the signature, then blows lightly on it to stop it from smearing when she closes it over. She takes a deep, satisfied breath, clutches the book briefly to her chest, then reaches down and slips it into the side panel of the briefcase. She straightens again, then moves forward slightly and places her hand lightly on the sleeve of Ivan's jacket. 'Can I ask you something, Mr Connor?'

'Ye-yes, of course.'

'Where *do* you get your ideas from?'

5

On a gloomy Thursday afternoon Ivan takes refuge in Pages, a small independent bookshop which he visits at least three times a week. It is a *Sgt. Pepper*'s length from his mother's house. Ivan's musical tastes are quite catholic, but when he likes something he plays it to death and then can no longer bear to listen to it. For the past month he has been listening to *Sgt. Pepper* while he walks to the bookshop, alternately speeding up or slowing down as he approaches the shop so that the last few bars of the final track fade out just as he pushes through the door.

He removes his earphones, then slips the disc out of the Walkman. He never wants to hear it again. He nods at Marcus, the owner of the shop, sitting forlornly behind the counter, then hands him the disc.

'I need something more cheerful,' he says.

Marcus, rotund, owl-faced, rifles under the counter for several moments, then produces a dozen CDs, none of them in boxes. 'Old or new?' he asks.

'What do you think?'

Marcus nods, then removes the newer discs from his collection and replaces them under the counter. 'Okay,' he says, 'that leaves the Stones' *Get Yer Ya-Ya's Out!* or Pink Floyd's *Dark Side of the Moon.*'

'Stones,' says Ivan.

The shop is not large. The books are new, but smell musty. Or it could be Marcus. He has no staff, never goes on holiday, he has no wife or girlfriend. The shop is his life. It's not much of a life.

'What's wrong?' Marcus asks as Ivan parks himself on a bar stool on the opposite side of the counter.

Ivan shrugs.

Marcus sighs. 'It's this business,' he correctly interprets. 'It's killing us.'

It is a familiar refrain, and normally one Ivan would choose to ignore. The business wasn't killing him at all until a couple of days ago; in fact, now he realises he was relatively happy with his lot. But since Year Zero dawned at Winfrey his fingers have become frozen. He cannot write at all. Who's to say it's a temporary blip? Perhaps he has written his final words.

'Been thinking about dropping the genre shelves,' Marcus says, 'just lump them all in together. I mean, you can't tell any more. Is Grisham Crime or Literary Fiction? Is Trollope Romance or General Fiction?'

'Anthony Trollope?'

'Joanna.' Ivan sighs. 'I'll just make it A to Z. Or Zee. It's all Zee these days. That is zee truth, Ivan!' He smiles, then says: 'Do you know there's no word for irony in German?'

62

'I've been dropped by my publisher,' Ivan blurts out suddenly.

'Oh dear,' says Marcus. He sniffs up. 'It was coming,' he says eventually.

'Meaning what?'

'Look at this place. Nobody reads novels any more.'

'Of course they do.'

'No, they don't, Ivan. Not your sort of novels, anyway.'

'What do you mean, my sort?'

'You know what I mean.'

'You'd better explain yourself or I'll take my custom elsewhere.'

'Ivan, you haven't brought any custom here in years. We swap CDs. I should open a record shop. I'd get more business from you.'

Marcus produces a bottle of wine from beneath the counter, then reaches below again for two glasses. As he pours, Ivan wonders if he does this with all of his customers or only with him; he has no real idea because there never seem to be any other customers, at least when he's there. Then he wonders if Marcus provides the wine because they're friends or because he's an author and it's theoretically good to have an author hanging around your shop. This leads naturally to Ivan wondering if he is actually still an author at all because he doesn't have a publisher. Has he reverted to being a typist?

'Ivan, Ivan,' Marcus says, pauses to sip his wine, then wipes his lips with the back of his hand, which he then waves around the shop. 'Don't get me wrong, the trash still sells, but nobody reads what you would call literary fiction.'

'Of course they do.'

'No, they don't.'

'Yes, they do.'

'Let me clarify: they might buy it, but they don't read it. Anything over a hundred pages, who the hell has the time?'

'You don't know what you're talking about.'

'Open your eyes, man. You're in a bookshop. Anything over a hundred pages – it's a coffee-table book. It sits there. I know this to be true.'

'*Because* they're over a hundred pages long?'

'Yes! And no. Ivan, it's a known fact, there simply aren't any good long novels.'

'There aren't any good long novels?'

'Exactly.'

'My novels are long. They get excellent reviews. For about three weeks I was the heart of a generation.'

'Don't take this personally. I'm speaking generally here.'

'Speaking generally, I'd say you're off your rocker.'

Marcus pours them both another glass, then looks up hopefully as the shop door opens, but it's just someone looking for directions to the nearest tube. Marcus explains patiently with the aid of a guidebook, and the young woman departs. He sighs. 'A better businessman would have sold her the guidebook,' he says.

Ivan nods.

'Tell me,' Marcus says, 'what is your definition of a great book?'

Ivan thinks for a moment. 'A book that is admired by the critics – and by the public – and which stands the test of time.'

'Exactly. Proving my point that there are no great long books.'

'I don't follow.'

'*War and Peace*, great book?'

'Yes, of course.'

'Ever read it?'

'Not exactly.'

Marcus nods confidently. 'Okay. Let's stick with the Russians. *Anna Karenina*? Read it?'

'Yes, actually.'

'And now the truth.'

'Well, halfway.'

'Okay. Now, let me give you an example of a great book. *Animal Farm*.'

'Agreed. Great book. A classic.'

'Read it?'

'Yes, of course.'

'See, short book, you've read it, long book you haven't. And it sells by the cartload. Now, *Animal Farm*, *The Old Man and the Sea*, *The Snow Goose* – read them?'

'Yes.'

'*The Brothers Karamazov*, *Les Miserables* and *A Suitable Boy* – read them?'

'Well . . .' Ivan takes another drink. He has to admit there is a certain logic to what Marcus is saying. But he won't, of course. 'What about Charles Dickens? You can't say *David Copperfield* and *Nicholas Nickleby* aren't great.'

'Possibly. You've read them?'

'Yes.'

'You think the public have read them?'

'Yes.'

'Or just watched the television series?'

'Well . . .'

'I'll tell you what Charles Dickens' only great book is – and by great I refer to our definition of great as being well reviewed and widely read and standing the test of time.'

'What?'

'*A Christmas Carol.*'

Ivan sighs. 'Because it's short and—'

'Now you're getting it. Ivan, I know how it is, believe me. People come in here all the time and they buy one of our big, cheap compendiums of Charles Dickens novels because they think they need some classics in their life, but they don't want to spend more than a couple of quid. Then they get it home, and if they pick it up at all, you know what they read? *A Christmas Carol* because it's short and because they know the musical. To be honest, I don't think he's a great writer anyway.'

'Oh God,' Ivan says, 'here we go.'

'I'm serious. Problem with Dickens is, he's too tall. You can't be a great writer and be tall as well. It doesn't work. Writers are, by definition, short. Shortness signifies struggle, oppression. If you're too tall you don't have to struggle.'

Ivan arrives home, already bored with the Stones. His mum is sitting in the conservatory reading; he waves through to her and shouts that he's going to make the dinner as a special treat and she waves back, although she isn't sure that that's how she would describe Ivan's efforts in the kitchen. Still, it will take his mind off his work.

He puts Vivaldi on the music centre and begins to prepare his favourite pasta dish. He uncorks a bottle of red wine and sips steadily. He quite enjoys cooking. When it's ready, he drains the pasta into the sink, then calls for his mother, but there's no response. He adds the sauce, mixes it in, then turns the music down and calls again, but still there's no sign of her. He sets the pan down on the worktop then walks through to the conservatory; he stands in the doorway and smiles down at her. Her nose is still buried in her book.

'Mother! Dinner is served!'

She nearly jumps out of her skin. 'Yes, d-dear,' she stutters and quickly closes the book. She tries to distract him by smiling up and flicking at her hair while she slips the book beneath the cushion she's been resting her elbow on. 'Didn't realise the time!'

Her cheeks are flushed. She's like a teenager caught with a dirty book. Ivan laughs and strolls across the polished wood floor towards her, wagging his finger. 'Mother, what are you reading?'

She puts her hands to her face, half-masking a look of genuine trepidation. He reaches under the cushion to remove the book, which is quite an effort as she is now sitting on it. He gives it a tug and it comes free.

'Oh dear,' says his mother.

'Jesus, Mother! How could you!' She has been reading *Insanity Fair* by Francesca Brady. He immediately turns on his heel.

'Ivan! I'm so sorry!' She jumps to her feet and gives chase.

'Oh, the shame of it!' Ivan brays as he crosses the hall and enters the lounge.

'Ivan, please! What's got into you?'

'What do you think!' He hurls the book into the roaring fire. There's an immediate, spitting explosion of sparks. 'I will not have this trash in my house!'

'It's not your house!' Mother shouts as she pushes him firmly to one side and kneels down by the fireplace. She lifts a set of tongs and deftly reaches into the flames to remove the smouldering book. She batters it against the hearth to extinguish the few tiny licks of fire that have taken hold, then feverishly pats it down with an old cloth that she keeps on a small hook to clean up occasional avalanches of soot. Then she raises the book and examines it, tutting. The cover is burned and the edges of the pages inside are blackened, but there's not enough damage to render it unreadable. 'Oh you silly boy,' she says.

'How *could* you?' Ivan whines. He slumps down into a chair.

Mother sits on the armrest and shakes her head indulgently at him. 'Because,' she says, 'I was curious. And it's actually quite good. *Very* good, I might be tempted to say.'

'Nobody's tempting you.'

'To tell you the truth, Ivan, it wouldn't do you any harm to take a leaf out of her book.' She gulps. She puts a hand to her chest. 'There,' she says, 'I said it.'

'What *exactly* do you mean?'

'Well . . .'

'Well *what*?'

'Well, she makes the most of herself, doesn't she?'

'Your pasta is ready.'

'Oh Ivan.' She puts a soft hand to his immobile face, and manages to leave an imprint of soot. 'Please, you're my son and I love you and you're a brilliant writer, and I'm so, so proud of you. But . . . well, the world doesn't owe you a living. If it doesn't want what you're selling, then you have to sell it in a different way. She knows that. And what about Tina Turner?'

'*What?*'

'She was a washed-up old boot until Sonny left her.'

'Mum, that was Cher.'

'You see? You're so pernickety and precise and olde worlde. Ivan, you have to start shaking some ass or you won't get anywhere in this world.'

To prove the point, she gives a little shimmy of her own. Then she reaches up and kisses his black cheek. 'Now,' she says, 'that spaghetti smells gorgeous.'

He's pacing, pacing, pacing, and that's quite difficult to do in a study as small as his. He's mad. He's anxious. His heart is racing. He's drunk. He's been a writer all his life, he can't give it up now. What would he do? The *humiliation*. He is working his way steadily through a cardboard box containing a dozen bottles of home-made wine he was presented with for appearing at a tiny literary festival in Dundee. No money, just home-made dandelion wine. *I'll bet Francesca Brady doesn't get paid in fucking wine!*

Still, it isn't bad.

He glares at his mother's copy of *Insanity Fair* – she finished the rest of it off in a couple of dedicated hours after dinner while he fumed and drank – sitting on the windowsill like . . . like blue mould on a crusty loaf, like a rotting haddock making a guest appearance at the top table of a society wedding, like . . . He picks it up.

Flicking through the partially scorched pages, he reads excerpts aloud in a funny voice. He discovers three separate scenes featuring lesbian sex; he learns more than he ever needs to know about designing a hat; there's a bloody suicide with all the gory details. There is more drama in one chapter than there is in the whole of *The Last December*. Doesn't she know anything? Drama has to be earned! This isn't a soap opera! He hurls the book across the room, then slumps down in front of the computer. He has *The Last December* open on the screen before him. He scrolls through it. So much time, so much effort. And it's good, he knows it's good, but what the hell does that matter? Nobody will publish it.

It's not fashionable! It's not trendy! And it's probably too fucking long!

He takes another long swig of his wine, then looks at the page count – four hundred and ninety five. Well fuck that!

With several quick strokes of his mouse Ivan deletes pages 101 to 495. There you go, there's your one hundred pages. Now it's a classic in the making!

He laughs his leg off.

Page 100 now ends abruptly halfway through Chapter 15. Nothing resolved! Nothing even fucking started! But who cares – at least it's short! He types *The End*.

Two can play at your game, Francesca fucking Brady. You think I can't write trash with the best of you? You think I can't earn five million?

Ivan's on a roll now. He clicks on *Find & Replace* and types in Neville, the name of his modest, guilt-ridden hero; he ponders for a moment, then decides on Noreen. He clicks *Replace*, and hey presto, 200 references to Neville become 200 references to Noreen, and with one fair stroke Neville's romance with Lucinda, the highly strung young lady of the manor, has become a hot lesbian affair.

Ivan laughs his other leg off.

He is now completely legless.

Come and read this, Mother! Is this right up your street now? Ivan cracks open another bottle of dandelion. *Isn't this really the sort of crap you're looking for, Mr Winfrey? Something that makes no sense, with added lesbians?*

A title, a new title. *The Last December* is far too stuffy. Something new and fresh, something – what would his father have said, God rest his soul – something *fruity*. *The Last Lesbian* – no, too direct, too obvious. *The Last Supper*, *The Last Kiss*, *Last Kiss with a Lesbian*, *Lipstick Kiss*, *Kiss Me Deadly*, *Kiss My Arse*, he cackles, *The Lady and the Tramp*, *The Tramp*, *Kissing a Tramp*, *Kissing Cousins* . . . *Kissing Cousins* – lesbians with a hint of incest yet it sounds a bit like a musical. Perfect!

Ivan happily types in *Kissing Cousins* by . . .

By . . .

He sits back. He scans the room. Book jackets – that's where he usually finds the names of his characters, amalgamating the names of authors, but he needs something different for this. His eyes fall on the *Sports Illustrated Swimwear Calendar* 1988 which Raymond Carver left him in his will. (It's a long story and knee-tremblingly embarrassing.) He should have taken it down a long time ago, but then he should have done a lot of things. Ivan half-stumbles across to the dusty calendar and lifts it off its hook. He flicks through the pages, an idea battling through the fog which is now starting to roll in fast and thick across his study, and his brain.

Kissing Cousins by . . .

April . . .

May . . .

Kissing Cousins by April May.

He sits back, satisfied.

He saves the novel, then rubs his hands together excitedly. He clicks onto the Internet. This is it! This is it! He has it now! He's going to expose them for the hypocrites they are. He's going to send them *Kissing Cousins* and they're going to adore it, and . . . and . . . then he'll call all the newspapers and vilify them for the capitalist devil spawn they really are!

He spends ten bleary minutes locating the e-mail address for Julia Malone, Chief Editor at Winfrey Books – my God, in all the time he's been published he's never received so much as an e-mail from her! What lack of care! What ignorance! Just a word of encouragement here and there might have made all the difference. Not that he ever uses it himself, e-mail – the nail in the coffin of literary composition. Nobody writes letters any more. It's all about instant communication, instant gratification. But it's so *right* for April May! She's a child of the Web! She will communicate exclusively by e-mail. She's an e-chick!

Ivan types rapidly.

Dear Julia, My name is April May. I am 23 years old and I work as a dancer. It paid for my time in college. I have a degree in Physics, but my first love is literature, so I'm sending you this little old novel to see what you think. He pauses for a moment, looks at the calendar again. *I am also sending you my photo, in case it's of any interest. My friends say I remind them of Madonna.*

Ivan, drunk, forgetful that the calendar – intact and signed, as it is, has not only been a true inspiration to him over the years, but is probably worth more than the advance for his last but one novel – tears the photograph of the model posing in a leather thong on a beach for the month of April, out of its spiral binding, and then tears it again three times along the edge of his desk until he is left with a head and shoulders – *lots* of shoulder – which he places onto the small scanner which goes with his computer and scans it into his e-mail.

Now he will send the lot to Winfrey and sit back and wait to see how they deal with April May – how they faun over someone who's all teeth and tits.

He sits with his finger on the mouse, ready to press *Send*.

Send.

Send it.

Make fools of them.

Make a fool of . . . yourself.

And abruptly his shoulders are shaking and tears begin to cascade down his face.

Oh what a sad bastard you are, he thinks. Washed up. Hopeless. Reduced to desecrating your own work. Reduced to cheap, tatty, sexist jokes.

I was an author! A novelist! The heart of a generation.

Ivan reaches for another swig of dandelion wine, but he's so far gone he knocks the bottle over. The sweet liquid sprays across his computer keyboard. He jumps back in panic, then begins to swat at the keyboard, trying to stop the alcohol soaking into—

Fuck!

There's a hiss and all sorts of jumbled figures are cascading across the computer screen and then there's a distinct smell of burning and then suddenly . . .

BANG!

And the screen itself explodes with enough force to spray glass across the study, glass which might have ripped him to pieces or given him a nasty scratch, if he hadn't already sought refuge under the desk. A coward morally, physically, his desecrated work up in smoke, his life a disaster, no wife, no job, a kidnapper, a fantasist; he doesn't even feel drunk any more. He feels empty, alone; he is the literary equivalent of one of those bottles of wine. Cheap, home-made, lacking flavour, desperately unfashionable but undeniably alcoholic. And like the bottle before him, completely empty.

He crawls out from under his desk and shakes his head wearily at the smouldering ruins of his life.

From the hall comes his mother's voice – she knows better than to enter. 'Ivan, what are you doing in there?'

'Nothing, Mother,' he says, and then adds wearily, 'and I've been doing it for years and years.'

6

Julia Malone arrives at Winfrey Books at around ten each morning, bearing coffee, doughnut and the *Guardian*. People who know her outside of work, if they're honest, might describe her as being rather cool and self-contained, but also a lady who enjoys a drink and is inclined to become bubbly and flirtatious with it. Sometimes, when drunk, and talking to someone who doesn't work in publishing, she will admit that she was the model for *Bridget Jones*, even though it's a complete lie.

At work she's not so much cool and self-contained as Ice Queen, and she never, ever drinks on duty. She's not happy at Winfrey, and it shows. She was seduced, metaphorically speaking, away from Macmillan five years previously with the promise that Winfrey, the sad old man of British publishing, was finally getting its act together and really going places. Well, that lasted for all of about three weeks. She'd come from a company where she'd had three top-five hits in six months; here she'd struggled into the nether regions of the top fifty twice in the past year. She would leave tomorrow if she wasn't sleeping with the boss, Carson Winfrey, Managing Director, heir to the fast dissipating Winfrey fortune, married, kids, the usual story. Julia's in love. Carson's in lust. Usual story, part two. Sometimes she thinks she'll write a book about it, but she knows she hasn't the talent. 'That's why I became an editor,' she cracks to anyone who'll listen.

She drinks the coffee, eats her doughnut, examines the media jobs in the *Guardian*. She almost, *almost* applied for a job a month ago, but balked at the thought of going for an interview. She feels she's reached a certain stage in her life where if she's going anywhere, she's going to bloody well be headhunted, not have to go through the humiliation of applying for a job. Her real problem is that she's thirty-eight and her get up and go long ago got up and left.

Her desk is a mess. She looks at it and tuts. She's been letting things get away from her of late. Sometimes she thinks it's the air conditioning or the pollution or something seeping into the building from the sewers below, some kind of invisible fog which invests everything with gloom and doom. She has half a dozen manuscripts awaiting her attention, but she hasn't the energy to apply herself to them. The most pressing is a novel written by a British-born Hollywood actress; Carson paid half a million for the British rights without setting eyes on the manuscript, then discovered with horror that it was unpublishable – and it has to be pretty damn awful for that to happen.

'But it's not bad if you consider she's dyslexic,' Carson whined when his folly was discovered.

'Dyslexia is an excuse used by cretins who can't read or write to cover their tracks, Carson, you know that,' Julia stormed. 'She isn't dyslexic, she's fucking illiterate. And you're innumerate for paying that much fucking money just because she smiled at you.'

'She didn't smile at me.'

'Yeah.'

It will be saved. They'll apply a ghost writer to it and they'll slap a boob-heavy pic on the front and the critics will destroy it and a few thousand teenagers of all ages will buy it after she's bared her soul and a large part of her cleavage on the TV chat show circuit. It will sell averagely, like everything Winfrey has published of late. And averagely is no longer good enough.

Julia switches on her computer and then clicks onto her e-mail. Most of it is junk these days i.e. unsolicited manuscripts. She curses e-mail sometimes, because once someone has hold of your private e-mail address they can circumnavigate all the usual channels, including the stormtroopers at reception, and put something directly on to your personal computer. As a rule Julia never opens these manuscripts, which come in the form of attachments – well, she has twice in the past, once to find some very hardcore pornography staring her in the face and once to find a virus which crashed the company's entire system for four days.

Today there are half a dozen routine messages which she quickly deals with, and one e-mail with a file attachment. Another no-hoper with a dodgy manuscript. But although she doesn't recognise the e-mail address, the subject is described as *Kissing Cousins* and her first reaction is, *Christ, someone in the family has written a novel. How embarrassing.* The least she can do is open the e-mail and then make her excuses: the perilous state of publishing, the pitifully small remuneration first-time authors receive, the fact that he/she should go and do something worthwhile like organising a concert for Bolivian Indians or weeding gypsy tarmac. She knows she has to reply in some manner, or else she'll be collared at a wedding or dragged across the graveyard at a family funeral and beaten about the head with a ceramic vase.

She opens the e-mail and beholds the photo of April May. Her breath is taken away. My God, Marketing will love this, is her first thought, and then she sighs, because that says it all, really. Teeth over talent.

She reads the e-mail and laughs. Someone with a sense of humour *and* a smile.

Her finger hovers over the attached file. April May, whoever you are, I'm about to blow your cover. She clicks and the manuscript appears on screen. Julia lifts her coffee, checks her watch and decides against her better judgement to give *Kissing Cousins* five minutes of her valuable time.

Carson is lambasting some hapless agent on the phone when Julia appears in the doorway looking flustered. It's a little after lunchtime and he hasn't seen her all day and he's thinking maybe she hasn't forgiven him for the misunderstanding about the olives in bed the previous evening. But no, she's waving at him to get off the line.

'What can I say, Liam?' he barks into the phone. 'The punctuation is great. The paragraphs are nicely symmetrical. But there's no story, nothing fucking happens!'

'He's a stylist, Carson, the last great—' the agent is bleating.

'I want a stylist, I go to the hair salon.' He cups his hand over the receiver and looks at Julia.

'Check your e-mail,' she says.

He nods and clicks it on. Liam continues to whine in his ear. 'Carson, come on, you have to give me a break here. You were best man at my wedding. I can't go back to Martin and—'

Carson puts the phone down. He has just seen the photo of April May. 'Who is *this*?' he asks.

'Isn't she gorgeous? It's probably all make-up, but still . . .'

He turns his attention to the e-mail. 'Oh, my. I thought maybe she was PR – but a novel. *Excellent*.'

'It came in on my private address, so she's obviously agented. I've tried responding but my mail keeps getting returned.'

Carson runs a finger lightly over the picture of April May on his screen. 'Julia, we can sell this. *This* we *can* sell. Find out who the agent is and set up a meeting.'

'You haven't even looked at the manuscript, Carson.'

'I don't need to. If she has an agent then somebody likes it, and that's good enough for me. Besides, look at her. It'll be like selling sand to the Arabs.'

'Don't you mean water to the Arabs?'

'Get off your high horse, Julia, and phone the agent.'

She flushes. She won't stand for other people talking

to her like that. In fact, they wouldn't dare – but there's something about the way Carson humiliates a girl that makes her feel all warm, inside and out.

Campbell arrives at Ivan's house at a little after three. It's a cold, autumnal day and the air is full of the smell of burning leaves and the burning unpublished ramblings of a formerly published author. Ivan's mother shows him through the house and then gestures forlornly down the garden to where Ivan is standing incinerating old manuscripts, story ideas, letters and reviews. The remains of his computer have also gone on to the fire, creaking and shrieking as they bent and buckled in the heat.

'How's he doing?' Campbell asks.

Mother shakes her head. 'I hope you've come to cheer him up,' she says.

Campbell rolls his eyes and goes out of the kitchen into the long, well-maintained garden with a path of stepping stones leading down to where Ivan's staring into the flames. Campbell comes up beside him and stands, also staring into the flames.

'I can't hear the birds singing any more,' Ivan says. 'It's like Auschwitz.'

'No, Ivan, Auschwitz was a concentration camp. This is Peckham. What you're hearing – or not hearing as the case may be – is migration.'

'I was being metaphorical.'

'Well, I probably guessed that.' Campbell smiles wanly, then points at the flames. 'So what're you up to?'

'The heart of a generation just expired. This is the cremation.'

Ivan looks pale and tired and drawn. He's stubbled and red-eyed. Campbell feels a pang of compassion. Ivan picks up another handful of pages from a large cardboard box at his feet and throws them onto the fire.

'I own ten per cent of those,' Campbell says.

'Fifteen on foreign sales.'

They look at each other and smile. Campbell reaches into his jacket and removes his wallet. He flips it open, peers inside, then removes half a dozen small business cards. 'Campbell Foster, Literary Agent,' he reads, then flicks them against his fingers for a second before tossing them into the fire. 'It's the end of the road, Ivan,' he says.

'I admire the solidarity, Campbell, but won't your other clients be upset?' Campbell looks at him with sad brown eyes, and Ivan realises. 'Oh,' he says.

'I was thrown out of my office last week,' Campbell tells him. 'My landlord's another one who puts money before art. It's just no fun any more.'

Ivan puts a hand on Campbell's shoulder and squeezes. 'Have you ever,' he says very seriously, 'tried dandelion wine?'

Julia is at her desk, looking frazzled and frustrated. She's on the phone to yet another agent.

'What's the name again?'

'April May. The book is *Kissing Cousins*.'

'No, sorry. Not one of ours. What's the panic?'

'Oh nothing, just lost track of it. Usual hack job. Thanks anyway.'

She dials again. And again. And again. There are a lot of ten-percenters out there.

'Julia, good to hear from you. You're calling about *Kissing Cousins*, aren't you?'

A sigh of relief – *inward, don't give the game away*. 'Yes, I am. We've a couple of thousand left in our fiction budget for this year, Tony – thought I might take a gamble on it. Either that or I lose the money to Education, and we can't have that.' She forces a laugh. 'So what do you say? I'm willing to take a shot at—'

Tony sniggers.

'Okay,' she says, 'we're reasonably serious about it.'

'Sorry, Julia. We don't have *Kissing Cousins* or April May.'

'Then what the fuck—'

'Look, the wires are burning up with *Kissing Cousins*. This is the third call I've had about it this morning. Every publisher in town's desperate to get a copy of it and nobody's admitting to having it. But *you* have it.'

'Yes, of course I have it.'

'What's it *like*?'

'It's okay.'

'Julia, the truth.'

'I am telling the truth.'

'I hear it's the best thing anyone's read in twenty years. I hear it redefines the novel. I believe the sex is fantastic. I believe April May is a stunner. Whoever has her is going to make a million overnight in commission alone . . . but you have the book Julia, why don't you know who her agent is?'

'Blip in our computers. I just thought you were the most likely. I'll sort it out in a minute.'

'If she doesn't have an agent, she needs one, you know

that; she needs to be protected. I can do that. I'll even do it for five per cent. Do you hear me, *five*. I've never gone that low in my life.'

Julia says she'll see what she can do and hangs up.

When she checks her voicemail there are calls from forty-three other agents. She checks them off against those whom she has already called, and then examines her list of agents again. There is only one agent in London she hasn't yet contacted and only one agent who hasn't called her seeking to represent April May. *Of course.* She sighs again, and picks up the phone.

Ivan is wearing his big winter coat, and Campbell his summer sports jacket. Both are in deckchairs set out before the dying embers of the fire in Ivan's mother's back garden. They have drunk three bottles of dandelion wine between them and were both adamant that it was having no effect on them whatsoever until Ivan fell suddenly asleep and then Campbell, in trying to wake him up, lapsed into a coma mid-sentence.

Campbell is only brought around by the vibration of his mobile phone. He opens his eyes, trying to locate the source of the annoyance, and then gradually his half-frozen hand snakes into his jacket pocket and removes the phone. He barks a gruff, 'What?' into it.

'Campbell? This is Julia Malone at Winfrey . . .'

The connection is reasonably good, but Campbell has dandelions in his ears. He gets to his feet and bellows, 'Whaaat?!' into the phone.

Julia, at the other end, is girding her loins, about to mount her version of a charm offensive. April May. She's jittery with adrenalin and coffee. She knows big things will come of this if she can just reel Campbell in. She'll be back at the top of the tree. Number one on both sides of the Atlantic. The word is already out. And it's all her own work.

'Campbell, before you say anything, I just want you to forget our last little upset. That's all water under the bridge as far as I'm concerned. In the words of the blessed Margaret, "tomorrow is another day", but I say there's no time like the present.'

'What the—'

'I've only two words to say to you. April. May.'

Campbell, with one finger in his ear, trying to clear the fog, gets that much at least, but it still makes no sense.

'And I've only two words to say to you, Julia. Fuck. Off.'

He kills the line, then looks at the phone for a moment. He laughs gently to himself, then tosses it into the fire. When he turns back he sees that a loose page has blown across and set fire to Ivan's coat.

Carson is standing at his window, with its fine panoramic views of London, thinking about his wife, his lover, his children, his business – about ten seconds apiece, perfect time management – when his office door flies open again and there's Julia looking hot and bothered and excited – and he hasn't even laid a finger on her. He chortles quietly to himself.

'Campbell has it!' she shouts. 'He's playing hardball!'

Carson waves a calming hand at her. 'Shhhh,' he says. 'Settle down. Take a seat.'

'But Carson—'

'Sit.'

She sits.

'Let's have a drink to celebrate,' he says coolly.

'Celebrate?'

'Well, if Campbell Foster has her, then we can do a deal. Campbell's an intelligent man. He knows which side his bread is buttered on.' He's pouring a couple of Cointreaux.

'You don't understand, Carson – we have to get on to this! Word's out – the pack's after it.'

'Yes, so I heard.'

'You heard?'

'Mmmm. I had Felix on from New York. He's keen as mustard. Already talking to the coast. Says he got a fax back from Dreamworks seven minutes after he called them.'

'Christ.'

'Exactly. But the fact of the matter is, Julia, that we mustn't rush into this. We are, are we not, the only company to have been sent this masterpiece?'

'As far as I'm aware.'

'Well, what does that tell us?'

'That we're getting preferential treatment.'

'Exactly.'

'But why would Campbell give *us* preferential treatment?'

'Because, Julia,' Carson says, bringing the drinks across, 'Campbell is a romantic. He's not in publishing for the money, he's in it because he's cultured and educated and thinks he's helping the cause of English Literature by acting as wetnurse to any number of struggling artists – like Ian Connor. In Winfrey Books he sees the last of the great family-owned British publishing companies, and even though we've had our run-ins, he recognises the importance of giving us a leg up in our time of difficulty. He's not thinking of himself, he's thinking of the greater good of British publishing. Do you know what that makes him, Julia?'

'A fool?'

'Right first time. And we must exploit that mercilessly. Julia, my dear, this company is going back on the map, all the way to the top of the tree.' He places a loving hand on her knee, then kisses her moist lips. Just as she starts to respond he breaks off. 'However, despite being a fool, he's not a complete idiot. Just because he's offering us first bite at the pie, doesn't mean he's going to give us the whole melon. We have to hit him with a huge pre-emptive offer, something he won't be able to vacillate over. We'll start at one, we can go as high as three.'

'Million?'

'Of course. We can't afford to let this get away.'

'But *three*? Won't the accountants . . .'

'Bugger the accountants, as they are buggering me. We'll spend this money and we'll make it back tenfold.'

'What if we don't get it back?'

'Then we're buggered anyway. Julia, *everything* is resting on this. We have to make it work.'

7

Julia has every confidence in Carson; if anyone can make this work, he can. He can be an ogre, but he can also turn on the charm like a tap, and in such a way that it doesn't feel as if it's being turned on like a tap. They take a cab across town to Campbell's office. As they sit in the back he rests his hand on her thigh, and although she doesn't look around she smiles as she stares out of the window.

Campbell's office is on the third floor of a four-storey building in Golden Square. The lift isn't working. Carson marches directly up the stairs, not waiting for Julia, who's struggling in her heels. When she finally catches up with him he is standing in an open doorway shaking his head. As she comes up beside him she understands why. The office is empty. Completely empty. No furniture, no anything. Just bare space.

'Christ,' says Julia.

'He's moved offices on the strength of a book he hasn't even sold,' Carson whistles.

'What balls,' Julia says.

'It's not enough,' Carson decides.

'What isn't enough?'

'One to three. We'll have to go to four.'

'Carson . . .'

'What choice do we have?'

His voice is anguished. She feels such compassion for him. He's strong but weak. One half Rock of Gibraltar, one half marshmallow. She loves him dearly. She puts her arms around him.

'Don't,' he says, brushing her away. 'We have to get to Campbell.'

Julia's not hurt by it. He's a man of action. She understands. She pulls out her mobile and calls Directory Enquiries for Carson's new office number. She draws a blank.

'Christ, he's confident,' she tells Carson. 'Most people playing hard to get would go unlisted, make us chase them, but not too hard. Campbell's not unlisted, Carson, he's *disconnected*. There's no account anywhere. I called Bernie at the Groucho – he hasn't seen Campbell in weeks, heard he's gone out of business.'

'God, he's clever.' Carson taps his fingers against the office door. 'Okay. If Mohammed can't dial the mountain, then Mohammed will have to go and see him. Where is he?'

'Where is he what?'

'Where is he living?'

'Christ, Carson, I don't know. He's an agent, I don't socialise with him.'

'Well, maybe you should think about it. Look what

he's got – April May. Julia, you should know this kind of stuff. Campbell may be itching to give us *Kissing Cousins*, but what if somebody gets to the author before we do our deal? *She* may not support art over money, you know.'

'I'm sorry, Carson.'

'Get Campbell's home address. We're going there now, and we'll wait all night for him if we have to.'

Eventually they have to let the taxi go, so they repair to a wine bar just around the corner from Campbell's house. Every twenty minutes Carson makes Julia click-click around the corner to see if there are any lights on. After her fourth trip she finally protests.

'Why don't you go for a change?'

'Because if I start hanging around outside people's houses they'll think I'm a pervert or something.'

'While it's okay for me to look like a prostitute?'

'You don't look like a prostitute. And even if you did, I'd pay good money for you.'

'Carson, I know you're trying to compliment me, but please don't. I am in charge of our Feminist list.'

'Not for long.'

'What's that supposed to mean?'

'Feminism went out with the ark. Just look at April May. Women don't care any more. They're as likely to pick up a book with breasts on the cover as a man is. Feminisim is irrelevant, and a Feminist list is doubly irrelevant.'

'I've spent three years building that list.'

'And it doesn't sell shit. I'm sorry, Julia, I know I'm

being brutally honest with you – but I feel I can be that with you.'

'As opposed to being honest with your wife.'

'Now there's no need for that.'

Julia takes the manuscript she printed off her computer from her bag and sits reading it. They've been in the wine bar for four hours, but they haven't had any wine. Carson thinks it would make a bad impression to go in even smelling vaguely of alcohol. This is the most important business deal of his life, and he has to be on top form. So they've been drinking Diet Cokes and farting quietly.

Carson checks his text messages, then stares out into the gloom, into the early-evening traffic. He's the Managing Director and major shareholder of the most famous name in British publishing; he shouldn't be sitting in a wine bar in Peckham at the beck and call of some lucky bastard agent. He glances across at Julia, lost in the manuscript, then back at the traffic.

'God damn him!' he says suddenly and slaps the table. 'Where the hell is he?'

Two questions, loud, and Julia doesn't even look up.

'Julia?' he says. Still no response. He reaches across the table and touches her arm, and she jumps.

'What?'

'You're miles away.'

'Sorry – the manuscript.'

'Don't worry about it. We can *fix* it. You think *Catch 22* arrived fully formed? You speak to Felix. His dad edited *Catch 22* and you know what that was when it came in – dull as dishwater and as funny as a fire in an orphanage. Felix's dad told him, "Stick some jokes in" and Bob's your uncle. I'm telling you, we'll get somebody decent on to *Kissing Cousins* and then—'

'Carson, there isn't a problem with the story. It's really good.'

'*Seriously?*'

'Seriously. It's sensational. I mean, it's unlike anything I've read before.'

'You mean difficult. I can't be having any of that *Captain Corelli* nonsense.'

'No, it's not difficult. It just kind of draws you in – it's so refreshing. And so . . . I hate people who use the word zany, but it *is* zany – and whoever heard of a zany historical novel before? I mean, it's about these lesbians, okay, but one of them keeps talking about her penis—'

'Get down!' Carson bellows suddenly, and ducks beneath the table.

'Carson?'

But then Julia glances out of the window and sees Campbell labouring along the pavement outside with several shopping bags. She quickly lifts a menu off the table and holds it up to her face. In a moment he has passed, looking nowhere near the wine bar. Julia watches him go. He's an agent, all right – might be sitting on a fortune, but likes to give the impression of being a sad divorcé with two cents to his name. Without knowing that she has struck the nail firmly on the head, she puts the menu down, then tidies the manuscript.

'It's okay to come up now,' she says. 'He's gone.'

'I was just admiring the view,' Carson says as he rises slowly, and Julia blushes.

*   *   *

Campbell, with a same-day hangover, arrives home at a little after 9 p.m. clutching the groceries he has spent an hour over in Safeway's, groggily pushing his trolley along the aisles while fully aware that he has plenty of food in the house but he has *nothing else to do*. Chief amongst his purchases are various titbits for his two Jack Russells, Ben and Jerry.

He owns his terraced house, although he has never felt that he really does own it – certainly the 10 per cents he makes couldn't have bought him this large a house – because he was left it in his father's will. There is something about earning a house that gives you more pride in its upkeep. He has had it for twenty years, no paint, barely cleaned, and he's now as old as his father was when he dropped dead from a heart attack. This worries him, although not enough to stop him drinking like a fish and eating all the crap of the day.

There's a ring at the door. The dogs fly towards it, barking. Campbell shushes them, slips a finger through Ben's collar, then pulls Jerry over and slips another finger through his so that he's holding them both with the one hand, then opens the door with the other.

'Hello, Campbell,' Julia says.

Campbell blinks at her, then at Carson. Ben and Jerry are yapping and straining, desperate for a bite at a publisher.

'Not tonight thanks,' Campbell says, then shuts the door.

Except Carson puts his foot in the way and the door scrapes a line across the front of his expensive Oxford brogue. 'Campbell, please, we have to talk.'

'You've got the biggest balls in town,' Julia adds.

Campbell stares at her.

'We just want five minutes,' Carson says urgently.

'I'm not interested. It's over.'

'Two million,' Carson blurts.

'What?'

'Two-five.'

'We will kill for this, Campbell,' Julia says.

'I don't know what you're talking about.'

'Chicks with dicks!' Carson shouts, now hardly able to contain himself. 'Three million, that's our absolute final offer!'

'I honestly don't—'

'Four!'

Carson says it with such desperation that Campbell hesitates, then sighs and shakes his head. 'Okay,' he says, opening the door fully. 'You've got five minutes.'

'Yep. That top one. Just open it up and put it in the dish.'

Campbell is sitting at a small table down in the basement, while Carson is opening a tin of dog food for Ben and Jerry, and Julia is filling their bowls with water from the tap. Campbell's enjoying this. He no longer has anything to lose.

Carson puts the food down in front of the dogs, but then hesitates before joining Campbell at the table. 'Might I suggest adjourning to somewhere more conducive to—'

'Dogs and publishers stay in the basement,' Campbell says dryly.

'Oh Campbell,' Julia says, taking her seat, 'you're so wicked.'

Campbell smiles without humour. 'Well?' he says, then glances at his watch and looks expectantly at them.

'Well,' Carson repeats, and then for a moment he's lost for words. He's not used to being in this situation.

Julia steps quickly in. 'We love April.'

Campbell nods. 'So do I.'

Carson now leans forward across the table. 'April May is something very special.'

'Yes. It's a wonderful time.'

'For all of us I hope,' Julia says.

Campbell finds the conversation profound, and confusing. He examines his fingernails. Julia glances at Carson and nods.

'We can't go beyond four, Campbell, but I promise you this, we will pull out all the stops on this one. We will put everything we have into April.'

'What about May?' Campbell asks.

Julia thumps the table, making them both jump in surprise, not to mention the dogs, who bark, but then quickly return to their food. 'God dammit Campbell, stop playing with us. April May has everything, she's the double whammy we've been praying for. She's beautiful and she writes like a tarnished angel. I would work on this for nothing. Campbell, please, I've waited my whole career for *Kissing Cousins*.'

Carson stares at Julia, and then at Campbell; Campbell stares at Julia, and then at Carson, and then back to Julia. Then *he* thumps his fist down on the table and all three of them jump, not to mention the dogs, who bark again. 'Right,' says Campbell, getting to his feet. 'I've had enough of this nonsense. I don't know what kind of drugs you're on, or what sort of a joke you're trying to pull, but I'm not falling for it, I'm out of this sordid little business, I don't have to deal with corpulent fucks like you any more. I want you out of the house right now!'

Julia, astonished by the confidence of Campbell's brinkmanship but also distraught that she might really be on the verge of losing *Kissing Cousins*, and beginning to believe that he could just possibly be extracting some sort of perverted revenge for their previous rejection of Ivan Connor, suddenly opens her handbag, pulls out the manuscript and slaps it down on the table. 'This is dynamite, Campbell!' she shouts. 'Please forgive us! We must have it!'

Campbell is surprised, but he is an agent through and through and knows enough not to betray his emotions, even in marriage. He runs his fingers through his hair, he blows air out of his cheeks, then sighs and gives them a roll of his eyes that says, *Okay, you're on your final, final chance*. He sits down again, and Carson smiles at Julia in relief.

'Thank you, Campbell,' Carson says. 'I know we can work something out. This really is an unutterably wonderful book.'

Campbell lifts the manuscript. 'I can't remember whether this is an early draft I sent you,' he says.

Julia is salivating. 'You mean there's a better draft? Oh, I'm coming out in goosebumps.'

Campbell reads the title aloud. '*Kissing Cousins*. Good story?' he enquires innocently.

'Brilliant,' Julia says.

'Defies description,' adds Carson.

Campbell turns to the opening page and begins to read. His eyes flick up to Carson and Julia. He reads some more, then turns to the next page, a smile of recognition gradually unfurling across his face. He begins to laugh, a slow chuckle at first, but then quickly building into a big, comic-book guffaw. And the more he laughs, the more distressed his visitors look, and the dogs begin to whine.

'We can work something out, can't we, Campbell?' Carson says hesitantly.

Campbell shakes his head in disbelief. 'Oh you blithering idiots. Don't you realise what you have here? It's—'

'Six million!' Carson bellows. Julia looks at him in shock. 'Final, final, final offer, Campbell. I know we've messed you about in the past, but we need this, we *must* have this.'

Campbell looks to see if he's joking or not, but the look is so deadly serious, his eyes are so enlarged, the veins pulsing out of his temples – and Julia has her mouth open and her cheeks flushed, and her hand on her chest as if her heart might explode.

They're serious.

They're deadly serious.

Campbell slowly clasps his hands before him. 'Well,' he says after a suitably dramatic pause, 'it's certainly an interesting opening offer.'

8

Campbell doesn't sleep a wink, of course. He opens a bottle of red wine and thinks and thinks and thinks, and he finally crashes into bed at about four but he can't stop his head from spinning.

What is Ivan trying to pull off?

And why didn't he consult me, his dearest friend for twenty years? Campbell pauses. *His dearest friend who can't get him published any more. Has he betrayed me, or is he trying to shield me from the consequences of being involved in such a charade?*

Campbell has been an agent for twenty years and has never negotiated a deal that came anywhere near what Winfrey are now offering for the mysterious April May. His commission on six million is six hundred thousand pounds! And that's just for British and Commonwealth rights. That still leaves the rest of the world!

It was never about money – but still.

He's up and dressed for seven, then takes the dogs for a quick walk. Once he's sorted them out with food he's away to Ivan's with as much speed as he can muster in the traffic. He parks outside and when Mrs Connor answers the door she looks surprised to see him. 'You've never been here before lunch before, Campbell. What's the emergency?'

And she knows it is important because he doesn't joke the way he usually does.

'Nothing,' Campbell says bluntly. 'Is he in?'

'No.'

'Damn.' *He's with another agent.*

'He's over at the pond.'

Campbell glances across the road. He can just about see Ivan in the distance, crouching down by the side of a pond.

'I hope he's not planning to do anything silly,' his mother says.

'Ivan?'

'He's been very down.'

'Well,' Campbell says. 'I'll have a word.'

He waits for a gap in the traffic, then hurries across to the green. As he draws close he sees that Ivan has half a loaf of bread, which he's breaking up and feeding to the ducks. He glances up as Campell approaches, but there's no greeting; no good mornings, no how are you's, they know each other too well for that. It is a good measure of their friendship that they can be happily silent with each other. But you don't need a friend as an agent, you need a Rottweiler. Campbell knows this. He has been thinking about it overnight. He's been everyone's friend for too long – now he has to show what he's made of.

Ivan throws more bread into the pond. 'In the summer,' he says, 'kids come and throw bread in every day. Too much. The ducks get fat and bloated and can't eat any more, but they keep throwing more in. It just rots. Come the autumn and the kids are away back to school, then nobody but me comes and feeds them. I think they love me. I'm an honorary duck.'

'Your mum's worried you're going to throw yourself in.'

'Mother?' He glances momentarily back at the house. 'Is that why you're here? Because if you're a rapid response unit from the Samaritans then I'm in deeper trouble than I thought.' He smiles weakly; he stares for several moments into the murky pond. 'Don't worry about me, friend, I'm much too shallow to drown.'

'I didn't say I was worried.'

'Do you know why I have two children?'

'What?'

'Do you know why I had two kids, instead of one?'

'No, Ivan.'

'Because I wanted a second in case something happened to the first. Or vice versa. What do you think that says about me?'

Campbell shrugs. 'I buy half a dozen tins of beans when I go to Tesco's in case I run out. I buy twice as many sausages as I need in case I get caught short. You're not so strange.'

'Children are not beans and sausages.'

'Well, there's two schools of thought on that.'

Ivan finishes the last of the bread, then stands. He thrusts his hands into his long coat, which is badly burned around the hem, then smiles down at the ducks quacking happily in the water, and also at those braver few pecking around his feet.

'You need a job,' Ivan says.

'What, like you, Defender of the Ducks?'

'You'd need to get your own pond. This is mine.'

'I have a job. I'm a literary agent.'

'I thought you gave that up.'

'I did. But I have a new client.'

Ivan nods for several moments. 'I'm not hurt or any-thing, if that's what you're thinking, if that's why you're here. You were entitled to start again once you got rid of the dead wood.'

'It's not like that, Ivan.'

'I don't mind.'

'It's only the one client.'

'That's fine by me.'

'Her name is April May.'

Ivan blinks for several moments, while Campbell watches him closely.

'Who?'

'April May. She wrote *Kissing Cousins*. You may have heard of it.'

Ivan's brow is completely furrowed. It's like the vaguest kind of déjà vu. April May? *Kissing Cousins*?

'I quite understand why you did it,' Campbell con-tinues. 'I know I wasn't getting you the business. You had to show me the way, but now I've seen it, and they've seen it, we can do this together if you'll give me one last chance.'

'What the hell are you talking about?'

'Ivan, we've been friends for twenty years.'

'I know we have, but how do you know about April May?'

'Ivan – *everyone* knows about April May.'

'But—'

'She's the talk of the publishing world.'

'But—'

'My phone is ringing off the hook, and I don't have a phone.'

'But—'

'It's the most talked-about book in London. Not to mention New York.'

'Campbell, are you winding me up?'

'Why would I wind you up?'

'Because April May is a figment of my imagination. She doesn't exist.'

'Yes, I know.'

'I was only doodling. I was drunk. I didn't print it out or anything. She went up in flames, I—'

'You did something.'

'I was only messing. I was going to send it to Winfrey for a laugh. But then I caught myself on and I didn't send it.'

'Somebody did.'

'No, it was never printed, it was just on my e-mail, and then . . .' *Christ*. He remembers the wine spilling clearly enough, the computer short-circuiting. Surely it couldn't have just sent it itself, a reflex action before it exploded. He slaps the top of his own head. 'Oh God,' he says.

'Oh God indeed.'

'I'm so embarrassed. They must think I'm such a sad fool.'

'Au contraire.'

'I'll never be able to hold my head up in a public library again.'

'Winfrey love the book, they're determined to publish.'

'But it doesn't make any sense. They can't have read it – it's gibberish.'

'They've made a pre-emptive offer of six million pounds.'

Ivan blinks for several moments. Then pats his pockets. 'Do you have a pen?'

They repair to a small café – next to a wine bar – around the corner. It's too early for wine, or even champagne, neither of them are that bad. It's a workers' café. They order big fry-ups and strong coffee. Ivan's down in the dumps again after an ecstatic five seconds when he pictured himself the richest and most successful author in the world, a girl on each arm and a best-seller on either side of the Atlantic. Now he realises the stupidity of even thinking about it, and the absolute certainty that even if they did think about it, they couldn't possibly get away with it.

'Campbell, you're getting carried away. I did something stupid when I was drunk. You should just tell them.'

'But it's a stroke of genius! It's subversion, anarchy, it makes a mockery of the whole publishing business. It exposes its inherent hypocrisy, its championing of image over content, shiny teeth over polished prose.'

'Okay, so maybe we – I – have exposed something that we knew all along. It's hardly front-page news.'

'Six million for a first novel is!'

'But it's not a first novel, it's—'

'It's *April's* first novel.'

'She doesn't exist!'

'Yes, she does! You created her!'

Ivan sighs and drums his fingers on the table.

'It's one million on signing,' Campbell says, 'two million on hardcover publication and three on paperback.'

'Less ten per cent.'

'Fifteen for overseas.' He smiles. 'Ivan, this is too great an opportunity to pass up. You'd regret it for the rest of your life. And it's still your creation. April May and *Kissing Cousins* – they're both yours, they're living proof of your genius. We must run with this!'

'I just don't—'

'Ivan, they're desperate! We're going to be rich beyond our . . . and of course we'll be subverting the system, and we'll be striking a blow for authors everywhere.'

'You're getting carried away. I mean, even if I condoned this . . . outright *fraud* . . . you'd have to be a blind man in a coal mine not to realise I'm not exactly April May.'

'But you can be!'

'This isn't *Tootsie*.'

'Yes, it is! Look, Ivan – celebrities, actors, sportsmen, they hire ghost writers, then pass books off as their own, and nobody accuses *them* of fraud, do they?' Ivan shakes his head warily. 'Okay, so what if we just reverse the process a little bit. We hire some – for want of a better word, and in a strictly non-sexist sense – babe to pretend to be April May. We tie her into a secrecy agreement, slip her some cash and everyone's happy. It *could* work.'

Ivan looks at him doubtfully. 'But then *I* will be a fraud. I poured everything I had into that book,' he goes on, 'all of me. Now it's just a mockery of what I intended. It doesn't even make sense. I mean, the lesbians have—'

'Dicks – yes, I heard. But that's the beauty of it.' He suddenly grasps Ivan's hand across the table. It's not the sort of place where men grab each other's hands, so Ivan quickly pulls his away. 'Look, Ivan, think about it. So many things that we have come to regard as works of genius either don't really make sense either, or happened by accident.'

'For example?' Ivan asks doubtfully.

'Like . . . penicillin! What was that, but a mouldy old fungus! Do you think he – whoever the hell he was – started complaining about his slides or his plates being messed up by fungus? No, he went with it, he changed the world by accident. Or photography, a complete mistake, you know that story. And if we're talking books – *Finnegans Wake*. I mean, what's that all about?'

Ivan is about to say it's a classic, but then he realises it's a bit long.

'I'll tell you what it is!' Campbell exclaims, warming to his subject. 'Old James Joyce was going blind, so he dictated the whole thing to his girlfriend. She was not only over-scxed and stupid, but dyslexic as well. So this manuscript, absolute gibberish, goes to the publisher, he doesn't understand a word of it . . . so what does he do? Throw it in the trash or hail it as a new art form?' He raises an eyebrow at Ivan, who nods submissively. 'Exactly! Ivan, you've stumbled upon something, something profound, so don't walk away from it. Be proud. You're a genius. And you're also going to be very, very rich indeed.'

Slowly, slowly Ivan nods.

'Less ten per cent,' he says.

'Fifteen on foreign,' Campbell replies.

9

Carson is drawing up the contracts personally – well, he's supervising the man who's supervising the drawing up of the contracts – while Julia is working twenty-two hours a day editing the manuscript of *Kissing Cousins*. And it's such a joy for her. A wonderful, original, barrier-busting fresh daisy of a book – and one *she* has discovered. An air of elation now permeates Winfrey Books, even though the project is officially being kept strictly under wraps, at least for the next few days. But everyone knows and everyone is smiling because happy days are here again. Soon they'll host a press conference to launch April May and her book on the world. Normally a novel can take more than a year to meander into print, but they'll pull all the stops out for this one. They'll have it on the shelves in two months, max – *not that it will remain on the shelves for long!* Word of mouth is already causing booksellers to besiege central ordering. It could become the first novel to sell a million before it's even published! Christ, they're making Amazon look like a stream! Carson is smiling all the time now, and has told Julia he will definitely leave his wife if the book is a hit. She somehow construes this to be a wonderful confirmation of their love.

But God love her, she's happy.

Poor Ivan, he lacks confidence in the masterplan. But Campbell's fired up.

They make an odd sight, sitting in Ivan's lounge, interviewing actresses for the position of April May, bestselling novelist.

Campbell's small advert in *The Stage – Beautiful Actress Required for Difficult Undercover Role* – has elicited some one hundred and fifty replies. Acting, as ever, is a precarious occupation. All of these responses include a standard head and shoulder shot, known in the agenting trade as 'a mutton', and a cv, which Campbell has been advised to treat with a bucket of salt.

Ivan catches on fast. 'So, when it says *starred with Bruce Willis in* Hudson Hawk, it actually means *was in crowd scene in* Hudson Hawk, *which ended up on cutting-room floor.*'

'Exactly.'

They've been interviewing all morning and Ivan is already slumped down in his seat in despair.

'This is never going to work.'

'Yes, it will. As soon as we find the right girl.'

'We're never going to find the right girl.'

'Yes, we are. Some of them have been very beautiful.'

'Yes, they have.'

'And some of them have been very bright.'

'Yes, they have. But we're never going to find the one that has the other.'

'It can't be that difficult. There are thousands of bright and beautiful women out there.'

'Yes, and they're all working. We're left trying to sort the chaff from the chaff.'

The door opens and Mother, who has been persuaded to wear the closest she has to a smart business suit, though in fact she looks like she's going to a wedding, comes through with the next actress on the list. 'Mona Kildare,' Mother says.

'Mona, have a seat,' says Campbell, smiling.

Ivan studies her photo, then passes it to Campbell. He wonders why Mona has sent in a photograph of her daughter. Ivan picks up her cv.

Mona is twenty-three going on thirty-eight. She has worked on stage in Manchester and Glasgow; she has played several small television roles in *Brookside* and *Taggart*. She takes a seat and crosses her legs and smiles. Her hair is dirty-blonde and her complexion is pale with exaggerated worry lines.

'I'm sure you're wondering what this is all about,' Campbell says.

'I'm intrigued.'

'Well, you've signed the confidentiality agreement, haven't you?'

'That was the—'

'The form my moth— Office Manager asked you to sign.'

'Oh right, is that what it was?' She laughs. 'Didn't really read it. I'll sign anything, me. Apart from a cheque.' She giggles.

'Well, in simple terms, we're looking for a bright and vivacious personality who can act as the public face of our company.'

'I see. Well, that's a change. I thought it might have been the porn again.'

'Excuse me?'

'Oh you wouldn't believe what's out there. I was all ready to give you both a blow job the moment I walked in. It's such a relief not to have to.'

'I . . .' Campbell begins, red-faced.

'See, I've been caught out before, being offered jobs like this. You give the guys a blow job, then they turn round and say you're not quite what they had in mind. Of course I've learned my lesson by now. One swallow doesn't make a summer, if you know what I mean.'

'Yes, of course,' says Campbell, clearing his throat.

'I see from your cv,' Ivan begins, desperate to contribute something, 'that you've performed in Manchester and, er, Glasgow. What were you appearing in?'

'The buff, mostly.'

'I'm sorry?'

'Manchester was *Flashdancers* and Glasgow was *Soho Nights*.'

Campbell and Ivan both look blankly at her.

'Lapdancing.'

'Ah.'

'Right.'

'Strictly no touching.'

'Of course.'

'Touch my arse and the bouncers rip your head off.'

'I'm sure it must have been . . .' Ivan trails off, not quite
sure what it must have been.

'Anyway,' Campbell says, 'this position requires . . .'

'I don't regret any of it, got me my big break.'

'Your . . . ?'

'I was dancing for this guy, a real gent, said he was a
movie producer – adult movies he said, told me right up
front. I like that in a man, no messin' about.'

'Commendable,' Campbell says.

'So he gave me this audition, right there and then.'

'Anyway,' Campbell says, 'this position requ . . .'

'Made me get down on the floor and fake this massive
orgasm. It's my party piece now. That cow Meg Ryan
doesn't have a clue.'

Mona suddenly starts moaning. She throws her head
back, she runs her fingers through her hair.

Campbell looks at Ivan, who is staring steadfastly at the
ground.

'Mona, please,' he tries.

'Pleeeeease,' she purrs in reply.

Her breathing becomes faster, she's letting out little grunts. Her hands are on her legs but not moving,
in fact she's sitting remarkably still. It's only her head
that's lolling forward, twisting around, being flung back.
Campbell isn't sure whether she's a wonderful free spirit
of an actress or psychotic.

Now her mouth is open and her tongue is shooting in
and out. She's barking.

Literally.

The lounge door opens and Mother looks in. She looks out again.

There's sweat rolling down Mona's brow, her hair is growing damp; even though her body remains still, the chair she sits in begins to vibrate. Then she suddenly lets go with a massive howl, which freezes Campbell and Ivan in their seats. She throws her head back one final time, then slumps forward, breathing hard.

There are several long moments when nothing can be heard beyond Mona's heavy breathing and the slight tick-tock of the clock on the mantelpiece.

Slowly Mona raises her head and looks from Campbell to Ivan and back. She smiles, almost sweetly.

'Well,' Campbell says, 'thank you for coming.'

They're not all like that, of course. Mostly they're eager young actresses looking for their break, any break, and this might just be the one.

Ivan is terribly depressed by it all. 'Nobody reads books any more,' he says.

'Nonsense,' Campbell comforts.

'How they even read scripts baffles me. They haven't a clue, Campbell.'

'Suzie Major,' Mother says, showing another one in.

Campbell smiles at the actress as she takes her seat, but before he can launch into the niceties Ivan launches into his own.

'Do you read many books, Suzie?' he asks.

'Oh yes,' she says, her hair in plaits. 'I read all the time. All the time.'

'What about *Finnegans Wake*?'

'I'm sorry, I didn't even know he was dead.'

If she'd followed it with a laugh, it would have been just about bearable, but she just smiles, eager to please. When Ivan thinks it can't get any worse, she adds: 'Were you very close?'

Ivan jumps up out of his seat and stalks into the kitchen.

'Ivan!' Campbell calls after him.

'Oh dear,' Suzie says. 'I'm always putting my feet in it. Was it very sudden?'

'Ivan!'

At about four in the afternoon, twenty-three girls interviewed and rejected, Ivan and Campbell sit in the kitchen around a pot of tea.

'Pointless,' Ivan says. 'Pointless and stupid.'

Campbell nods grimly. 'I have to admit,' he says, 'it has been a bit of a let-down.'

'Who do we think we are?'

'I know.'

'We're messing with things we know nothing about. We built ourselves up like Cameron Mackintosh but ended up Walter Mitty. I've never, ever got away with anything in my life. Tube tickets, double yellow lines, cheating on a girlfriend, I always get caught. We're being ridiculous.'

'We're amateurs.'

'We're pathetic. Porn producers have more self-esteem.'

'And they don't get embarrassed. I've been embarrassed all day.'

'I've been embarrassed all of my life.' Ivan shakes his

head sadly. 'And I've got a cracking headache.' He leaves the kitchen to go upstairs to liberate some headache pills. When he comes down Campbell has opened a bottle of wine.

'We'll drink this,' Campbell says, 'then I'll phone Winfrey. Admit all.'

Ivan nods. He lifts his glass. 'It would have been a wonderful adventure,' he says. They touch glasses. 'Except neither of us has the stomach for it. Face it – we're useless.'

'Exactly,' Campbell says.

As they clink, the doorbell sounds. They hear Mother stepping briskly along the hall. A few moments later she's back in the kitchen doorway. 'Your four o'clock is here.'

'Tell her we're closed,' Campbell snaps. 'And to buy a watch.'

'Tell her the part is filled.'

'Tell her to go to hell.'

'Why don't you tell me yourself?' the most beautiful woman either of them has ever seen says, stepping into the doorway behind Mother.

It could have got things off on the wrong foot, but she's above it. She steps, smiling, into the kitchen, full of apologies for being late, brimming with sympathy for all the hard work they must have put in that day; her smile is beguiling, her handshake soft yet somehow firm as well, her eyes keen, her eye-contact keener. 'I'm Shona,' she says.

After some moments of shuffling their files, Campbell

and Ivan realise that they have no Shona, nor indeed any record of a four o'clock appointment.

'I know I'm chancing my arm,' Shona volunteers with an embarrassed shrug. 'My agent was holding out for a movie, but I like to work. I've come under my own steam because I like to keep busy. I hate wasting my mind, and hey, good looks don't last for ever.'

She laughs, they laugh with her. She's lovely.

'Have a glass of wine,' Campbell says.

'Have mine,' Ivan trumps, pushing his own across. 'I can get another.'

She takes it, and then looks quizzically at him before she takes a sip.

'What?' Ivan says, flushing under the scrutiny.

'Aren't you Ivan Connor?'

'I – well, yes.'

'I've read all of your books.'

'Oh,' he responds, fluster building on flush. 'You're the one.'

'I was in publishing before I became an actress.' She leans forward. He finds it hard not to examine her chest as she does this; she catches the flit of his eyes and there's the merest sparkle from her own in response; appreciative rather than admonishing. 'I must tell you,' she continues, 'you are so highly regarded in the industry. Such a unique talent.' She leans back again and smiles. 'This is all very mysterious, isn't it?'

'Well,' Campbell begins, 'not so much mysterious as . . .'

'Only I was very nearly not going to come – there are a lot of dodgy people about. But if it's you, Mr

Connor, I'll tell you now: if I'm lucky enough to be offered the job, whatever it is, whatever is required of me, the answer is yes.'

Ivan's voice goes up a couple of notes as he forces himself to ask: 'Do you know, ah, *Finnegans Wake*?'

Shona laughs abruptly. 'Know it? I did the thesis for my Masters on it. Although, between you and me, I think Joyce was probably pissed when he wrote it.'

10

Ivan is up at eight, shaved and showered, having his breakfast downstairs. Mother is suitably impressed.

'This wouldn't have anything to do with a certain beautiful young woman, would it?' she asks innocently as she cuts his toast into soldiers.

He pulls his side plate away from her. 'Mother,' he says, 'I'm old enough to butter my own toast,' and now she looks not only impressed, but shocked.

'My God,' she says, 'it's like when you took your first steps.'

'Mother.'

'It was a Friday, your father was at work.'

'*Mother.*'

'Nobody else to see it but me. I cried my eyes out. Of course, today you'd have a video camera. Back then I just had words, and when I described it to your father, he burst into tears too. I expect it's where you get your facility with words from.'

He sighs indulgently. 'Mother, I'm not sure if you're being ironic or sarcastic or entering your dotage. It's just toast.'

'It's just a girl. I haven't seen you light up like this since you first met Whatshername.'

'Avril, Mother, Avril.' Mother shrugs. 'Did I ever tell you that you're a daft, vindictive old biddy?'

'Did I ever remind you that you live here rent free?'

'I pay for just about everything, Mother.'

'Yes, you pay for some incidentals, but you don't pay rent.'

'Mother, I'm your son. You don't charge your son rent.'

'I shouldn't have to ask.'

He sighs, not so indulgently this time. 'Is this a festering sore, Mother, or are you just winding me up?'

She looks sternly at him for several moments, then smiles. 'Winding you up, of course. But she does seem lovely.'

'Who does?'

'This Shauna.'

'Shona. She's just an actress.'

'I don't approve.'

'Of her being an actress?'

'Of this whole scheme.'

'Well, you should have said that before you agreed to take part.'

'I didn't really have a choice.'

'You're an accomplice now. Albeit in a soft, Ronnie Biggs kind of a way.'

'Your father would turn in his grave if he heard you comparing me to Ronnie Biggs.'

'I expect,' Ivan says carefully, 'that he has been turning for quite some time.'

Mother nods thoughtfully for several moments, then smiles. 'I just want you to be careful,' she says. 'With this girl.'

'I've only met her. It's strictly a business arrangement.'

'You bought her new clothes.'

'Campbell and I bought her new clothes. For the part.'

'You took her out to an extremely expensive restaurant.'

'Campbell and I took her out to an extremely expensive restaurant, to check her social skills. And she made us feel like culinary philistines.'

'You've been looking for somewhere to live together.'

'We've been looking for somewhere to act as her base. When the press come snooping and find she reports here every morning, the game will be up.'

'You've still been spending an awful lot of time with her.'

'*We've* been spending an awful lot of time with her. She has to be completely familiar with the book, she has to understand what went into it, what shaped it. She has to spend time with us to understand that.'

'She stays on when Campbell goes home.'

'She likes to unwind after a long day. We have a glass of wine. That's it.'

'I hear a lot of footsteps from your study.'

'We're just having a laugh. We dance. She likes to dance.'

'Your father and I used to dance.'

'Yes. I know.'

'I just don't want you to get hurt.'

'How could I get hurt?' He reaches across the breakfast table and places a reassuring hand on her arm. 'Don't worry about me,' he says. 'I'm made of titanium. And it really is just business.'

Ivan gulps as the doorbell sounds. 'That's her.' He jumps up and examines himself in the dining-room mirror. His hair is all over the place. Mother reaches up to flatten it down, but it bounces back up. She licks her hand then goes to smooth it again; Ivan ducks away. 'Mother, please, I'm not four.'

'No,' she says, coming after him, laughing, 'you're not that old.'

He shakes his head, then stops, turns, places his hands on her shoulders and kisses the top of her head. 'Don't worry about me,' he says, 'I'll be fine.'

Campbell is spending the day at Winfrey, studying the contracts, talking about marketing and tour schedules, so Ivan takes Shona for a drive, then they have a nice lunch. He's so relaxed in her company now, he doesn't feel any pressure at all. She's just so nice – beautiful, yes, but also friendly and interesting and funny and she really listens when he talks about his books and the difficulties he has had writing them, and then, later, in publishing them. And she has a way of looking at him and touching him as she speaks that just sends a shiver through him. They feel so *right* together. They haven't so much as kissed, yet he knows it is inevitable. He hasn't felt this strongly about someone since he first met his wife – and maybe not even then.

They browse through a Waterstones in Hampstead and Ivan glows when he finds that several of his previous novels are in stock. Shona admires them, then drifts off to look at some books for herself. Ivan lingers by his own small display, and is finally rewarded when a member of staff approaches and asks him if he's Ivan Connor.

Ivan shrugs bashfully. ''fraid so,' he says, his face colouring.

'Would you mind signing your books for us?'

'No, not at all.'

Ivan dutifully signs the books, removing them one by one from the shelf, and taking at least a minute over each copy, flourishing the biro ceremoniously so that the other customers in the shop can't fail to notice that there is A Genuine Author on the premises. As Shona escorts him out of the shop he's gratified to see several of the customers hurrying across to examine the signed copies.

They're strolling down Hampstead High Street, Shona with her arm slipped through his, when Ivan says: 'You went and found that boy in the shop and told him who I was.'

She smiles bashfully. 'I thought it would cheer you up.'

He smiles. 'Yes, it did. It was very thoughtful. Do you think I need cheering up?'

'I think you're the saddest man I've ever met.'

'Sad as in the great artist suffering from an inner turmoil and an innate melancholia caused by struggling with an unrealised genius, or because I come across like Johnny-no-friends?'

119

'A bit of both,' she says straight-faced, but then quickly bursts into laughter.

'Well, at least you're hon—'

But before he can finish she's up on her tiptoes and she kisses him lightly on the lips. Before he can fully respond, she's turning away, laughing. 'Come on,' she says, 'let's go and eat again.'

Later, in the afternoon, they sit on a wooden bench in the garden, Ivan sitting straight, Shona with her legs up, resting against him. He puts a protective arm around her and she snuggles against him. He's studying his notes for *Story of the Blues*, she's studying the manuscript of *Kissing Cousins* intently and every once in a while purring with satisfaction.

'You are a genius,' she says.

He smiles.

'This is just unique. I'm so proud to be involved in this. It's a grand adventure, isn't it?'

He nods. He hasn't the heart to tell her that *Kissing Cousins* is an accident, a nonsensical folly.

Because he doesn't want to lose her.

And because working away at him is his growing belief that perhaps Campbell has a point. That sometimes works of great genius do happen by happy accident. That subconsciously this is how he meant *The Last December* to turn out all along. That somehow he shifted himself to a higher plain and willed *Kissing Cousins* into existence when his own, normal self, couldn't create it. And he begins to believe that if the book really is hailed as something wonderfully original, that he will one day reclaim it as his own, and take the praise that is due to him. In the same way that the Brontës wrote under male pseudonyms, so he will write as a female. In their day it was impossible to be a woman and be treated seriously as a writer. Today it is the women who call the shots – but in time, he will come to be recognised as—

'Daddy!'

Ivan is shaken out of his reverie by Michael, *sans* hood, and Anna, dashing across the garden towards him. Shona swings her feet off the bench as they approach.

'Did I mention my children?' Ivan says, mildly panicked. 'I hardly ever see them.'

'Your last book was dedicated to them,' Shona says.

Anna and Michael stop at the bench, give their daddy a hug, and then step back to examine Shona.

'Michael, Anna, this is Shona. We're working together.'

'Working?' Anna says doubtfully.

'Yes. Working.'

'Granny says you're going to marry her.'

Ivan blushes. Shona laughs and claps her hands.

Ivan glances back up at the house, where Mother is standing in the kitchen doorway. 'Don't pay any attention to Granny,' Ivan says, 'because she's OLD AND MAD.'

Ivan introduces the kids properly to Shona and she chats away quite happily to them about school and cartoons and what books they read. Ivan sits back and basks in the warm glow of his inner happiness. Eventually Michael and Anna skip away. Michael rescues a half-deflated football from the garden shed and begins to kick it around the grass while Anna goes inside to watch TV. Shona snuggles back beside him and picks the manuscript up again.

Michael has been watching Liverpool on TV and thinks he's Michael Owen. He shouts and roars as he scores imaginary goals.

'Michael,' Ivan says, 'keep the sound down, we're trying to concentrate.'

He quietens for all of thirty seconds, then he's yelling again.

'Michael,' Ivan repeats.

'Sorry.'

He smiles apologetically and kicks the ball away. He charges after it. Ivan returns his attention to his notes. Her body is warm, soft, against his. His arm is around her now, passing beneath her shoulders, resting just below her neck and above her breasts. Every once in a while she lets out a little *hmmmm*.

Then the ball cracks against the base of the bench and they both jump.

'Michael!' Ivan scolds. 'I told you!'

'Sorry!' He grabs the ball and dashes off.

Ivan sighs. 'Sorry,' he says.

'It's okay.'

He removes his arm. 'How about I get us a glass of wine?'

'What about a hot toddy, chilly day like this.'

'Perfect,' Ivan says. 'You hang on here, I'll be back in a minute.'

He hurries back into the house. 'Mum, can you make us a couple of hot toddys?'

'Would. But being old and mad, I can't remember how.'

'Mum, come on. Don't be daft.'

She huffs off upstairs.

Outside, Michael storms up and down the grass, kicking the ball before him. He's seven, and he's about to score the winning goal in the FA Cup Final. He strikes the ball cleanly, and it sails through the air; he's just raising his arms in triumph as the sodden, grassy ball slaps against the side of Shona's head.

She drops the manuscript and lets out a shout.

Michael lets his arms fall. 'Sorry,' he says weakly.

She glares at him for several long moments, then sighs and gives half a smile as she rubs at her face.

The ball is sitting at her feet. His eyes flit down to it, then back up to Daddy's girlfriend. She has picked up the manuscript and is now giving it her full attention again. Her cheeks are flaming red.

Michael cautiously approaches, one step at a time. He stands for a moment right in front of her, but she pays no attention. He breathes a sigh of relief, then bends to retrieve the ball.

Just as he touches it, her hand shoots out and grabs his wrist. Her face is in his and her eyes are as cold and hard as the witch in *The Lion, the Witch and the Wardrobe*, which his mummy is reading to him at night.

She squeezes his wrist. He feels tears welling up. 'You think that's sore?' she hisses. 'That ball comes near me again and I'll *break* your fucking wrist.'

Then she lets go. Michael staggers back, dazed, forgetting the ball, massaging his wrist.

'And if you tell your daddy, I'll break the other one.'

Then Daddy is coming down the garden with two steaming glasses in his hand. 'Here we go,' he says jovially, handing one to Shona, 'just what the doctor ordered.' She smiles lovingly at him as she takes the glass. 'What are you two up to?' Ivan beams.

'Michael fell and hurt himself. I was just kissing him better, wasn't I, love?'

Michael stares at his daddy, absolutely certain that he'll see through this monstrous lie.

'Are you okay, son?' Ivan asks. 'Why don't you have a game with Shona?'

Michael can't believe it. The tears begin to roll down his cheeks; he turns and races back towards the house.

'Michael!' Ivan calls after him. 'What's got into you!' But he's away. Ivan turns to Shona. 'Sorry,' he says.

She smiles. She crinkles her nose up. 'He's just embarrassed.' Then she kisses Ivan gently on the lips again. 'Your lips are warm,' she murmurs, 'you've been sampling the goods.'

'Chance would be a fine thing,' he says, too quickly, then blushes.

Three days later and this flirty-kissy relationship is threatening to send Ivan off the deep end. He would have been content to continue with the little pecks for ever and a day, but last night when she was leaving she stopped in the hall and kissed him again, but this time her mouth opened and her tongue sought out his and for all of thirty seconds they were going at it passionately. Then her moist lips slipped along his cheek and nibbled at his ear and she whispered something that was too breathy and lustful for him to fully comprehend. He had thought at the time that she had said quite a lot, but on reflection the only word he could recall was 'soon'. Then she'd hurried off into the night and he was left with an erection that would not go away.

Now it's D-Day, the meeting with Winfrey and the signing of the contract. The troops are being marshalled in his mother's front room. Cups of tea are poured. Battenburg cake is sliced. Ivan's too nervous to eat, and he's not even going, not even to linger outside. Too dangerous, Campbell says. Ivan is nervous for Shona, but she's her usual self, confident, funny, inspiring; she's in a designer outfit, and she's wearing a blonde wig which makes her look almost identical to the photograph of April May. He's nervous also for Campbell who looks pale and serious and won't sit still. Mother shuffles about, being Mother. She puts a slice of cake on a side plate and offers it to Shona with a smile; Shona returns the smile, takes the plate, but sets it down again without touching it.

'I'm sorry, Campbell – you were saying?' she says.

'That the important thing is not to say too much. Be enigmatic. You don't have to explain art, art is just what it is.'

'It's more than art, Campbell, it's perfection.' She gazes at Ivan. 'You really understand women.'

Ivan shrugs bashfully as Mother snorts. He is getting more and more into this unconsciously-I'm-a-genius thing.

Campbell's new mobile rings, and he excuses himself.

When he steps out of the room, Shona puts a hand on Ivan's knee.

'How do you do that, Ivan, get inside a woman?'

'I . . . well. It just comes out.'

Campbell returns. 'That was Winfrey, just checking our ETA. They're really nervous. This is great, having them on the back foot like this.' He rubs his hands together. 'Okay. Let's get this show on the road.'

Campbell and Shona pull on their jackets as Mother lifts the plates and cups onto a tray and then stands with it. 'Well,' she says, 'good luck, my dears. I'll come and visit you in prison.'

Ivan rolls his eyes at Shona. She is looking astonishingly beautiful. Her eyes twinkle at him. He wishes he was going with them – not, he realises with a sudden gulp, because he wants to be in on the sting, but because he's jealous that Campbell is going to be alone with her.

Get a grip!

He shakes Campbell's hand and wishes him good luck. When he turns to Shona he suddenly becomes embarrassed, unused to showing affection to her in front of either Campbell or his mother. She solves it by coming forward and giving him a hug and pressing her warm lips against his cheek. He glows. She steps out of his arms and turns to follow Campbell, who's standing with eyebrows raised, by the door. Then she stops.

'Oh,' she says, 'just one thing before we go.'

Campbell glances at his watch and sighs. 'What?'

'It's just the money.' She gives a shy little laugh. 'I've been thinking about the money. You've said five hundred pounds for each public appearance. It's really wonderful.

I mean, as this is going to be so high profile, why, there could be maybe fifty or a hundred public appearances a year. It could be as much as fifty thousand pounds.'

'Yes, indeed,' Campbell says.

'Time was,' Ivan says, 'when I would have given my right arm for fifty thousand pounds.'

Mother, fussing in for the rest of the plates, says, 'Don't be silly, dear, how would you have typed?'

'Shona, we need to go,' Campbell says, as Mother moves past him, shaking her head and tutting at the same time.

'I know, I know. It's just – well, no point in beating around the bush. Dress it up how you please, but what you're doing is basically fraudulent, isn't it? And you're making me an integral part of that.'

'It's not fraud, Shona,' Campbell says. 'It's . . . deception.'

'Whatever it is, I'm the public face of it.'

'Yes, and you're being well rewarded. Now can—'

'To all intents and purposes, I am April May. If she takes off in the way you envisage, then she's going to be with me every day. As far as the publishers, the public and the media are concerned, I *will be* April May.'

Campbell has moved back inside the door now. He pushes it closed and looks grimly at Shona. Ivan, not at all sure where this is going, lowers himself back down into his chair.

'Shona?' Ivan says. 'Are you having second thoughts?'

'I think it's only right that I should be paid accordingly.'

Campbell's eyes have narrowed. 'What are you suggesting?'

'Thirty-three per cent of all monies paid to April May either in publishing advances or royalties. Thirty-three per cent of all movie options, screenplay agreements, principal photography payments.'

'Is that it?' Campbell asks.

'One hundred per cent of all fees paid for public appearances, readings, television interviews, endorsements and merchandising containing my likeness. A retainer for being on call, a clothing allowance, an apartment for my exclusive use, health cover, pension contributions.'

Ivan begins to laugh. 'Shona, come on, you're not—'

The look she fixes him with is cold, and he suddenly feels a heaviness in his stomach and a chill on his spine.

'Of course I'm serious. Boys, I used to work in publishing. I know what you're trying to pull off and I admire you for it, but if you think you're going to fob me off with fifty quid a day you've another think coming.'

'But Shona . . .' Ivan begins again, then trails off, not knowing how to continue.

'These demands are not excessive, gentlemen. Any best-selling author would expect them as a matter of course.'

'You haven't *sold* any books!' Ivan suddenly explodes.

'And neither have you!'

Oh, God, how wrong I have been. She's as cold as a fish. As lethal as a shark. She's played me like a mandolin.

Ivan looks despairingly at Campbell, whose mouth has fallen half-open. Shona has her hands on her hips now. Her eyes are narrowed and cruel.

Oh Christ!

'Well?' she says. 'What's it going to be?'

Campbell and Shona are approaching Campbell's car. Ivan stands in the doorway and watches, seething inside. She's walking differently now, he fancies. She's walking – triumphantly.

He and Campbell had discussed it for three turbulent minutes in the hall while Shona waited inside. They cursed her up and down, albeit in whispers, but their anger was mostly directed towards themselves for being sucked in. They should have seen her coming. A smooth operator. She has taken them to the brink, and now it's too late to go back. Too late to recruit someone else. Winfrey is waiting. The money is almost in the bank. Surely two thirds of something is better than all of nothing. They have no alternative.

There's a slight movement to his right and Ivan turns to find Michael standing beside him. He puts an arm around his son's shoulders and squeezes.

Campbell looks back up towards the house and gives a helpless shrug as he opens the passenger door for Shona, who doesn't even look back.

He had been dreaming of sex and money. Now he is convinced there will be no sex, and less money. He sighs as Campbell pulls the car out of its parking space.

'Daddy,' Michael says.

'Hmm?'

'I don't like her much.'

Ivan nods slowly. 'No, son,' he says, 'neither do I.'

11

He's barely put a foot back inside the house when there's an almighty crash, a sickening screech of metal against metal, a shivering shatter of glass.

He races down the garden, leapfrogs the privet hedge and then he's dashing around the corner of the street. There's Campbell's car, steam or smoke pouring from it, the bonnet stoved in, the windscreen shattered, another car firm up against it, slightly bent at the front but otherwise not obviously damaged.

'Campbell!' Ivan shouts as he races around to the driver's door. 'Campbell!'

He pulls the door open and Campbell's sitting there holding his forehead, looking dazed. He turns groggily towards Ivan and gives him a half-smile. 'Reckon we're going to be late,' he says.

'Moron!' Shona bellows from the passenger seat, one hand cupping her face, though it's not clear whether she's addressing Campbell or Ivan or the driver of the vehicle, who so far hasn't shown his face.

Ivan helps Campbell out of his seat belt, then out of the car. He sits him down on the kerb.

'Are you okay?'

'Just . . . shocked. My heart's thumping like billyo.'

Ivan squeezes his shoulder, then hurries across to the other car. As he approaches he sees that the driver's forehead is resting against the steering wheel and for a moment Ivan contemplates leaving him where he is, convinced that he's going to be dead of a broken neck, and that's all he needs. The upset of it could stop him writing for days. But then he's quite pleased with that thought, because it means he's still thinking like a writer and so he decides, sure, hell, it's all research, his first encounter with a real live dead body, go for it. So he takes a deep breath and opens the driver's door.

'Are you okay?' he asks tentatively.

The driver turns her head towards him. 'Hello, Mr Connor,' Donna says.

For a moment he doesn't quite comprehend. He recognises the pale elfin face, the short spiky hair cut, the lively eyes, but it's so out of context.

'Donna?'

'I was just coming to see you.'

'Donna, are you okay?'

'You promised you'd help me with my poetry,' she says vaguely, 'or someone did.' She rubs at her brow. 'Wow. I feel a little . . . *fuck*.'

She scrambles out of the car, and throws up against the kerb.

Ivan thinks that maybe this is a sign of massive internal organ damage, or that she's suffering a stroke. Behind him, Campbell's back on his feet and standing looking at the damage.

'Christ,' he mutters, swaying visibly. He turns angrily towards the retching Donna. 'What the bloody hell were you playing at?'

Donna spits up some more, then wipes her mouth on her sleeve and looks forlornly back. 'I'm sorry, I'm really sorry. I was looking for Mr Connor's house. I only took my eye off for a . . .' She turns to vomit again.

Campbell throws his hands up in angry frustration. 'What the fuck are we going to do now?'

Ivan shakes his head. He looks down at Donna again. 'Have you escaped or something?' he asks.

Donna spits again. 'Parole.' Spit. 'Out on licence.' Spit. 'Good behaviour.' Spit.

Campbell wags a finger at her. 'I don't know who the hell you are, but I'll tell you one thing, we're going to sue you for everything you have.'

Donna's head snaps round angrily. 'Oh why don't you just fuck off?'

'Don't you speak to me like th—'

'We had an accident. We'll sort it out, okay?'

'*You* had an accident. I was merely—'

'Will you just leave it? For fuck's sake, I'm puking my guts up here.'

'Campbell, Donna,' Ivan says, raising placatory hands. 'It's not as bad as it looks. We can sort this out.'

Campbell looks incredulously from Ivan to the state of his car. 'It's a write-off, Ivan,' he glances at his watch, 'and we're supposed to be at Winfrey's by now.' He sighs. 'Oh well.' He finally looks back down at Donna with some modicum of sympathy. 'Are you hurt?'

Donna pushes herself up from the kerb. 'No, I just felt sick.'

'Can you stop talking to that *imbecile*?'

They turn towards Shona, forgotten in the excitement, finally emerging from the passenger seat. She staggers slightly as she crosses towards them. 'We're going to need a cab. Can you call a cab?'

But they don't move. They're staring at her.

'Look, there's a lot of money at stake here, will you stop standing around like idiots and call a cab!' But they're still staring at her. '*What?*' she demands. Then her brow crinkles as she realises that their eyes aren't meeting her own, but are concentrating slightly lower down. And she's aware of the throbbing in her face that's been growing steadily since that little tramp pranged their car, but surely it's nothing more than a scratch. She bends down to Donna's car and stares at her reflection in the wing mirror.

The most beautiful girl in London's nose is bent almost completely to one side. She lets out a scream of horror.

'Oh my God! Oh my God! Do something! Somebody do something!' She has her hands over her nose now to prevent anyone from seeing it. She begins to run about in a blind panic. 'My nose, my nose!' And the crazy thing is, it's not even bleeding, it's just that when she runs north, it points east. If she's running for Scotland, it's sniffing out Poland.

'Shona,' Ivan begins.

'My fucking nose! Look what you've done to my

fucking nose!' She kicks out at Donna, but the kick falls short and her stiletto heel flies off and through the open window of Donna's car. Shona lets out another scream. She hobbles about on one shoe, crying. 'Help me, somebody help me!'

Granny and Michael have come running up now, but neither of them venture anywhere near her.

'Shona, please settle down. We'll get you to a hospital.' Campbell looks at his watch. 'We'll call an ambulance.' He looks at Ivan, then at his watch again. 'What are we going to do about the meeting?'

Ivan feels he's been up to the top of the mountain, and then been hurled down the other side. So many times, in fact, that he doesn't know whether to laugh or cry.

'Help me, someone!'

'Shona, just settle down,' Ivan snaps.

'Christ, Christ, Christ,' Campbell says, beating his hands against his legs.

'I'm really sorry,' Donna says.

'It's okay,' Ivan replies insincerely.

'It's not okay! I'm not even fucking insured!' She is close to tears.

'Look, that's not—' Then he stops, and he looks at her, and she's so surprised by his suddenly intense gaze that her hand goes to her own nose as if it too might be pointing east.

'*You* can do it!' he exclaims.

'I can do *what*?'

'Campbell? *She* can do it!'

'Eh? What the hell are you talking about!' Campbell looks incredulous.

'She can be April May!'

'She looks nothing like April May!'

'We have no choice! We've to sign the contract in twenty minutes.'

Campbell raises his hands in desperation. Shona is staggering back towards them, still crying for help.

Ivan suddenly grabs Donna by the shoulders. 'Donna, you've wrecked our car, you're not insured; we need you to do something for us, and we'll forget the damage.'

'Do what?' Donna asks apprehensively.

'We just need you to sign a piece of paper for us. Look at that poor girl, look at her nose – *you've* done that, Donna, and because of that we stand to lose a great deal of money, and you stand to go back to prison. Now all we want you to do is to pretend to be someone else for ten minutes.'

'WHAT!' Shona bellows. She's up beside them now, one hand still cupped over her nose, which is now swelling out around her fingers.

Ivan ignores her. 'Donna, we need you to become April May.'

'NO!' Shona cries. '*I* am April May!'

'Who *is* April May?' Donna asks.

'It doesn't matter – you have to do it.'

'We're going to have to use your car as well,' Campbell says. 'There's hardly a scratch on it.'

Donna looks a little dazed, but nods. 'Okay, as long as I don't have to pay.'

'It'll be fine,' Ivan says. 'Now let's just go!'

As they turn to the car, Shona cries, 'Stay where you are! You can't do this! I'll sue you for every penny! I'll tell the press! You'll go to prison!'

Campbell hesitates, then comes back around the car to stand before Shona. He looks sympathetically at her. He places a hand on either shoulder. 'Shona,' he says softly, 'we thought you were really nice, but you tried to fuck us over.'

'I—'

'Shhhhhh.'

'Don't you—'

'Shhhhhh.'

She quietens.

'Now,' Campbell says, 'you signed a confidentiality agreement. If you so much as breathe a word, we'll sue you, and we'll have the money to do it. So let's just call it quits, okay?' There are tears rolling down her swollen cheeks. 'And next time,' he adds, reaching up to smooth her hair, 'wear a seat belt.'

He gives a sudden yank and her wig comes off in his hands. He races across to Donna's car. 'Now let's go!' he yells.

There's a sustained screech of untwisting metal and the sad crunch of glass being reduced to powder as Donna throws the car into reverse. Then she straightens up and leapfrogs forward.

Shona lets go with a howl of, *'Bastards!'* shaking her fist after the car, but it's gone. She turns to find Ivan's mother and the little boy standing looking at her.

'Can you please,' she says tearfully, 'phone for an ambulance?'

But Ivan's mother puts her arm around Michael and leads him away. Michael glances back, and gives her the finger.

*   *   *

137

All the way there, Donna's not happy. Understandably.

'You think I'm crazy or something? I'm out on licence and you're asking me to impersonate a *writer*?'

'Why not?' Campbell jokes. 'Ivan's been doing it for years.' He laughs, then winces. His head is pounding. 'It'll be okay. Just sign the contract. Say as little as possible.'

'Christ,' Donna says, 'what the hell was I thinking of? I should have stayed in bed.'

Campbell raises an eyebrow. 'If only you had, then we wouldn't be in this bloody pickle. Ivan, support me please. This was your idea.'

'I didn't think you'd take me seriously,' Ivan grumbles. 'This is never going to work.'

Campbell rolls his eyes. 'Your bloody problem is you blow hot and cold. You never stick with things.'

'I stuck with you.'

'Oh that's rich. And the moment you come out from under my protective wing, look what happens.'

'At least it happened.'

'Maybe I should pull over and you two can discuss—'

'Keep driving!' Campbell cries. 'We're going to be late as it is. We can't stop this now. It's like a snowball gathering moss. We have to go through with it, you *have* to be April May. Though frankly you look more like Mother Teresa.'

'Cheek of it!' Donna is outraged.

'Look, I just mean, make-up, perfume – woman things. That's what they'll be expecting.'

He holds out Shona's wig. Ivan takes it from him and carefully fits it over Donna as she drives. 'There,' he says.

Donna shakes the hair out of her eyes, then glances doubtfully at herself in the mirror.

'That's grand,' Campbell says. 'Now make-up.'

'I don't wear it.'

He reaches to the floor and lifts her handbag. 'You may not wear it, but you have it. You all do.' He empties the bag at his feet.

'Just watch what you're doing!' She can't grab it back because of the traffic, and anyway, he's already rifled through the contents and is holding up some of her cosmetics.

'Soon as we stop, you get as much of this slap on you as you can. You *will* look like April May by the time we're finished with you. You have to.'

'I am never going to look like that woman,' Donna says steadily.

'No you won't,' Ivan agrees. 'But at least your nose will be pointing in the right direction.' He and Campbell exchange a nervous giggle.

Donna glares at them. 'You were horrible to her.'

'She deserved it,' Ivan says.

'You abandoned her in the middle of the road. She was hurt.'

'She was trying to rip us off. She was a monster in the skin of a model.'

'And to think you nearly fell for her,' Campbell says.

'I did not,' Ivan protests.

'You were all over her like a rash.'

'You're talking balls.'

'Do you think you two could shut up for a minute? I don't want to do this. I'm on licence.'

'Yes,' Campbell says, 'we heard you the first time. Now stop bleating about it and get on with the job. You've written off my car. It'll cost me thousands.'

Ivan, sitting in the back, puts a reassuring hand on her shoulder. 'You'll be fine.'

She glances back. 'If I do this, will you help me with my poetry?'

'Yes, of course,' Ivan manages to say without the barest sliver of conviction. 'Let's just get this out of the way first.'

They park around the corner from the Winfrey building, then Ivan and Campbell lean on the bonnet for five minutes while Donna gets on her make-up and straightens her wig.

Campbell lights a cigarette. Ivan swallows a couple of headache pills.

'We're mental,' Ivan says, 'even trying this.'

'What else can we do? Might as well go down fighting.'

'They'll see right through her. She's pretty enough, but she's not April May.'

'April May would have screwed us into the ground. Metaphorically in my case, and literally in yours. And then she would have walked off with our money, and your balls in her pocket. We had a lucky escape. Everything else is gravy. I'm going through that door with my head held high and I'm going to bullshit them into giving us six million quid.'

The car door opens and Donna steps out. She looks nervous. But she also looks great.

'You clean up well,' Ivan says.

'You're so kind,' she replies, heavy on the sarcasm.

'No really, you look great.'

'Now,' Campbell says, 'let's all just settle down, be calm. Remember, Dolly . . .'

'Donna.'

'Donna – April. Don't say too much. Less is more.' Campbell clears his throat. 'Okay,' he says, clapping his hands together. 'Let's go for it.' He leads off. Donna glances at Ivan, raises her eyebrows, then follows.

'Good luck,' Ivan says after them. Then adds for Donna's benefit, 'Break a leg,' although he regrets it immediately, because she probably will.

12

'Everyone's looking at me.'
  'Yes, they are. Smile.'
  'But everyone's looking at me!'
  'Smile.'
  'They look disappointed.'
  'They look impressed.'
  'They think I'm mutton dressed as lamb.'
  'No, they're wishing they were you. They're jealous.'
  'Yeah.'
They're standing in Winfrey's vast airy atrium as the staff on three open-plan floors stare down. Campbell is basking in the attention. Donna examines her shoes and scratches at her wig.
  'To carry this off,' Campbell whispers, 'you're going to have to appear more confident. You look like you're waiting to be sentenced.'
  'That's easy for you to say. This wig is driving me fucking demented.'

'Decorum, please. You have to at least give the pretence of quasi-sophistication.'

'Can I have that without the fucking marbles?'

'Stop swearing, and don't spit on the floor.'

'I'm dying for a fag.'

'This is a non-smoking building.' Campbell sighs. 'This is probably the wrong time to ask you what you were inside for in the first place.'

'Yes, it is.'

'If you have any tattoos, try not to expose them.'

Donna rolls her eyes and the receptionist makes the mistake of thinking she's making eye-contact and smiles back at her.

Donna barks, 'What?' at her.

'I . . . it's just that I hear the book is marvellous. Well done. We're all very excited.'

Donna nods tersely and the receptionist looks quickly away as the lift doors open and Carson Winfrey appears. He strides purposefully across the atrium while those watching from above duck down and then slip back to their work stations.

Julia walks with Carson. Well, behind him. It's only right. April May might be her discovery, but he's the boss.

Campbell sucks in his breath. This is it. The moment of truth. Get past this, and we're flying.

'Campbell! Good morning!'

It's the afternoon. Campbell takes this as a good sign. *Carson's nervous*. 'Afternoon, Carson.'

But Carson has already let go of his hand and is now beaming down at April May. Is there a shadow of doubt crossing his eyes? Is he thinking that she looks nothing like her picture? But he must know that nobody looks like that picture, not even April or May. It's all make-up and computer wizardry.

'Carson, this is April May.'

He takes her hand, and clasps it between his. 'April,' he says, 'I'm so excited.'

'Not too excited, I hope,' April purrs, and Carson lets go of her hand with a great *Carry On* guffaw.

Jesus, Campbell thinks. The girl is *acting*.

'Julia, this is April.'

Julia extends her hand and this time April clasps it between her own. 'A pleasure,' April May says. 'I've heard *so* much about you.'

Julia is blushing. Only Carson has done that to her before.

They walk together to the lifts.

'I can't tell you what a thrill it's been, working on *Kissing Cousins*,' Julia says. April smiles politely.

'Oh we have big plans,' Carson adds. 'Big plans.'

They rise to the third floor.

'It's only once in a generation that a book like this comes along,' Julia says.

'Thank you.'

'Are you working on another?'

April's eyes flit quickly to Campbell, but he's not in a position to whisper, indicate or mouth anything.

'Well,' April says, 'I've been writing some poetry.'

'Oh how marvellous,' Julia says. 'We have a poetry imprint as well.'

April nods. 'Perhaps I should show you some of it.'

145

'We'd be honoured.'

'Poetry,' Campbell says, 'doesn't really sell.'

'Oh the author shouldn't have to worry about sales,' Carson says. 'He, or she, should write exactly what he, or she, wants. It's up to philistines like us to make it sell.'

Campbell smiles at Carson, quite impressed by his willingness to humiliate himself in front of April May. He feels like shouting, *Liar, Liar, Pants on Fire*, but suspects it might be construed as being somewhat childish.

As the lift doors open, Julia says, 'Everything's set up in the boardroom.'

Carson walks ahead with April, while Campbell follows behind with Julia.

Julia says, 'She's very petite.'

'All great writers are small,' Campbell says. Ivan has told him this, and he sees no reason to disbelieve it, though of course he made it clear to Ivan that he was the exception to the rule.

'She doesn't look much like her photo.'

'Who *does*?'

'She's still very pretty.'

'I know.'

'I'm not sure about the wig.'

'It's a wig?'

'Campbell, *please.*'

'She's very attached to it.'

'So it stays. Campbell, this is going to be great.'

April and Carson have stopped by the boardroom door.

'Julia,' Carson says, indicating the door, 'I think the honour should be yours. You did, after all, bring April to my attention.'

Julia *glows*. She could almost swoon in his arms, but contents herself with a friendly-dismissive, 'Oh, Carson,' and promises herself to swoon later in the privacy of their hotel room. She puts a hand on the door-knob, smiles at April and Campbell, and then twists it and pushes the door open.

They are immediately blinded by camera flashes.

The boardroom is crammed with press. There are television lights, there are at least thirty-two photographers.

'Ladies and gentlemen,' Carson says, stepping into the room. 'Miss April May!'

'Jes-us fuck,' Donna hisses, and tries to take a step backwards.

But Campbell stops her, and at the same time puts a hand on Carson's arm and whispers urgently, 'What the hell is this? We're only here to sign a contract.'

Questions are already being shouted by reporters. Carson shrugs off Campbell's hand, keeps his smile in place, but says quietly out of the corner of his mouth: 'Biggest advance for a first novel in publishing history, too damn right we're going to exploit it. Now smile.'

Carson takes a reluctant April May by the hand and leads her across to a table set out at the top of the boardroom. She's followed all the way by camera flashes and photographers calling on her to look their way. She looks dead ahead.

'Oh she's so confident,' Julia whispers to Campbell.

Carson pulls the chair back for April, and she sits. For a moment she looks completely lost. Then Campbell crouches down beside her and whispers in her ear. 'I'm sorry,' he says, 'I didn't know this was going to happen. But you can do this. You really can.'

Donna looks doubtfully up at him.

Carson raises his hands and calls for quiet. 'Ladies and gentlemen,' he says, 'I'm sure I don't have to tell you that Winfrey Books is the oldest and most respected of British publishing houses, and dare I say it, the last one still in private hands. Perhaps it has been our downfall, but we have always prided ourselves on being known as the writer's friend: the work has always come first.' Campbell clears his throat. 'That is why authors seek us out, because they know that they will be cared for and nurtured as artists should be. Every once in a while, perhaps once in a generation, a new voice emerges in British literature, a voice that is so unusual, so refreshing that it demands not merely to be published, but almost worshipped. This moment, this signing of a talent as incredible as April May's, alone justifies my entire career. I know that when the history of publishing comes to be written, my name will be in there not as the Managing Director of Winfrey Books, not as the man who has published almost five thousand novels over the past ten years, but as *the man who signed April May*. But why am I saying all this, when April is more than capable of speaking on her own behalf? Ladies and gentlemen, we're going to sign the contract now. Take as many photographs as you desire, then feel free to talk to the one and only . . . April May!'

There's a round of applause, another volley of flashes, and then Carson hands April a pen and indicates where she should sign the contract. Donna looks to Campbell, who nods, and then she begins to write her name.

'Look up, love,' a photographer shouts, and she does. She smiles.

It's a great smile. But the eyes are those of a rabbit caught on a motorway on a busy night. The camera lights are so hot. The back of her blouse is soaked in sweat. The wig feels like it's biting into her head. She's going to be on TV, in dozens of newspapers.

Oh shit on a stick. I'm just digging a deeper and deeper hole.

'How does it feel to become a millionaire overnight?'

Her mouth drops open, slightly. *What?* She glances at Campbell. *Protect me from this.* He shrugs.

She shouldn't be here. She should be at home – no, not at home, not there, but somewhere nicer. In the park. Feeding the pigeons. Working in a shop or a pub. Christ, her head feels like it's going to explode. What do all these people want? Don't they know? Can't they tell? She's not a writer, she's a little girl who's fucked up her life.

'How does it feel to become a millionaire overnight?'

'I . . .'

Flash, flash, flash, flash.

'How does it feel?'

'Fucked if I know!' she shouts suddenly. 'I didn't ask for it!'

Laughter peals around the room as she looks about her in desperation. The publisher, the editor, the agent, their faces all seem engorged, distorted, they're laughing along as well, but it's not just laughter, it's like a tidal wave of sound.

'What's the book about?'

'Don't know – haven't read it yet.'

'But you wrote it!'

'Well, I was probably drunk.' She needs a drink. A great big fucking vodka.

'Do you think all this hype is justified?'

'What hype?'

'Is it true the book's about lesbians?'

'I haven't a clue.'

'Are you a lesbian?'

'Not yet.'

Calm down. Be sensible.

'Are you married?'

'Yes . . . no.'

'Are you or aren't you?'

'What the fuck has it got to do with anything! Read the fucking book!' And with that she jumps up out of her chair. 'I'm out of here,' she says. She points an accusing finger at Campbell. 'I didn't ask for this shit, I was only trying to help!'

Campbell looks impotently at her, and then at Carson, who's standing with his mouth open. Julia is gripping Carson's sleeve tightly, like a child lost in a supermarket.

Donna charges across the boardroom, holding her hands up over her face as the flashes flash again and the reporters lob their questions like grenades at Stalingrad.

Outside, Ivan is sitting in the car going through the glove compartment for clues. He hasn't learned much beyond the fact that the log book shows that it's registered to one Jon Teckman with an address somewhere he's never heard of, and that he's the third owner. The tax disc on the window is out of date, the ashtray is full of butts and the driver's musical tastes, at least according to the CDs carelessly scattered at his feet, consist of groups like Eminem and Destiny's Child.

Luckily he happens to glance up in time to see Donna hurrying along the pavement and he's able to scramble the log book back into the glove compartment before she opens the door and plumps herself heavily down onto the ripped upholstery of the driver's seat.

She blows air out of her cheeks and says, 'Fuck.'

He looks at her and waits. She reaches into her handbag and pulls out a cigarette and lights it. She inhales deeply, glances at him and says, 'Fuck.'

'It didn't go well,' Ivan says flatly.

'No, it fucking did not.'

'They guessed. I knew the wig was a mistake.'

'It wasn't the wig.'

'The clothes then. I mean, they're fine, but not really what a writer would wear.'

She glares at him. 'What the fuck are you talking about? Are there special writer's clothes or something? Do *you* go to a special writer's clothes shop? And was it fucking closed when *you* went?'

'Sorry. I can see you're upset. I'm sure you did your best. Maybe it was the shoes.'

'Would you ever shut the fuck up? It wasn't the fucking outfit, okay? It was the fact that the world's press were waiting to ambush me.'

'Oh.'

'Oh in fucking deedy.'

'You mean they knew all along? Winfrey set this whole thing up to show what a desperate has-been I am?'

'No, they set this whole thing up to get fucking April May plastered all over the papers so that they can sell a cartload of fucking books.'

'Well, isn't that what we wanted?'

'It might have been what *you* wanted, but you didn't fucking warn *me*! I'm on licence – I can't have my noggin all over the papers.' She takes another drag and squashes the half-smoked cigarette into the overflowing ash tray. Then she lights another.

'We were stuck,' Ivan says weakly. 'It was an emergency. But it sounds like it went off okay.'

She sighs and rubs at her brow. 'It didn't go off okay. I lost my fucking bottle.'

But before he can ask her what she means, there's a tap on his window; it's Campbell, looking grim-faced. Ivan opens the door for him, then clambers into the back of the car. Campbell slips into the vacated seat, and it's his turn to blow air out of his cheeks.

'Sorry,' Donna says, looking straight ahead.

Ivan reaches forward and squeezes Campbell's shoulder. 'Let's go and get a drink. You can tell us all the gory details then.'

Campbell nods slowly. Then he reaches into his jacket and removes a piece of paper. 'Do you think,' he says, holding it up, 'that they'll cash a cheque?'

13

They are so ridiculously drunk, sitting at a table in the White Hart, in front of a roaring fire, drinking cider like kids. Donna's still in shock from the press conference, but it's been cushioned by Campbell writing her a cheque for one thousand pounds, and Ivan trumping it with one for one thousand one hundred and twenty-seven pounds. Neither of them have that much money in the bank, but they will soon.

'How's about that, Donna m'girl?' Campbell says, reverting to the Scottish accent his family dropped five hundred years ago when they moved south. 'Not bad for half an hour's work.'

Donna smiles happily. Two thousand one hundred and twenty-seven pounds for crashing her car and then making an arse of herself in public. She hasn't had nearly as much to drink as Ivan and Campbell. The car's sitting outside, she should go while she can. Now isn't the time to mention her poetry.

'I really thought I'd blown it,' she admits.

'*I* really thought you'd blown it,' Campbell replies. 'But they lapped it up! They bloody lapped it up! See, the press, they're used to dealing with manufactured pop stars and mollycoddled actresses, so it's a breath of fresh air when . . .'

Ivan leans forward. 'Some dodgy trollop with attitude gives them grief.'

Donna forces a weak smile.

'You gave them a mouthful – they just loved it,' Campbell beams. 'Carson couldn't get the cheque into my hand quick enough.'

'We are *the* men!' Ivan shouts suddenly.

'We are the *men*!' Campbell bellows in response.

'Could the men get the feet off the table?' the barman enquires.

Campbell points at him. '*You're* the man!'

Ivan follows. 'You *are* the man!'

They move their feet off the table. Ivan gestures at Donna. 'And *you're* the lady.'

'You *are* the lady!' Campbell adds.

'Yes, well,' Donna says, 'the lady should get going.' She stands and lifts her jacket. 'It's been great.'

Ivan points suddenly at the fire and she looks there. Distracted, he grabs her coat out of her hands. 'You're going nowhere, we're celebrating. Sit down. My round.'

'No really, I should go.'

'Balls. Have a drink, you've earned it.'

'Yes, well, I've been paid.'

She makes a grab for the jacket, but he holds it away from her. 'C'mon, stop messin',' she says, and makes another grab. Ivan tosses the jacket to Campbell. When she goes to him, he throws it back to Ivan. 'Mr Connor, please.'

'Call me Ivan.'

'Ivan, please, I really have to—'

He throws the jacket back at Campbell, but Campbell has moved to pick up his drink and instead it lands on the fire.

'Jesus Christ!'

Ivan and Campbell can't help but roar as Donna dives past them and pulls her coat out of the flames. She drops it on the ground and stamps on it.

'Now that's what I call a smoking jacket,' Campbell says, and that sets them off again.

Donna lifts her coat, and they all see the large hole melted in the back of it. The air is now rich, or possibly poor, with the aroma of melted synthetics.

'What the fuck did you do that for!'

'Was only mucking about,' Ivan says, then looks at the damage critically. 'It's a cheap old thing. I'll buy you a ming coat.'

'*Mink*,' Campbell corrects.

'You are both such fucking arseholes.' She throws the coat in Ivan's face and storms out of the bar.

'Yes!' Ivan shouts after her. 'But in the morning I will still be ugly!'

The pub door slams.

'Do you think I should go after her?' Ivan asks, then belches. A moment later he adds, 'Or should I go to the bar?'

They nod as one.

When he comes back with more cider Campbell says, 'I was thinking, I should have taken her phone number. We'll need her again.'

Ivan nods sagely. 'We are so fucking crap at this.'

Campbell shakes his head and removes the cheque from his jacket. He holds it up for inspection. One million pounds. Made out to Campbell Foster. He is of course aware, somewhere in the back of his mind, that he is only entitled to 10 per cent of it. That he will be passing on fully £900,000 to Ivan in the coming days, or indeed weeks. But for now he ignores this. He feels the texture of the paper, traces the outline of his name, circles the series of zeroes with his little finger. Wonders how someone can just type some figures into a computer, and suddenly he's a rich man. He has made the deal of the century. 'Not *that* fucking crap, Ivan.'

'No,' Ivan says, 'not *that* fucking crap.'

He collapses into his seat. Within five minutes they are both asleep.

There is something spectacularly awful about a cider hangover. It makes death seem like a pleasant day out at the seaside.

Ivan spends the next morning throwing up, dreaming feverishly, holding his head and calling for his mother. He hasn't the strength to crawl out of bed for his headache pills, nor the stomach to hold them down. He is suffering so much. A horse would be put down in his condition. Although a horse probably wouldn't drink as much cider.

'You've only yourself to blame,' Mother says from the doorway.

'Go away.'

'Can I get you an egg?'

'GO AWAY.'

'Campbell phoned.'

'Mother . . .'

'He was on the news. April May was on the news. The newspapers are downstairs. They're raving about her.'

'Mother – I don't care. I'm dying.'

'You've only yourself to blame.'

She leaves him be. He falls asleep. He dreams about being chased by crabs on a desert island. He wakes in the early afternoon and finds a glass of orange by his bed and two of his mother's headache pills. Bless. He manages to get them down and hold them down, then pulls the quilt up over his head. He tries to remember how he got into this state. He remembers waiting outside the Winfrey building, Campbell producing a cheque – Christ, a million pounds – they did it, they really did it. They suckered them, they pulled off the con of the century, they're made, they're the men . . .

We *are* the men.

Setting fire to Donna's jacket.

God.

Mortification.

At four the phone rings downstairs and his mother shouts up to him. He staggers down in his underpants and lifts the receiver. 'Morgue,' he croaks.

'Must be a different morgue from this one,' Campbell says.

'I'm never drinking again,' Ivan says.

'We're millionaires.'

'I know. One more drink to celebrate.' He laughs dryly, very dryly.

'We pulled it off,' Campbell says.

'We did.'

'Have you seen the papers?'

'I haven't seen daylight yet, Campbell.'

'April's all over them. My phone's ringing off the hook, and I have two of them now. Everyone wants to meet her.'

'What did you tell them?'

'That she's gone to ground. Working on her next book. Look, we have to talk to Donna. Sort out some kind of contract. This is only a down payment. We have to keep it up until the book comes out.'

'I set fire to her coat.'

'I know. You'll have to apologise. That was well out of order.'

'You were just as bad.'

'I didn't set fire to her coat. Or call her a trollop.'

'I called her a trollop?'

'Amongst other things. You've a lot of grovelling to do.'

'You're my agent, that's what I pay you for.'

'No, that's a slave you're thinking of. I'm your literary agent. I do the deals, you do the apologising.'

'You can't make me.'

'No, I can't.'

Ivan sighs. 'Okay. All right, I'll speak to her. Give me her number.'

'I don't have her number. She's your friend.'

'She's not my friend. Give me her address.'

'I don't have her address. She doesn't know me from Adam, and she probably doesn't know Adam. Why don't you call your friends at the prison? They'll know where she is.'

'They're not my friends.' He tuts. 'Okay. I'll do it in the morning.'

'You'll do it now.'

'I'm not well.'

'Tough. Call me back when you know what's what.'

Ivan puts the phone down. He asks his mother to look up the number of the prison for him, and she tells him to do it himself. He says he's half-blind and his head is dizzy and she says she left headache pills by his bed. He sits at the bottom of the stairs and laboriously works his way through the telephone directory until he finds a listing for the prison. He dials and asks to speak to the Governor.

'You mean the Chief Executive.'

'Yes. Whatever.'

'Who will I say is calling?'

'The Late Charles Dickens.'

'And what company are you from?'

'The Mutual Friends.'

'Is that an insurance company?'

'Yes.'

'Hold on.'

A moment later the familiar voice of Barbara Cohen comes on. She says, 'Charles Dickens, Mutual Friends, I suspect an alias.'

'Got me first time, Guv'nor.'

'It's Chief Executive.'

'If you're Chief Executive, does that mean there are lots of little executives running about?'

'Of course.'

'But still popularly known as warders?'

'Who is this, exactly?'

'Ivan Connor.'

'Ivan. What a pleasure. But sorry – two creative-writing classes a week is our absolute limit.'

'It's not about that. I need to ask you a favour. I'm trying to track down that girl Donna, from my class.'

Barbara Cohen sighs. 'Yes, dear,' she says. 'Aren't we all.'

Five minutes later, hangover forgotten, Ivan's screaming down the phone to Campbell: 'She's escaped from prison! She's on the run!'

'Who?'

'Who the fuck do you think?! April May! Donna!'

'You mean she's—'

'I mean she's escaped from fucking prison. She told us she was on licence or parole or whatever the hell you call it. But she wasn't! She escaped! She's on the run! Oh holy fuck, I can't take much more excitement. I should go and lie down.'

'This isn't good,' Campbell says.

'It's bloody awful. Jesus, Campbell, have you any idea what this will look like when it gets out?'

'No, Ivan. Why don't you explain it to me?'

'There's no need for sarcasm.'

'Well, don't state the bleeding obvious then. Christ. This is all we need.'

'We're accessories!'

'We're not. We're fraudsters. We'd nothing to do with this.'

'That's right, one moment she's behind bars, the next we've given her a disguise and milked some company for a million quid.'

'*And* we gave her a couple of thousand for her trouble,' Campbell reminds him.

'Did we? Shit! It'll look like she's part of our gang. We're all going to prison!'

'We're not going to prison.'

'Christ, we're lucky to even be alive.' Ivan shudders.

'What're you talking about now?'

'Donna – you know what she was inside for? *Stabbing* someone. And I burned her coat. She probably wasn't coming to talk poetry at all. She was coming for me – to cut my throat. Christ, I need a drink.'

'Pub?'

'Pub.'

They meet in the Speckled Goat forty-five minutes later. Campbell sets the drinks down and says, 'It's important that we look at this soberly. I was thinking about it on the way over. There are a number of alternatives. One, we go directly to the police, and confess all.'

'They won't believe a word. Not with my record.'

'You have a record?'

'I'd rather not talk about it.' The man who put the *kid* in *kid*napping.

'It's important right now that we're honest with each other.'

'It was a misunderstanding. I wasn't charged.'

'Then it isn't a record.'

'Elephants and the police never forget. You said a number of alternatives. Hit me with them.'

'Two, we track Dolly down ourselves.'

'Donna.'

'Donna.'

'You mean finding her where the police and the prison service can't? I think not.'

'I disagree. They'll hardly be breaking a gut looking for her. City this size? We've as good a chance as they have. We need her, Ivan. We've only received the first payment, and they can take that back if we don't fulfil our obligations.'

Ivan sighs. 'So what if by some miracle we do track her down?'

'We exploit her ruthlessly, then if it looks like there's any chance at all that we'll be rumbled we hand her in to the police and say she hoodwinked us as well.'

'That's pretty cold and calculating.'

'Hey, I'm an agent.'

'You've never been cold and calculating in your life.'

Campbell smiles. 'Why thank you, Ivan.'

Ivan raises his drink. 'Christ,' he says.

'Well,' Campbell says, 'you'd better get moving.'

'What?'

'If you're going to track her down, you'd better get moving.'

'Me?'

'I told you before, I'm the agent. I do the deals and the paperwork. You do the writing, the apologies and the tracking down. Ivan, this is too important for you to waste time drinking in a pub. Get out there and find her. I have to cover for April May, I can't be scouring the backstreets of London looking for her. She's practically an industry now, and I've got to protect that. Now get your arse in gear.'

Ivan glares at his agent, then raises his pint and downs it in one. He wipes the back of his hand across his lips, then stands. 'I'll bet you wouldn't treat Oscar Wilde like this.'

'Ivan, I wouldn't treat Marty Wilde like this, but we're desperate. Now go and find Dolly.'

14

He's not Sherlock Holmes. He's not even *Basil, The Great Mouse Detective* or *Inch-High Private Eye*. He's hopeless, but he has an idea. And there's nothing worse than a hopeless man with an idea.

He rushes around to Pages where he finds his friend Marcus actually serving a customer. This is not Ivan's normal time for visiting the bookshop, so it might be as busy as this every day at 4.30 p.m., but he's so desperate for help that he actually feels affronted that Marcus doesn't get rid of his customer immediately in order to devote his complete attention to him – a real author, the heart of a generation etc. Marcus doesn't even feel the need to point out to the customer that an acclaimed author has entered the shop. He just nods at him over the customer's shoulder and rolls his eyes. The customer doesn't notice, he just whitters on about this title and that title and then another, none of them in stock, none of them even in print.

Ivan paces up and down, glancing at his watch, letting go with a sigh every so often to indicate his displeasure.

Eventually Marcus himself reaches the end of his patience and finishes the conversation with a curt, 'I'm sorry, sir, but you had your time in the sun, the public is so fickle.' The customer nods sadly and shuffles out of the shop. Marcus shakes his head after him. 'Of course your situation is entirely different. You were built for longevity, Ivan. Your books will be in print long after you're dead.'

'I'd prefer them to be in print while I'm alive.'

'Yes, well, it's not a perfect world. Besides, *I* have them all on my shelves, the complete works. What other bookseller can claim that?'

'This is depressing me, Marcus. Let's move on.'

'Oh Ivan, you would find a downside to heaven. Be happy that they're here at all. Now, what has you in here at this time of day?'

'I'm looking for a woman.'

'Have you tried King's Cross?'

'Please. She's an escaped prisoner.'

'Author turned bounty hunter . . . interesting.'

'I can't tell you the whole story, but she must be found. I need your help.'

'Ivan, you've come to the right place. For a book. Now please tell me what you're on.'

'I'm serious. I've to find this girl or – well, I prefer not to think about the *or*. You have to help me! I'm your most loyal customer.'

'You're my most loyal *visitor*, which is a different thing entirely. Why me?'

'Because when you don't have customers you read

nothing but detective books, and apart from this recent aberration, you don't have customers, so you must have read every detective novel on the go. You'll know where to start. You'll know how to crack a case like this. I'm hopeless. I've been on it for four hours and the most I've managed is a call to Directory Enquiries – and that was a waste of time. Tell me what to do, Marcus. Please – tell me what to do.'

Marcus looks suitably thoughtful. Then he reaches under the counter and produces a bottle of wine. He pours two glasses. Before either of them are touched he says, 'Two hundred quid a day, plus expenses.'

'What?'

'Two hundred quid a day, plus expenses. That's what I charge for my PI work.'

'What're you talking about? *What* PI work?'

'Everyone has to start somewhere. Okay, I'll give you a discount. One fifty, plus expenses. Seeing as how you're my first case.'

'I'm not your first anything. I just want some pointers in the right direction. I don't want to hire a PI. Or a bookshop owner, for that matter.'

'Okay. Please yourself.'

'So what do you think?'

'About what?'

'About where I should start. Looking for her.'

'I'm afraid I'm not at liberty to talk about it.'

'Marcus, for fuck's sake.'

'Marcus PI, if you will.'

Ivan sighs. He takes a drink. Marcus takes a drink. They eye each other up.

'One hundred a day, plus expenses,' Marcus says.

'What kind of expenses?'

'Well, I don't really know. I haven't really thought about it. Lunch.'

'One hundred all in. No expenses, no excuses, you find Donna Carbone and bring her in.'

'One hundred all in, no expenses, no excuses, I'll help you track her down.'

'What's that supposed to mean, you'll *help* me?'

'Well, for a start I've only a provisional licence for my car, so I'll need a qualified driver beside me.'

'Christ.'

'And then you'll have to be there anyway so you can make a positive ID. You wouldn't want me pouncing on some dame, drugging her with chloroform, throwing her into the boot, bringing her back here, only to discover I'd picked up the wrong floozy, would you?'

Ivan summons the latest in a long line of sighs. 'Marcus, she's not a dame, or a floozy, and I don't want anyone chloroformed. I just want to find out where she is and have a chat. Now, why don't you stop the fannying around and start working out how you're going to track her down.'

Marcus nods slowly. He takes a sip of his wine. 'So you've tried Directory Enquiries?'

Ivan doesn't intend to tell Marcus anything about the great April May, but he's not only panicked by the consequences of not finding Donna, he's also kind of proud of having thought up such a daring scheme and pulled it off – six million pounds, remember – so that before he's halfway through his third glass of wine, he's spilled the beans.

Marcus refuses to close the shop until exactly 5.45 p.m., despite the gravity of the situation and the fact that there is nil likelihood of any other customers. 'It's a matter of appearance,' he says. When the shutters are finally down he issues a very overdue, and suitably impressed, 'Christ, Ivan, I didn't know you had it in you. You're a dark horse, aren't you? Six million. My God. You could start your own publishing company. Or a chain of bookshops.'

'No, and no. Let's stick to the case.'

Marcus asks him to relate every single detail he can recall of his previous encounters with Donna Carbone, from the first day he really became aware of her in his prison writing class, to her storming out of the pub after her coat was burned.

'So what do you think?' he asks when he's sure he's told him everything relevant.

'I think there's probably a love-hate thing going on here. You're sure there's nothing happened between—'

'Marcus, please.'

'Okay. First of all, the cheques you and Campbell wrote for her. If she's just out of prison, she's probably short of cash. Shouldn't be overly complicated to track down where she cashed them. Most probably a bank. Should give us the general location. But could take a couple of days to come through.'

'We don't have a couple of days.' He pauses. He realises he's slipping into detective speak. 'Well, yes, we probably do, but I'd really like to get this sorted out.'

'Okay, then, second, were you aware of anything unique about her ensemble?'

'Ensemble, Marcus?'

'Her clothes. Designer labels. We could possibly track her down through a particular shop . . .'

'Look, she's on the run from prison, not going to a royal wedding. Christ.'

'Don't get narky with me, you've hardly given me anything to work on. Was she wearing a particularly memorable type of perfume? Or smoking an unusual brand of cigarettes?'

'I've changed my mind, I can do better than this myself.'

'What about her car? A number plate, a garage sticker . . .'

'It was stolen, Marcus.'

'Oh. From the prison?'

'I don't know.'

'Could you find out?'

'Not really. I don't understand the relevance.'

'Well, she's a girl. She's probably not very good at stealing cars. I mean, my sister Bernie's been driving for twenty-five years and still can't put petrol in by herself. Says she can't get the petrol cap off, and then she feels embarrassed standing there with this big—'

'Marcus.'

'What I'm saying is, seventy-five per cent of murders and serious assaults are carried out by a close relative, you know – they're domestic.'

'Nobody has been murdered.'

'I know, but the same probably applies to stolen cars, if you factor in the fact that women are traditionally crap at stealing them. So if you could remember a licence plate or a—'

'Log book,' Ivan says suddenly.

'Log book, even better.'

'I looked at the log book. I was bored.'

'And nosy.'

'Whatever. I read it. I remember thinking at the time, I wonder who owns this because it wasn't in her name.'

'Whose name was it?'

Ivan shakes his head. 'I can't remember.'

'You read it, you must remember. Name, address. Think, man! It could be vital.'

'That's not going to help me remember.'

'Well, what *is* going to help you?'

Ivan wakes the next morning with a tremendous hangover. He's sick in the bathroom, his mother asks him if he wants an egg, he staggers downstairs and lifts the phone. It is 11.15 a.m. He calls Marcus.

'I've remembered.'

'Fantastic.'

Marcus has been in the shop since the stroke of nine.

'I can be there in twenty minutes,' Ivan says. 'Make that an hour.'

'No can do.'

'No can do what?'

'I can't go with you. This is my busy day.'

'What are you talking about? You don't have busy days.'

'Wednesdays, always. Can't do it, Ivan.' Ivan hears a dinging sound down the line. 'Uh-oh, better go, here's a customer.'

'Marcus, there's no customer, you've just tapped a spoon against the glass in front of you.'

'I did *not*,' Marcus says, outraged. And then several silent moments later: 'It's not a spoon. It's a pen.'

'Marcus.'

'I'm sorry, Ivan, I can't. I've been warned off. Four big guys came into the shop and said if I had anything more to do with the case they'd break my legs.'

'Now you're being pathetic. You've never had more than two people in the shop at any one time. The *Guinness Book of Records* would be on to you. Now what's the real reason?'

Marcus sighs. 'Dentist.'

'Marcus.'

'I'm serious. I'm having two teeth crowned. It's costing me nearly a thousand quid. It's either crowns or I lose them, and I don't want to lose them. I've been waiting months for this appointment.'

'You didn't mention it yesterday.'

'I wasn't getting it done yesterday.'

'Marcus.'

'I'm sorry. I just hate getting injections. I hate being numb, and slobbering everywhere. I'm very nervous. But it must be done. If you wait until Friday, I'll be right as rain. Thursday's no good, but Friday's fine. What do you say?'

'I can't wait until Friday. I told you, this is urgent.'

'I suppose I'm more of a bookshop owner than a detective.'

'Oh well.' Ivan sighs. 'It's nothing to be ashamed of.'

'I wish you every luck in your quest.'

'Thank you, Marcus.'

*　　*　　*

He's driving to Tower Hamlets. Looking for Jon Teckman. The name came back to him in the midst of his drunken thrashings in bed; and wonder of wonders, the address too. It's such a wonderful thing when you assault the unconscious mind with large amounts of alcohol. Obscure facts cascade out, novels of the calibre of *Kissing Cousins* are created. Sure, you might forget a thousand things from the night before, but a good blow-out on the sauce almost always produces some nugget of long-lost information – although generally it's of the completely useless variety, like the capital of Honduras or the square root of anything. But on this occasion he has managed to dredge up a real hidden treasure. The only thing missing now is the exact house number – but that shouldn't be much of a deterrent.

Tower Hamlets.

Jon Teckman.

Sherlock, put that in your pipe and choke on it.

He knows nothing about Tower Hamlets beyond the fact that he probably won't be instantly recognised there as the author of *Chapter & Verse*, as he would be in, say, his own house.

The address he remembers is Verdant Manor, but long before he finds it Ivan realises he's probably not looking for a manor house swathed in ivy. These are either shabby tower blocks or shabby terraces, with even shabbier people. He feels quite excited, really. He has lived in a leafy suburb for too long. He needs to get out more, experience life, live on the edge, dance with the devil.

Verdant Manor is a huge grey block of flats. Not even an American or an estate agent would risk calling such monstrosities apartments. He thinks *monstrosities* is perfect – *monstros*, and *cities* – put them together and you have the very definition of Verdant Manor. Even from where he sits in his mother's Fiat Uno, trying to affix the security bar to the steering wheel, he can sense that each of Verdant Manor's two hundred plus flats will be small, decrepit and dangerous. If these flats were human, he thinks, they would be like Barney Rubble on crack cocaine. (He loves this analogy so much he writes it down for future use. Perhaps in *Story of the Blues*.) He has deliberately not shaved this morning. He's wearing his long black coat with the burned bits around the bottom. He has undone his top shirt button and has a used match jutting out between his lips. He fancies he looks like The Man With No Name, although in fact he looks like The Man With No Money, Sense or Lucrative Publishing Contract. You can take the man out of his culture, but you can't take the culture out of the man.

He walks away from his mother's car, glancing back every ten metres or so to check that it isn't being interfered with.

When he enters Verdant Manor he is immediately assailed by the stench of – well, he'd expected urine and degradation, but it actually smells of disinfectant and fresh paint. When he reaches the stairs leading to the first-floor flats he sees orange-suited council workers hard at work painting over graffiti. He smiles at them and they nod sullenly back.

He takes the steps to the first floor three at a time, and then pauses to get his breath back outside the front door of No. 1, Verdant Manor. Before he knocks, he glances over the balcony to check that his mother's car is still okay. Reassured, he raps on the door, and in a few moments an elderly black lady opens it a fraction and peers cautiously out.

'I'm so sorry to trouble—'

She closes the door.

He tries No. 2.

'I'm awfully sorry—'

The door is slammed.

'I'm—'

Slam.

'—'

Slam.

Before knocking on No. 16, he pauses for a moment of reflection. Clearly he hasn't got the approach quite right. It's a psychological thing. A mind set. An attitude. He might think he looks like Clint Eastwood, but he comes across like Noël Coward on his uppers. He's a big enough man to realise this and do something about it. He needs to toughen up. This is clearly one of the most dangerous and deprived areas of London: he needs to think bookies, not bookshops.

He takes a deep breath and tries to will himself into hardness. He rolls his neck like Tyson. He bunches his fleshy hands into fists, then puts one inside his jacket like he has a gun and lets the other hang loose at his side, ready to strike; the impression of hands of death, when they're really hands like feet.

Don't mess with me, motherfucker.

Don't fuck with me you motherfucking motherfucker.

He strikes No. 16 hard, three times, then bares his teeth.

An elderly woman with a boiled egg in an egg-cup in one hand answers the door.

'Excuse me, but you wouldn't happen to have any idea where Jon Teckman lives?'

'Jon Teckman? Oh yes. Number thirty-two, I think.'

'Oh great. Thanks awfully.'

She nods and closes the door.

When he hears the bolts being drawn back across, he points at the door and whispers, 'Motherfucker.'

15

No. 32 is only distinctive because the front window is boarded up. This could be for any number of reasons. A child's ball or a misguided sparrow. Or it could just indicate a derelict flat. But he thinks more probably it's a crack house. *Crack flat.* Ivan has no idea what a crack flat might be. He only has a vague notion of what crack itself is. He has dealt with drugs in his novels, but these have mostly involved opium dens on the sub-continent in the heyday of the British Empire. He's not really street smart, Ivan. He's not knocking on the door because he's brave, he's knocking because he's naive; he realises this when the door opens suddenly and a big guy grabs a fistful of his shirt and drags him inside and slams him against a wall. There's an odour of Chinese takeaway. There's hardly any furniture, no TV, the tinny beat of a cheap radio, and there's an angry, spittle-mouthed face stuck into his, yelling, 'I've had it up to fucking here!' and he's slammed against the wall again. 'I'll fucking pay you when I can! I'm doing my best!'

Then the guy lets him go and Ivan slumps down to his knees, his head spinning.

Jon Teckman lets out a frustrated howl as he stalks away. He stands in the kitchen and drums his fingers on the draining board. He glares back at Ivan, who's cautiously raising himself. Teckman isn't actually as big as Ivan thought he was; in fact Ivan realises that he's probably taller, bulkier than Teckman is. The other guy is quite weedy. And small. But remembering fully the lesson of David and Goliath, Ivan remains where he is, leaning against the wall and looking worried. Hitler and Napoleon were quite small. Charles Manson wasn't exactly a giraffe. It's not the size of the man, it's the size of his violence. Somebody famous said that, and Ivan suspects it was himself. Teckman is wearing a white T-shirt and blue jeans; he has an earring in his right ear; his teeth aren't good; his fingers are stained with nicotine.

'Well?' Teckman growls. 'What this time? The bed? The fucking toilet? Fuck it, take what you want.'

Ivan clears his throat. 'I'm not sure if you quite understand why I'm here.' Teckman's little eyes get smaller. 'Have you ever heard of the Church of the Latter Day Saints?' Ivan asks weakly. 'We're going from door to—'

Teckman is charging across the room towards him, fists ready.

Ivan hurriedly spits out: 'I'm looking for Donna!'

Teckman stops suddenly, genuinely surprised, 'What?'

'Donna,' Ivan says. 'Donna Carbone.'

'What do you want with that cunt?'

Ivan clears his throat again. 'Well. It's important.' And then he's grabbed by the throat and pushed back up against the wall.

'You find that little bitch, you tell her I'm lookin' for her too. I'll rip her fucking head off, do you hear me?' Ivan can hear him. He nods loudly. He's on the verge of tears – he hasn't been manhandled like this since boarding school – so it comes as a considerable surprise when Teckman himself suddenly bursts into tears. He gives Ivan a final half-hearted thrust against the wall, then lets him go and reels away across the room, tears cascading down his face. 'That bitch!' he splutters. 'That fucking bitch!'

Teckman collapses into an armchair and buries his face in his hands. His shoulders move up and down. Ivan remains against the wall for several moments, then cautiously pushes himself off.

'Would you, um, like me to make you a cup of tea?'

Teckman shakes his head.

'It's no trouble.'

'They took the fucking kettle.'

'Oh.' Ivan nods sympathetically. 'What about a glass of water?' Teckman shakes his head. 'Who, um, would *they* be?'

Teckman's face reappears. 'What the fuck's it got to do with you?'

'Nothing. Nothing,' Ivan says hurriedly. 'Just making . . . anyway. Ah. Obviously – Donna – not in your good books.'

Teckman laughs sarcastically. He mimics Ivan. '*Good books*? Would someone who did *this* ever be in my good books?' and he suddenly pulls up his T-shirt and Ivan winces as he sees that Teckman's chest is criss-crossed by a dozen or more jagged scars. 'Impressed?' Teckman says as he lowers his shirt. 'The fucking surgeons were. Nearly lost me. Fucking bitch.'

'God,' Ivan says.

'Yeah, sure.' Teckman removes a crumpled packet of cigarettes from down the side of the chair, takes one, lights it, then offers the packet to Ivan, who shakes his head. 'So,' he says after taking a long draw, 'what's she done to you? Do you want to compare scars or something?'

'No – no, nothing like that. I'm just looking for her.'

'Steal your money, did she? What're you, Sugar Daddy number five?'

'No, of course not. I . . . you know she's escaped from prison?'

'Know – course I fucking know! Fucking police called round to warn me. Been living on my fucking nerves since I heard. Swore last time she'd finish me off, the fucking cow. Scared to go fucking outside.'

'So she hasn't been here.'

'Oh she's been here all right. Stole me fucking car, the bitch. Nearly broke the fucking door down. Woulda had me 'n' all if I hadn't phoned the filth.'

Ivan, without thinking, observes. 'You haven't got a phone.'

'Fucking mobile, you cunt.'

'Of course. Sorry. Were, ah, you two married or—'

'Fuck no. I lived with the bitch for a while, then I decided it was time to move on and she went fucking mental on me. Fucking Stalker of the Year, she is. She doing you as well?'

'Me? No. I . . . well, I teach in the prison and I was supposed to kind of be keeping an eye on her, helping her with her poetry.'

'Oh don't start me on the fucking poetry! Fucking psycho or what?!'

'Well, I—'

'I mean, get a life, go out and get a fucking job, bitch.'

'Yes. Of course.'

Ivan jumps as Teckman suddenly leaps out of his chair. But he's only turning round, lifting the cushion, and reaching underneath. He produces a notebook and holds it aloft triumphantly. 'This is what she's fucking after. The collected works of Donna Fucking Carbone. If I'd given this to her fucking psychiatrist, they would have thrown away the fucking key.' He flicks carelessly through the pages, tearing their edges as he goes, shaking his head. Then he pauses and his eyes, suddenly filled with an idea, flit up to Ivan. 'You want her back?'

'Yes, I do.'

'Then take this. She'll do anything for it.'

'Well, that's awfully decent of you.'

'Three hundred.'

'Yes, that's a lot of poems.'

'No, three hundred quid.'

'I'm sorry, I really don't think—'

'One hundred. Christ, man, look at the state of me, look at this fucking place. I've nothing to eat, nothing to watch, Jesus, I've two calls left on my mobile. That's one to the Samaritans and one for an ambulance, unless you help me out. Come on. You'll catch her with this. Swear to Christ.'

Ivan reluctantly removes his wallet. He turns away slightly as he checks his fiscal reserves. He has a hundred pounds.

'Fifty,' he ventures shakily.

Teckman throws the book at him. 'Done,' he says.

When he has stuffed the money safely into his pocket he shakes his head dismissively at Ivan. 'Fucking loser,' he says, 'paying fifty quid for that shit.'

'But it'll bring her back.'

'Yeah – and you'll regret it for the rest of your fucking short life.'

Ivan looks down from the balcony and sees a gang of kids gathered around his mother's car. He lets out a shout and they start running. By the time he's down the two flights of stairs and across the road he can hardly breathe, and the kids have probably been home and had their dinner.

He cautiously examines the outside of the car – no sign of damage. Four tyres. No obvious vandalism. Nothing scratched into the paintwork. He tries the driver's door. It is still locked.

He breathes a sigh of relief and opens the car. Inside – everything as it was before. He checks the radio, the tape player – she doesn't believe in CDs – and the glove compartment, which contains the log book, and a bag of boiled sweets. Ivan removes Donna's notebook from his coat pocket and stuffs it into what little space remains. He's trying to think positive – the car is fine, he has learned the truth about Donna Carbone, and it has only cost him fifty quid. He will call Campbell as soon as he gets home. They've both had a lucky escape; now the charade must end.

It's not particularly bright, but Ivan nevertheless removes a pair of sunglasses from his coat and puts them on. He has walked on the wild side and come out smelling of roses, and Chinese takeaway. He has stood up to violence, and come away with a result. Marcus would be proud of him. Ivan switches the radio on and turns the dial until he finds Classic FM. Vivaldi. He turns it up loud. He's willing to bet that nobody in Verdant Manor, or even Tower Hamlets, has ever heard Vivaldi at full blast.

Until now.

Ivan starts the car, moves forward. He puts his elbow out of the window. He's a pretty cool dude, Ivan Connor.

He's about a hundred yards down the road when he realises that he didn't actually wind the window down in order to put his elbow out. He's another twenty yards down the road when he realises those little bastards have stolen his side window.

He's at the garage, getting a replacement window, sitting in a cramped waiting room, running a thousand per-mutations through his head. How they can hold on to the money, how they can keep the con going, how to recruit a second April May and get away with it, how to reveal himself as the true author of *Kissing Cousins and* keep the money, how to rehabilitate his reputa-tion as a great author by presenting *Kissing Cousins* as the first post-post-modernist novel of the twenty-first century, but without all the fuss. He wants adoration and huge sales, but he also wants to be left alone to sit behind his computer screen and type. That's all. Maybe a modest little party once a year to celebrate the latest publication. And he would be quite happy never to see Donna Carbone again. He realises that he's touching his chest while he's thinking about her, that his fingers are tracing the outlines of imaginary scars.

Jesus, close call or what.

They tell him the car will be ready in half an hour. An hour later he peeks into the workshop on his way to the call box outside and sees the car still sitting there, untouched, with several others ahead of it in the queue. He sighs and phones Campbell.

It's answered on the third ring. 'Campbell Foster and Associates,' a female voice says.

Ivan is momentarily taken aback. 'Oh. Is that . . . is Campbell there?'

'Mr Foster?'

'Yes, Mr Foster.'

'Who will I say is calling?'

'Ivan.'

'Ivan who?'

'No, that's a novel by Walter Scott.'

'Excuse me?'

'Ivan Connor.'

'From?'

'What do you mean, from?'

'What company?'

'No company. Who the hell are you anyway?'

She puts the phone down. Ivan calls back. 'Mr Foster, please,' he says, in a slightly different accent.

'Who shall I say is calling?'

'Graham Greene.'

'One moment, please.'

Ivan hears her saying, 'Graham Greene,' and a moment later Campbell is on the line.

'Mr Greene?' he says.

'Campbell, what the fuck is going on?'

'Ivan. How're you doing? I've been trying to call you.'

'Who's the girl?'

'My receptionist? You should see her. She's lovely.'

'Yes, I'm sure she is. Since when did you need a receptionist?'

'Ivan, you've no idea what it's like. The press, other authors wanting representation, publishers wanting rights, I've never seen anything like it. We've a lot to thank April May for – and we've hardly started. Now, where are you?'

'I'm in a garage, getting my car fixed.'

'You don't have a car.'

'I'm getting my mother's car fixed if you want to be precise. And the fact of the matter is I haven't enough cash to pay for it.'

'Put it on your credit card.'

'Campbell, what I'm saying, in my roundabout way, is how can you afford a receptionist and a new office, and I'm presuming here it *is* a new office with tasteful decoration and plants and a water dispenser and a fucking coffee percolator, when I'm sitting in a dodgy backstreet car shop hoping to Christ I've enough money to pay for an extremely minor repair to my car. My mother's car. I'm wondering all this because I was under the impression that I got ninety per cent of the money and you got ten.'

'It's quite simple, Ivan. Yes, I do indeed have all of those things you mention – the water, the coffee – because in order to pass myself off as a successful literary agent I need to have the right trappings. All of this, and more, has been and will be attained on the basis of me earning ten per cent of what April May earns, and you earning ninety per cent, less the usual expenses.'

'The usual what?'

'Expenses.'

'Being what, exactly?'

'Ivan, for God's sake, don't worry about it. It's just paperwork, photocopying. God, you sound so paranoid.'

'I'm paranoid because I haven't got any money.'

'Ivan – *I* haven't got any money yet. It's all on credit. Have you any idea how long a cheque for a million pounds takes to clear? I have this lot on trust, Ivan. It'll be a couple of weeks before the money comes through, and then, I swear to God, you'll be rolling in it. Now, what about Dolly?'

'Donna.'

'Donna.'

'Christ, Campbell, what have we got ourselves into?'

'An awful lot of money. And money, as you know, can solve anything. So tell me about Donna.'

'She's a psychotic bitch from hell.'

'What?'

'She was in prison for stabbing someone about ninety times.'

'Oh dear.'

'Oh dear indeed.'

'So you found her?'

'No, but I found out about her. And if we never have anything more to do with her, then it'll be too soon. Do you understand?'

Campbell takes his point. Ish. He arranges to call over to the house later so they can talk it through.

When Ivan arrives home he doesn't mention the damage to the car – Mother would only worry. And besides, Donna Carbone is sitting in the kitchen, eating his dinner.

16

Mother is saying, 'Oh the poor little waif, I felt so sorry for her,' while Ivan finds himself almost hypnotically drawn to the cutlery Donna is using, and in particular, the steak knife. 'You know she slept in her car last night? The little darling is homeless.'

'That's what *Big Issue*s are for, Mother,' Ivan hisses from the doorway.

Mother sniffs. 'I would like to think that if or when you become homeless, somebody might have the heart to look after you, Ivan. Now show some compassion.'

He should tell his mother to call the police. But he doesn't, because Donna smiles sheepishly up at him and says, 'I hope you don't mind, Mr Connor. Your mother took me in. I'd nowhere else to go.'

Mother squeezes his arm and whispers, 'She's had a row with her boyfriend – left him. Sounds like a nasty piece of work.'

'No, of course not,' Ivan tells Donna. 'We were worried

about you, disappearing like that.' He pulls out a chair and sits opposite her. He glances expectantly at his mother.

'You're late,' she says, 'and she was hungry. You may make yourself a sandwich.'

'I don't want a sandwich.'

'Whatever.' She's pulling on her coat now, lifting her bag. 'I'm going to my salsa class. I'll see you later. Donna? Nice to meet you. I've made up a bed in the spare room.'

Ivan's mouth drops slightly open.

'Really,' Donna begins, 'there's no need—'

'Nonsense. Any friend of Ivan's is a friend of mine. Isn't that right, son?'

'Yes, Mother.'

'Well, thank you, Mrs Connor. Mr Connor.'

Mother laughs. 'Don't call him *mister*. You'll make him sound all grown-up. Call him Ivan.'

She smiles, and leaves. Ivan rubs at his brow and sighs. He gets up and goes to the cupboard looking for something to drink. All he can find is sugar-free Ribena. There's still some dandelion wine upstairs, but he's reluctant to leave Donna alone, or to give her the opportunity to follow him upstairs with a steak knife. Better here, in plain sight, with access to his own array of kitchen utensils. Although he isn't eating, he removes a knife and fork from the drawer and sits down with them before him. If she suddenly hurls herself across the table he can skewer her with the fork and drive the knife into her brain through her left ear.

She says, 'I'm sorry about running off like that, Mr Connor.'

'Ivan, please. I'm sorry about burning your coat.'

'It was an old coat.'

'Nevertheless.'

'I suppose you've been looking for me.'

'Did Mother explain?'

Donna smiles. 'She's very . . . what's the expression, "with it", for someone of her age, isn't she? Martial arts, salsa, and she knows all sorts of crap about the state of British publishing.'

'Yes, well, she has to listen to me a lot.'

'I told her I was on the run from prison.'

'Oh. Right.'

'For something I didn't do.'

Ivan nods.

'You don't believe me, do you?'

He shrugs. 'I'd like to believe you.'

'But every con says she's innocent.'

He shrugs again. 'Donna. We're in an awkward situation here. We really need you right now, for April May, but if we'd known about you escaping from prison . . .'

'I didn't escape.' She bites on her lip for a moment. 'I just didn't go back. I had a day release, but then I went round to my boyfriend's and we had a row and somehow I ended up drunk and then, and then . . . I just didn't go back.'

'They're all looking for you.'

'I know. But I'm hardly public enemy number one. Although I might squeeze into the top fifty.' She smiles, and it's quite endearing. He gives a short laugh.

'What are we going to do with you?'

She grins, then continues eating.

'Did you really sleep in the car?'

'There wasn't much sleeping involved.'

'Don't you have family?'

'Not that talk to me.'

'Friends?'

She shakes her head.

'What about this boyfriend?' He's fishing. 'No chance of making it up?'

She shakes her head again, and avoids eye-contact. She sets her knife and fork down. 'Did you see the papers with my face splattered all over them?' He nods. 'Pretty cool, wasn't it?'

He has to agree. She did look pretty cool. For a killer. Or as near as dammit.

The doorbell sounds, and Donna jumps. She looks at Ivan accusingly. 'You . . . ?'

Ivan raises his hands, half-placatory and half-defensive. 'Of course I didn't. Just sit where you are. Have some bread and jam.'

Ivan goes to the door thinking, What if it's the police, and they've surrounded the house with marksmen? What if they storm the house? What if they shoot first and ask questions later? He hesitates by the hall light. If I switch it on, will I be cut down in a hail of bullets like Butch Cassidy?

The bell sounds again. Mother has that stained glass cut in a diamond shape in the window, so he can't make out who's beyond.

He takes a deep breath, flicks the switch, then dives across to the other side of the hall, into a small cloak-room.

When after another ten seconds there's no indication of a violent assault by a heavily armed police unit, Ivan cautiously approaches the door. Standing well to one side of it he whimpers, 'Yes? Who is it?'

'The Count of Monte Cristo, who the hell do you think it is?'

Ivan opens the door. 'Campbell,' he says sheepishly. 'I forgot.'

'Jesus, Ivan, you sound like an old woman.' He strides past him into the hall and then on down towards the closed kitchen door. 'Your mum away dancing again, is she? Honest to God, I don't know where she gets the energy from. Anyway,' he says, opening the door, 'come on, make us a cuppa and let's work out how we're going to nail this stupid cow.'

Then he sees Donna, glaring up at him from the table.

'Not you,' Campbell says quickly, 'a different cow. Not that you're a cow. I mean – Ivan,' he turns red-faced to Ivan, who can barely stop himself from laughing, 'you could have told me.' His eyes return to Donna, and now *he* realises she's holding the steak knife in her hand. Campbell glances from her to Ivan and back. 'Christ,' he says, 'are you holding him hostage?'

'Sit down, Campbell,' Ivan says, 'and I'll make us all a nice cup of tea.'

'You've changed,' Donna says, looking from one to the other. 'When I did the April thing you were excited and nervous and enthusiastic – *and* condescending – but now you look, I don't know, scared.'

191

COLIN BATEMAN

'Publishing's a scary business,' Campbell says unconvincingly.

'I'm not talking about publishing. I'm talking about me. Mr Connor, Ivan – the moment you saw me you looked like you'd seen a ghost. And you, storming in like that! I mean, what's going on?'

Campbell gives a little shrug and keeps his eyes on the table.

Ivan says, 'Well . . .' and then trails off.

'Well what?'

'Well, you've escaped from prison.'

'And Ivan says you're a psycho,' Campbell blurts out suddenly, 'although I'm prepared to give you the benefit of the doubt.'

'I never said any such thing!'

'Yes, you did!'

'Okay!' Donna bangs the handle of her steak knife down on the table, and that quietens them. In fact, it freezes them. She looks at Ivan. 'You weren't scared of me in prison.'

'Yes, I was – you thumped me.'

'Well, you deserved that. But you weren't jumping every time I said something in class, and now you are. Okay, so I'm on the run, but that doesn't automatically make me,' and she glances at Campbell, 'a psycho.' Ivan shrugs and studies the table. 'Is that what it is? You think I'm stalking you or something?' Ivan remains silent. 'Christ. You think I don't have enough problems in my life that I have to stalk some washed-up hack?'

'He's not a hack,' Campbell says.

'And I'm *not* washed up. I'm . . . simply between books.'

192

'Whatever. Christ, you're so petty. The other night you thought the sun shone out of my arse.'

'The other night we didn't know you'd stabbed someone about ninety times,' Ivan says.

It sits in the air, cold.

Tears begin to form up in Donna's eyes. She looks away. She tries not to let them fall.

'Shit,' she says, and she pushes her chair back, and Ivan and Campbell push their own chairs back a fraction of a second later, both poised to run for the hills. But she merely goes and stands by the kitchen window, staring out at nothing. Ivan and Campbell look at each other. They relax, slowly.

'You've been talking to Jon, haven't you?' Donna says quietly.

'Who?' Ivan says.

'For fuck's sake! Tell me the truth!'

'Okay. I went looking for you. I traced your car back to—'

'He's a total shit, isn't he?'

Ivan shrugs. And then says, 'I suppose so.'

'What did he tell you?'

'Why you were in prison.'

'Which was?'

Ivan hesitates for a moment, then makes a criss-cross cutting action across his chest.

'Great,' Donna says, 'fucking great.' She pulls her chair out again and sits down. 'Look, I don't have to justify myself to anyone, okay? But I won't have him talking shite about me and fucking up the only good thing that's happened to me in months, all right?'

COLIN BATEMAN

Ivan glances at Campbell, then they both nod.

'Okay. Jon Teckman—'

'Who?' Campbell interrupts.

'The guy who owns the car,' Ivan says quickly. 'Go on.'

'Jon Teckman was a guy I met when I first came to London. I was just looking for fun, you know. I came down here and got a job in a bar and spent my time off clubbing and all that shit you do when you're young. Jon was a DJ and he was really happening for a while and we'd go to all the parties and get all the best drugs and it was great. I mean, I'd only see him twice a week and we were off our faces the whole time, so I never really got to find out what he was like in real time. Then we decided to move in together . . .'

'Tower Hamlets,' Ivan says.

'No, not Tower Hamlets. Notting Hill – he was making good money, and that's when it all started to go wrong. What I was doing recreationally, he was doing full-time, and what had been fun became a bit of a bloody nightmare, basically. He was getting into stronger and stronger stuff and I wasn't interested, and he was getting paranoid and jealous and spending all our money on drugs, and then he stopped getting work because he was always wasted, and we had to get out of the flat – and that's when we went to Verdant fucking Manor, and the moment we moved in there I knew I had to get away from him because he was into it all so deep. I mean, I thought I loved him before, but I knew pretty soon that I didn't at all, that he was just a good laugh. And then, after a while it wasn't a laugh at all, it was just sad and stupid, except I could see that and he couldn't and I wanted to leave, and he wouldn't let me.'

She's talking relatively normally, but the tears are now starting to roll down her cheeks. She's clasping and unclasping her hands; she's not looking at either of them, but between them.

'It wasn't just the drugs. After a while he just made me feel so small. I'm . . . I'm not stupid. I was always writing – you know, poetry, *lyrics*,' she smiles sadly at Ivan, and he smiles sympathetically back, then looks guiltily away, 'and I really wanted to do something with them but he'd just laugh and take the piss and rip them up or . . . I mean, one day I came home and he was using my poems for fucking roll-ups, you know?' She laughs. 'I mean, they probably deserved it, they were that bad, but still . . . Then after that, he wouldn't let me go out, so I lost my job, then he started saying I was going with other fellas, and I wasn't. When he became too wasted to even go out and score for himself, he wanted me to do it, and I did a few times, but it was scary and I didn't like it and I said no, but then he'd get angry and I'd do it, one last time, always one last time. And then, well, you can probably guess what happened next.'

Ivan and Campbell shake their heads.

'The money was gone,' Donna said quietly, 'and he started hinting that maybe I could find a way of earning some more, and that was the straw that broke the camel's back. I told him I was leaving, and he begged me to stay, did all the usual shit, but this time I was determined and I packed up, all the time him begging me to stay and saying that he loved me and couldn't live without me and what he'd do to himself if I left, but I knew I had to go right there and then or I maybe never would. That's when he took the knife and started cutting himself, all across his chest, to show how much he loved me, you know? The blood was pishing out of him. That's when I knew that he was right over the edge. So I hightailed it out of there. I needed to get away, I was going to go to Spain, just managed to scrape enough together for a flight, thought I was well out of it – then I got stopped at the fucking airport, *arrested* at the fucking airport – and you know what for?'

Ivan and Campbell look at her dumbly.

'Attempted fucking murder. He was that angry about me leaving he told the cops I'd tried to kill him, and they fucking believed him.'

'But surely—' Ivan begins.

'But surely nothing. When he wants to Jon can be very convincing. And he had cut himself to ribbons. I was fucking furious with everyone because I hadn't done anything and I was screaming and ranting, and once they found I had prior convictions . . .'

'You have?'

'I got caught buying dope for Jon a couple of times and was fined. But they just had me written off as a druggie, so nobody would make any effort. Everything went against me – shit Legal Aid lawyer, doddery old judge who thinks Disprin is a Class A drug, and there you go. I mean, thank Christ they didn't charge me with attempted murder in the end or I could have been put away for donkey's. They reduced it to causing GBH and I got three years.' She pulls at her short, elfin hair. 'I've served twelve months. I was due out on licence after eighteen, but they break you in gradually, let you out a day at a time. And I fucked it up. I was stupid. I had such good intentions. The one thing that's got me through being inside is my poetry; the Chief knew that – she gave me your address, said I should look you up, see if you could help me. But all the early stuff I'd written I left behind in my hurry to get out. I knew it was stupid going anywhere near Jon but I really wanted it. I couldn't go and see you without some of my stuff, could I? So I went round and he seemed all nice and sorry at first, but when he found out what I was there for he went mental again and chased me out of there. I shouldn't have done it, like, but he wouldn't give me my stuff, so I stole his car. It wasn't even *his* car – I paid for half of it. It's an old fucking jalopy anyway. I just lifted the keys and ran for it. That's why I crashed into your car. I was that upset by the whole thing, I wasn't paying attention.' She gives an embarrassed little shrug. 'And that's it, really. Donna Carbone, *This Is Your Fucked-Up Life*.'

Ivan and Campbell don't quite know what to say.

'It's just,' Donna says, filling the gap, 'it's just my life has been a complete disaster this last couple of years. Whatever could go wrong, did go wrong, and yet this thing with April May, it's given me a glimpse of what could be. I mean, it's not me, of course it's not me, and it freaked me out for a while when I was doing it – but the more I thought about it, and believe me, I'd plenty of time in that freezing bloody car last night – the more I realised that if I really gave it a shot, *became* April May, I could do it, become something really good and successful. It's about being someone else, and if it's got something to do with writing and literature, well, that's a world I never dared hope to become a part of. But now I really want to, and that's why I'm here. I want you to give me a second chance. I want to become April May.'

Ivan waits until the front door is closed behind them and they're walking down the driveway to Campbell's car, with Donna safe in the kitchen with a celebratory glass of dandelion wine, before he asks his agent what he really thinks.

'She's lying through her teeth,' Campbell says.

'You think so?'

'Of course she is. A farrago of lies from start to finish. Oh Ivan, you didn't fall for it, did you?'

'Well. I like to believe the best of people.'

'But I mean – he stabbed himself? A paranoid drug addict was able to convince everyone that she did it? Come *on*.'

'But miscarriages of justice do happen. I mean, I'm in Amnesty International.'

'Well, you should resign and join the British Fantasy League. Because that's what she's doing – spinning us a fantasy.'

'So all you said in there, about her becoming April May, setting up readings to build her confidence, that's all crap?'

'No, not at all. Jesus, Ivan, use your head. She stabbed that guy, but it's bloody obvious that it's what we used to call a crime of passion. She's probably perfectly safe to be around, unless you start snogging her.'

'You mean we really do keep using her?'

'Of course! We *need* her right now. We have commitments, and the good thing is, she's not completely barking. She can provide just enough of the kind of off-the-wall behaviour the press is gagging for without jeopardising the whole operation by going totally mental. It'll be risky, but I think she can pull it off. It buys us some time, at least until the book comes out. Then we'll need to think of a more satisfactory long-term solution.' He stops at the end of the drive and glances back up at the house. 'In the meantime,' he says, waving a warning finger, 'watch your back.'

Ivan groans. He raises his hand to wave goodbye to Campbell, who's now in his car and starting the engine. But he stops mid-wave and hurries across to the driver's door and raps on the window. Campbell looks round, then the glass descends smoothly.

'Since when,' Ivan says, 'did you drive a fucking Jag?'

'Since yesterday.' Campbell shakes his head wearily. 'Ivan, it's for the business. Image is everything. It's second-hand. Now go and talk to Dolly.'

Campbell has the window up and is shooting away before Ivan can correct him. He watches the Jaguar until it disappears around the corner, then inhales deeply of the crisp night air, and tramps disconsolately back up the drive.

17

They have just stormed along the platform to claim their seats on the train for Nottingham. Ivan is red-faced, out of breath and trying not to wheeze. Donna looks like she's just stepped out of a shower. He's flopped down in his seat, his coat stuck to his back. She has her face pressed to the window, her eyes wide with excitement.

'Nervous?' Ivan asks when he can finally manage it.

'A little bit,' she says, smiling at him. 'You ought to cut down on the fags.'

'And you ought to mind your own bloody business.'

'There's no need to be embarrassed because you're out of breath. You're no spring chicken.'

He desperately wants to find something bright and witty to fire back at her, but there's nothing there; his reserves of wit have long ago been exhausted. He has just endured days and days of severe mental pressure. Trying to be pleasant to the murderess. Watching his back. Keeping up the pretence. Imparting the wisdom of the great author to the lyric-writing jailbird. Giving her confidence. Showing her how to read aloud. How to project. How to bat difficult questions away. He has suggested books to her. He has changed her newspaper from the *Mirror* to *The Times*. He has tried to get her to slow down when she talks so that people can understand what she's saying; her accent is attractive but thick, and he tries to get her to soften it.

He generally keeps his temper, as he doesn't want her to lose hers, but sometimes he feels like smacking her in the chops. She tries, and is trying. When he describes it to Campbell he says Donna is the girl who put the *pig* in *Pyg*malion, but he doesn't really mean it. She's been very good, actually, and that is a pressure in itself. He wants to dislike her. He wants her to be bad at being good, but she's good at being good, although he always reminds himself that she's also good at being bad, and that her boyfriend has the scars to prove it.

He coughs and searches for a cigarette, but in the rush he's left them behind. Donna smokes, but he's not about to ask her for one. He'll wait until Nottingham. That won't be a problem. It's not that far. Not really.

'Okay,' Donna says, 'I'm more than a little bit nervous. It's not the reading, it's the standing up and answering questions.'

'You'll be fine.' He smiles at last. 'Really. My mother always used to tell me that thing, you know when you go for interviews and you're really nervous, that you should imagine that the people interviewing you are completely naked?' Donna nods. 'I used to do that,' Ivan continues, 'and I'd still be really nervous, but I'd have an erection as well. Didn't get too many jobs.'

Donna laughs, and Ivan's face reddens. He has never said *erection* in the presence of a woman he hasn't been married to. He tries to cover the blush with a sudden coughing fit.

Donna passes him the bottle of water she bought in WH Smith's. As Ivan drinks she says, 'I can't imagine you going for any sort of an interview. What were you before you became a writer?'

'I was always a writer.'

'Before you got paid for it.'

'This and that,' he says evasively.

'I always used to find it fascinating at the front of books when it said all the jobs a writer used to have. Y'know, deep-sea diver, shepherd, bullfighter, lumberjack. What were you really?'

'All sorts of things.'

'Like a soldier? Or a *mercenary*?' She giggles.

'Civil Servant, if you must know.'

'You mean like James Bond was a Civil Servant?'

'No.'

'Or Quentin Crisp was the *Naked*—'

'No.'

'You just checked paperwork and fiddled your flexi-time?'

'We can't all lead an exotic lifestyle, Donna.'

'Is that a dig at me?'

'Yes.'

She makes a face, but it's playful. 'I can't imagine

you just having an ordinary job. It must have been soul-destroying for you.'

'Actually I quite enjoyed it.' He gives a little shrug. She smiles. He likes her short *Jean Seberg is Joan of Arc* hairstyle and the way her eyes seem to smile as well. But he hates the fact that he has to be constantly on his guard in case she stabs him in the chest. He has told himself to relax on this trip. To be in good humour. It is important that she performs her function well. He will be her friend and give her as much guidance as he can; he fancies that he might actually be very good at it. In the same way that a mediocre professional footballer can sometimes make a great manager, so he might be able to instruct Donna on the art of giving perfect public readings without ever revealing to her that he was a bit of an arse at doing it himself.

She is wearing a new blue denim jacket with little stars above the pockets, and a white T-shirt. She is also wearing blue jeans and slip-on leather shoes. He has bought her all of these things, and many more besides, squashed into her cool new brand-name-to-the-fore suitcase in the rack above them, along with the new April May wig which fits her much better and doesn't make her want to scratch her head all the time. He has receipts for all the items and will claim them back from Campbell at the end of the tour.

The tour itself was Campbell's idea. Its main purpose is to get Donna toughened up, self-confident, ready to deal with an audience, the media, to be able to answer every question under the sun without getting flustered or bolshy. He is sending Donna Carbone on tour, but he wants April May to return. He wants a cool professional, not a nervous wreck in a scratchy wig. Marcus had the brainwave of avoiding the major book chains and instead setting up readings for April May across a loose network of independent bookshops in the provinces, the kind of small shops that are rarely visited by writers on their publicity tours, and which are therefore more likely to put a bit of an effort into an event. 'They'll love it!' Marcus enthused. 'It'll be like The Beatles playing the Cavern the night after Shea Stadium. In years to come people will say, "I was there"!'

'Yes, Marcus,' Ivan responded indulgently.

'I can get her into Nottingham, Derby, Sheffield and Coventry. We can do Glasgow, Edinburgh, Dundee – great little shop there . . . It'll be fantastic, and the best thing about it is she'll be able to make her mistakes off the beaten track. Then when she's ready, we can do the final night of the tour right here.'

'In London.'

'*Here* – in this shop. We can make a real event of it – food, drink, cocktail sausages. It'll be April May's coming out. We'll invite all the press, really go to town.'

'This is, of course, for April May's benefit, not your own?'

'Of course.'

But Marcus has actually been very good. Even Campbell is impressed with the way he has organised things, although admittedly he's not exactly dealing with a world tour by The Rolling Stones, but half a dozen small events in tiny bookshops, in out of the way places. He's shown enthusiasm not just in organising the events themselves, but in the rather more mundane practicalities: trains, planes and automobiles. 'Yes, he's doing great,' Campbell agrees, 'but if he thinks he's getting a piece of the action, he has another think coming.'

Ivan is inclined to agree, especially in the light of the first April May, who has thus far not shown her bent nose in public again.

'Well?' Donna says.

'Well what?'

'What was so great about being a Civil Servant?'

Ivan looks out of the window. The passing countryside is . . . well, green. He has never been one for the great outdoors. Feeding the ducks is about as wild as he gets. 'Ambition,' he says vaguely, 'is a dreadful thing.'

'What's this, *The Philosophical Minute with Ivan Connor*?'

'No, I just mean – Civil Service, do your job, go home, have your dinner, watch the telly. Writing – you never switch off, you never achieve what you set out to achieve. It's always a literary bridge too far. Unless you're bloody Francesca Brady or someone. And she's probably not truly happy either. I mean, she's conquered the world, but she's probably fretting about sales on Pluto or Mars.'

'That's not ambition,' Donna says, 'that's jealousy.'

'Isn't it the same?'

Donna smiles. The snacks trolley comes by and she eyes the sandwiches hungrily, but Ivan issues a swift no thank you and the woman pushes away along the coach. Donna purses her lips unhappily and stares out of the window. Ivan lifts his travelling bag down from the luggage rack and unzips it. He produces a plastic lunch box. From within he lifts two sets of sandwiches wrapped in tinfoil, and two apples.

'Mother . . .' Ivan begins.

Donna shakes her head. 'What age are you?'

'Old enough to appreciate it when somebody goes to the trouble of making me my lunch.'

'You're about twelve, I reckon. You're on a day out. A school trip.'

'You won't be wanting any, then.'

She makes a face, and lifts one of the tinfoil packages. Ivan unwraps his. She unwraps hers. She lifts one and sniffs at it, then curls back the bread for a closer look. She takes a hesitant bite. When she has finished her first sandwich she sits back and nods at him approvingly. He gives her a half-smile and looks out of the window again. Then he closes his eyes and feigns sleep. From time to time he flutters his eyelids to see what she's up to. She quite happily sits and studies the manuscript of *Kissing Cousins*, her thin fingers tracing the passages she intends to read later on. Ivan finds himself really drifting into sleep. He dreams of having his teeth extracted without anaesthetic, then wakes with a start, his brow caked in sweat and his teeth aching. Donna is looking at him intently.

'What?' he says.

'You were grinding your teeth.'

'Yes. I do that.'

'Are you worried about something?'

'Everything.'

'What are you, divorced?'

'Pardon?'

'Are you divorced?'

'Yes. As it happens. What tangent did that come in on?'

She shrugs. 'What happened?'

'I don't know that it's got anything to do with you.'

She nods, then looks out of the window.

He sighs and folds his arms.

She looks back quickly and says, 'Go on then, what happened?'

They have talked quite a lot over the past few days, but little of it has been personal. He has been reluctant to get into that particular arena because he knows that if he starts talking about himself, at some point he will feel obliged to say, 'Well, enough about me, what about you?' and he doesn't really want to know. He can talk about the boring details of his life until the cows come home, but frankly he doesn't want to open up the can of worms that has clearly been Donna's life. Stabbings, drugs, prison – what is he supposed to say? *Oh, that's dreadful, you poor dear, what a miscarriage of justice.*

In earlier, carefree days, about a week ago, he might have been fascinated by the sordid detail, but back then he was removed from it all. He had quite happily tried to cross-examine her in prison about lesbians and got a punch in the guts for his trouble, but that was okay, because he could walk away from it. It was an interesting encounter with a damaged low-life and he could put it down to experience and research. But here? He doesn't want to know about blood and needles and butch women. He doesn't need her breaking down or flipping out. She might give a passable impression of being an attractive young woman fascinated by his day job and sufficiently interested in him as a person to enquire about his marital status, but one slip and she could be in and then there would be no stopping her. If talking about himself keeps her happy, and their relationship on a calm, tranquil plateau, then he will do his best to keep it that way.

'We got married too young,' he begins.

'Yeah,' Donna responds. 'At one stage I thought I was going to—'

'We wanted different things,' Ivan cuts in quickly. 'She wanted love and loyalty and a Civil Service wage coming in. I could only offer her two out of three.'

'Which two?'

'Well, love and loyalty, obviously.'

'You left your job to be a writer?'

Ivan nods.

'Was she working?'

'No, she was looking after the children.'

'Ah. Right. I see. So she was angry that you left your job to pursue your dream, because she had nothing to feed the kids with.'

'Well, kid at that point, to be strictly accurate.'

'But you've published what, seven or eight books?' Ivan nods. 'But this was before the first came out?' He nods again. 'This doesn't add up. You have one child who's what, six or seven, and you've one who's at secondary school. If she kicked you out for leaving your job and your other child is only six . . .'

'Well, we got back together from time to time, which explains the younger one. We were divorced three years ago and I've been playing hard to get ever since.'

'You mean she met someone else.'

Ivan smiles sadly. 'Yes, several times.'

'And you?'

He shrugs. 'Who needs a lover, when you have a mother?' He blinks, surprised at himself for several moments. 'I didn't mean that to sound quite as . . . I suppose I'm just at an age where I've been married, had kids, it hasn't worked out and frankly I can't be bothered trying again.'

'Not when you have your mother to lift and lay you. Metaphorically speaking, obviously.'

Ivan returns his attention to the view, which is less interesting but not as worrying. He can feel her eyes upon him.

They're in a two-star hotel in the centre of town. They appear to be the only residents who are not asylum seekers. Ivan hasn't a racist bone in his body, but he nevertheless feels uncomfortable. This isn't what he had in mind when he explained to Marcus the minimum standards of mollycoddling a serious author requires when on tour.

He must complain immediately. Anything less would seem like weakness.

Marcus is in the shop, but when he answers the phone he says, 'Pages Books and Professional Author Promotions.'

Ivan immediately puts the phone down and calls Campbell. It takes him five minutes to get past the receptionist, and then only when he mentions April May's name.

Campbell says, 'Dr Livingstone, I presume.'

Ivan sighs.

'If you're calling to complain about your hotel, don't.

It's the best we can do, we're operating on a strict budget.'

'We?'

'Well, you. It's important not to draw attention to yourselves, Ivan, you know that. This is strictly low profile, to build up her confidence. Besides, outside London, the standard of accommodation inevitably slips.'

'Not this far. They couldn't take an imprint of my Visa because they don't accept credit cards. It's strictly cash. Hourly rates are available.'

'Yes, well. Just get a receipt.'

'Campbell, we're one step from *Midnight Express* here.'

'Well, Dolly should feel at home then.'

Ivan asks: 'This is all going to work out in the end, isn't it?'

'Yes, of course it is. Winfrey were on again today. They're really excited. They can't wait to get their hands on April May. They think this London launch is a great idea. They wanted to do Borders Piccadilly, but I talked them round to Marcus's. Unpretentious, sticking up for the little man in his little shop, that'll bring the *Guardian* mob in.'

'There's no mini-bar here.'

'Ivan . . .'

'There's no large-bar either. We're booked into a dry hotel. I'm surprised we're not in bunks. Just promise me one thing.'

'Anything.'

'This is all going to be worth it.'

'Of course it is. Now just settle down, try to relax. First night of the tour, of course you're a bit jittery. But everything is going to be fine. I called the shop, they've sold seventy-five tickets already.'

'*Sold?*'

'Sold.'

'But I never sold a ticket to a reading in my life. They were always given away. In fact, I think we paid some people to turn up.'

'Well, that's the phenomenon that is April May, Ivan. You'd better get used to it.'

He puts the phone down and lies back on the bed. He closes his eyes. That it should come to this, lying on a flea-ridden mattress in a doss house in the wilds of rural England, about to pass himself off as the literary agent for a writer who has never existed, reading from a novel that doesn't make sense.

18

The first person he sees when he enters the pub is Donna, sitting at the bar with a half-drunk pint of cider and a copy of the manuscript before her.

'I called your room,' he lies quickly, 'but you were already gone.'

She looks sheepishly at him. 'Sorry,' she says. 'Someone's headboard was banging against my wall. Had to get out.'

He raises an eyebrow.

She raises her drink. 'Okay, so I needed something to steady my nerves. Big night and all.' She pats the manuscript.

Ivan settles on to the bar stool and signals to the barman for a matching drink. Then he smiles indulgently at Donna. 'You'll be fine. Like I say, just look at the audience and imagine they're all naked. In fact, go one better, and imagine that all of the men have erections. Really small erections.'

She almost chokes on her cider. He's mentioned *erections* to her three times in as many hours, and now it doesn't even make him blush.

'What about the women?' Donna asks. 'How will I transform them?'

'Oh you don't need to worry about them. They'll hate you no matter what you do. Because they'll all be middle-aged and baggy and insanely jealous that you're not.'

'Is that some sort of a compliment?'

He clears his throat. 'Of course not. Mother Teresa is attractive compared to the women who come to readings. Well, my readings at any rate.' He takes a first sip of the cider that is now before him, then an appreciative look around the bar. It's mostly empty. There's a juke box playing Abba songs.

'Do you think anyone will turn up?'

Ivan shrugs. 'You never know with readings. Usually you'd get about two hundred, but because you're not that well-known, you might struggle up towards seventy-five.'

'It seems like an awful lot.'

'Well, it'll be a tiny little shop, so it might seem crowded. Seventy-five is pretty poor, but just right to get you started.'

She nods thoughtfully. Ivan, who can only dream of attracting seventy-five to one of his readings, gulps a good third of his pint down, then becomes aware that Donna is looking at him intently. He sets the glass down, then wipes his mouth with the back of his hand. 'What?'

'I . . . well, it's kind of embarrassing.'

He sighs his *what now?* sigh.

'It's *Kissing Cousins*. I've been going over the parts you suggested I read tonight.'

'And?'

'I'm sorry – maybe it's just that I'm too dense, but they don't really seem to make any sense.'

Ivan nods slowly. 'They're not supposed to make sense. They're *surreal*.'

'No, it's not that. They just don't make sense.'

'Like I say, they're surreal.'

'No really, it's not that, they—'

'I wrote them, Donna, I should know what they are.'

'Can you explain to me what they mean, then?'

'Donna, I don't have to justify what I write.'

'I'm not asking you to justify it, I'm asking you to explain.'

'I don't have to do that either. It's up to others to decide what they mean.'

'But what if I'm asked to explain them?'

'You say that you're the writer, and you don't need to explain them. They're not supposed to be clear. They're surreal.'

'But they're not surreal at all. They're just confusing and contradictory.'

'That's what life's like, Donna.'

'That's not what I mean, I—'

'Look, perhaps you didn't have the opportunity to take a class in literary interpretation while you were in prison, but take it from me, the extracts I have asked you to read make perfect sense, so just read them, will you?'

She looks away.

'I'm sorry,' he says, 'I didn't mean to snap.' He's hoping that she won't snap in response and carve her name across his forehead with her glass.

'I just get very protective. Of course you're right to ask, and I'm sorry I can't explain.' He raises a finger to his brow. 'It just all comes out of here, the writing, and I find it's best not to question what it all means. It's a style of writing called flow of consciousness. It doesn't always make perfect sense, but it's the purest kind of writing there is. James Joyce. Need I say more. Jack Kerouac.'

He raises his glass and clinks it against hers. 'Come on,' he says, 'cheer up. You're free, you're going to make a great deal of money, all you have to do is read some of my gibberish to cretins who wouldn't know an iambic pentameter from an Olympic event.'

He recalls vaguely that he may have put her down with this line before. But if she remembers she gives no indication.

She raises her glass, and this time clinks it against his. 'Okay,' she says, 'I'll knock 'em dead.'

Ivan feels she could have chosen a more appropriate turn of phrase, but he nevertheless smiles benignly at her and drains his glass. Then he orders another.

They arrive at the bookshop at 6.30 p.m., a good thirty minutes before the reading is due to start. Ivan is annoyed to find that there are already seventy-five people waiting inside, with several dozen others milling about outside, smoking. He thinks it is absolutely ridiculous that this many people should turn out to see an author who hasn't yet published anything, whereas he – the heart of a generation – has published seven novels and considers himself lucky to get seven people at one of his readings.

The name of the shop is Literary Classix, but he refrains from commenting on that. Instead he hurries April May quickly through to an office at the back where the owner, a rotund man called Bill, has thoughtfully provided several bottles of wine and a small buffet.

'We're so excited,' Bill says.

'So are we,' Ivan says, the corners of his mouth already building up sedimentary deposits of sausage roll.

'If you don't mind me saying,' Bill says, clasping April's hand, 'you do look absolutely fantastic tonight.'

'Why thank you, Bill,' April replies, squeezing his hand.

And she does look pretty good, Ivan has to admit. Wig, make-up, two hours in the bathroom getting ready. He'd look pretty good himself if he went to that much trouble.

Two hours he spent more profitably in the bar.

He's now pissed. 'Do you know why women wear make-up and perfume?' he asks loudly.

Bill shakes his head and looks nervously at April May.

'Because they're ugly and they smell.' Ivan cackles and turns to open a bottle of wine.

'It's a real treat to have you here,' Bill says.

'It's a real treat to be here,' April responds. She glances at Ivan, who has now turned back to them with a glass of wine in his hand.

Bill smiles at April. 'Would you like a glass of—'

'No,' Ivan says curtly. 'She can't have one. Don . . . April, it dehydrates you; you start reading and two minutes later your mouth is completely dry and all you can do is croak. That's what alcohol does to you. Avoid it at all costs. Drink water.'

'I'll just go and check on the audience,' Bill says. 'We don't have enough chairs.' He hurries away.

April glares at Ivan. 'What are you doing?' she snaps.

'What does it look like I'm doing?'

'You're pissed, and you're supposed to be here to support me.'

'I am supporting you. I'll cheer longest and loudest.'

'Ivan, please, don't do this to me. I need your help.'

And now that he looks at her properly, past the make-up and the hair, he can see that her eyes have shrunk to pinpoints and there's a frightened look about her.

He drains his glass. 'You'll be fine,' he says.

'No, I won't.'

'Yes, you will. We've worked out what you're going to say, and you know what you're reading. You've read it to me lots of times and, you sound great. It'll be easy-peasy. I can relax and enjoy the show.'

'Please don't drink any more.'

He puts the glass down. 'I won't, I promise. You're right.'

'Mr Foster?' Bill is standing in the doorway again.

Ivan lifts a sausage roll.

'Mr Foster?'

'*Campbell!*' April hisses, making eyes at him, and he remembers suddenly that he's supposed to be Campbell Foster, literary agent.

He turns quickly and smiles. 'Sorry,' he says, 'I'm a little deaf.'

'They're asking about autographs.'

'Autographs?'

'It's just that usually the author would sign a book and they'd buy that – except, of course, there are no books yet.' He grins at April. 'They're wondering if you'd mind signing anyway.'

'I'd be delighted,' April says, 'after the reading.'

As Bill is turning happily away, Ivan stops him with a, 'Just hold on one moment there.' Bill turns reluctantly. 'April, you have a heart of gold, but Bill, you know that's not how it works. She can't just sign autographs for nothing – that's like giving it away. You know as well as I do that an autograph isn't an autograph any more, like little boys used to collect them; there are serious collectors out there and they'll charge serious money when they come to sell it on.'

Bill's good humour is fading fast. 'What's your point, Mr Foster? That they should pay for autographs?'

'No, of course not. But they are all availing themselves of your free wine and nibbles.'

'We do this all the time. It isn't a problem. We have very loyal customers. What's your point?'

'My point, Mr . . . Bill, is that if they want an autograph they should purchase a book.'

'But there *aren't* any books!'

'Campbell, really,' April begins, but there's no stopping him.

'There may not be any of *her* books, Mr . . . Bill, but we do have other clients, and they need promoting as well.

I would suggest that you think about recommending to your loyal customers that they purchase a book by another of my authors, and then April May will be happy to sign that.'

Bill shakes his head in exasperation. 'This is most unusual.'

'These *are* most unusual circumstances. And remember, we could easily have gone to Waterstones. They would have killed to have April May's public debut.'

'Yes, yes . . . very well, have it your way. These other clients of yours . . . I mean, who were you thinking of?'

'Well,' Ivan says, 'there's Ivan Connor, for one.'

April rolls her eyes.

Bill's brows knit. 'Who?'

Ivan, with a slightly harder edge to his voice, says, *'Trader John*, he wrote *Trader John*. *Chapter & Verse* was his last big one.'

'Sorry,' Bill says, 'you've lost me there, and I know my stock backwards. Perhaps there's another author who . . .'

But Ivan has turned away and is now pouring himself another glass of wine. April steps forward, smiling broadly and kisses Bill on the cheek. He blushes. 'Don't worry about it, Bill. Honestly, these agents are such stick-in-the-muds. I'll be delighted to sign whatever autographs they want – and for free. If I'm nice to them, then they're bound to come back and buy the book when it's published, aren't they?'

Bill nods enthusiastically and backs out of the office. April immediately drops the smile. 'Why are you being such a wanker?' she hisses.

Ivan snorts. 'Years of practice, my dear, years of practice.' He sets his glass down, then lifts a three-quarters-full bottle of wine and stalks out of the office into the shop. 'Knock 'em dead, April,' he calls back. 'Knock 'em dead.'

He has to stand right at the back of the shop under a sign that says *Join Our Christmas Club*. The place is packed. There aren't seventy-five people here – there are at least one hundred and twenty. Ivan is sweating in his big coat, but not because he's hot, because he's angry. It's not even the number of people, it's the atmosphere. They're excited. The air is thick with anticipation. He has never encountered an atmosphere like this – even his run-in with Francesca Brady didn't have this kind of frisson. It's as if they're expecting the Second Coming. He sees Donna's pale face peeping out of the office, astounded by the size of the audience.

I should be in there helping her. I've deserted her.

Then: *she has done nothing to deserve this treatment from me.*

She has done nothing to deserve this audience, either.

She is nothing but hype and hysteria. They are here because she's the great white hope of English fiction, and she hasn't written a word in her life – except for some half-baked poetry.

They are my *words. My crazy bloody words.*

I have created a myth, and now it's turning into a legend. Help her! Guide her! Go to her!

But instead he is rooted to his place beneath the *Join Our Christmas Club* sign, his arm jostled as he tries to drink by April May's fans, crowding in with their pink, excited faces. No, he won't go to her – he is better off where he is, because once these cretins realise that April May is nothing more than a blonde wig and some confusing and contradictory prose, they will turn on her and pound her to death with mouldering copies of *Insanity Fair*.

They begin to applaud as Bill ushers April May out of the office towards the small lectern which has been set up at the top of the shop along with the regulation table and bottle of Evian water. There are even some cheers.

Ivan takes another long drink. He's hardly even listening as Bill introduces Donna; instead he's watching her and wishing dearly that it was he who was up there basking in the adulation.

Except she's not basking in it. She's nervous as hell. There's sweat streaming down her brow. Her cheeks are flushed red as she steps up to the microphone and tremulously thanks everyone for coming. She raises the manuscipt of *Kissing Cousins* and begins to read.

You can hear a pin drop.

Her voice is small, despite the amplification. Her intonation is far from perfect.

Ivan looks around the audience. They are giving her their complete attention. When she finishes her first section, they roar their approval.

These are my words. They love them.

Ivan takes another drink. *It should be me.*

He resists the urge to storm the stage and seize back what is rightfully his. Instead he backs out of the shop just as April begins to read her next extract.

He sits in a doorway across the road with the dregs of his bottle, thinking about what could and should have been.

About whether he really did get married too young and the fact that a big bloke called Alfred is having sex with his wife. He thinks about his children and how little he sees of them and of his mother and how she cuts his toast into soldiers. He thinks about how miserable he was in the Civil Service and how wonderful he felt when his first novel was published and how he has never had that feeling again and he wonders how he can ever recapture it.

He suddenly realises that he is sitting in the doorway of a branch of Dixons and that the plastic face of Francesca Brady is grinning out at him from half a dozen television screens. She is being interviewed on *Parkinson* and even though he can't hear a word, Ivan knows from their slick smiling faces that she is being witty and wonderful.

He finds that his face is wet and he knows that he must have been crying, but he can't for the life of him think why, because he's been miserable for years without ever having had to resort to tears, and then he notices that he's completely out of alcohol and he must do something about getting some more. He can't quite remember what part of London he's in but he's sure he'll find his way home okay. He has to get rid of the bottle, but there's no bin in the immediate vicinity so he does what any other reasonable person would do in such circumstances and hurls it straight at the laughing face of Francesca Brady.

It smashes loudly against the metal security grille, and he runs away.

19

A woman's voice says, groggily, 'Hello?'

'I'm sorry. I must have the wrong number.' He puts the phone down. He strains his eyes, then carefully pushes each number again.

The same voice answers, annoyed now: *'What?'*

'Campbell?'

'Hold on.' He hears her hiss *'Campbell'* and then realises through the fog that envelops him that even though she has only said four words, he recognises her voice; he has heard it at the end of a phone in Campbell's office. But this is Campbell's home number, and it is 4 a.m.

'What?' Campbell says, grumpy-groggy.

'It's me.'

'Oh. Shit. What time is it?'

'I don't know.'

'Where . . . what . . . did everything . . . ?'

'I don't know.'

'Hold on. Let me get the other line.' There's a bit of a

225

delay as Campbell pads out of the bedroom and down the hall to his small study. He lifts the phone and says, 'Okay, darling, you can put it down now.' There's a sniffy kind of a sigh and the other receiver is put down.

Ivan says, 'She's working late.'

'Mind your own business.'

'I can't. I'm not very good at that. Minding my own business, or any other sort of business. I think I've fucked things up.'

Campbell lets out a low groan and rubs at his brow. 'Ivan, what's going on? Has something happened to Dolly?'

'It's Donna. Her name is Donna.'

'Yes. Ivan. What has happened?'

'I got drunk by accident.'

Campbell inhales deeply. 'Tell me what happened.'

'It's all a bit of a blank. Except that now I'm in Sherwood Forest.'

'You're *where*?'

'I'm with Robin Hood and Friar Tuck and Will Scarlett.'

'Come again?'

'And I've just been sick over Maid Marian.'

'*Ivan!*'

He *is* sick and his head is throbbing and he's dreadfully confused and he dearly wants to be tucked up at home in bed with a boiled egg and soldiers to look forward to, not stuck in Sherwood Sodding Forest.

'Ivan?'

He's dozing off.

'IVAN!'

'What!'

'Stay with me, please.'

'I'm here. I'm *here*.'

'Okay. Now listen to me. Where is Dolly – I mean Donna?'

'I don't know.'

'Is she at the hotel?'

'I don't know where the hotel is.'

'You're in the middle of Sherwood Forest?'

'Yes. It's dark and I'm lost.'

'Ivan, listen carefully to me. You – don't – have – a – mobile – phone.'

'I know that.'

'So unless they've decided to install a phone box in the middle of Sherwood Forest, you are *not in* Sherwood Forest.'

'But the trees and . . . I'm with Robin Hood! And Will Scarlett! They *talked* to me.'

'Ivan, calm down. Calm *down*. Now I want you to describe to me very slowly exactly where you are. What you see.'

There's heavy, anxious breathing for several long moments and Campbell is worried that Ivan has drifted off again, but then he begins to speak and his voice is heavy and slurred and frightened. 'I'm in Sherwood Forest—'

'No! Ivan, *exactly* where you are? Are you sitting down?'

'Yes.'

'On what?'

'A . . . chair.'

'And is the phone on a table or a desk?'

'My God, *yes.*'

'So you're not in a forest?'

'I am in a forest. I can see trees, and Robin Hood spoke to me.'

'You're sitting at a desk, you are on a phone. You cannot be in a forest.'

'It's like *The Lion, the Witch and the Wardrobe.* I'm in an office, but there's no end to it. It stretches into a forest and there's Robin Hood and Will, and they spoke to me . . .'

'Ivan . . .'

'I was sick over Maid Marian. She said—'

'IVAN!'

Ivan is breathing hard now. 'I'm sorry. I don't mind telling you, I'm scared. It's like a dream, a nightmare and I can't wake up!'

'Okay, okay. Now just settle down and listen to me. You're in an office, . . . there's a forest as well, and you can see Robin Hood – right?'

'Yes.'

'Is he moving?'

'Yes, of course he's moving.'

'Okay. You're in a forest, you're with Robin Hood – how can you see him? It must be dark, is there a moon?'

'Yes, yes, I can see it through the window.'

'There's a window?'

'Yes, above the trees.'

'A window above the trees?'

'Yes, yes, a window above . . . Oh God, what's going on? Campbell, please, you have to get me out of here!'

'I'm trying, Ivan. I'm trying. Listen to me. Now – is

the phone fixed? I mean, is it hand-held? Can you walk with it?'

'I can walk with it.'

'Okay. I know you can see trees, I want you to walk towards them.'

'No, God, no! I don't want to go back there. They have bows and arrows.'

'Ivan – walk towards the trees!'

He takes a deep breath. 'Okay, okay. I'm going for it. I'm walking . . . I'm now walking. I don't like this. I—'

There's a loud crack, and the sound of a body falling, the phone clattering on a hard surface.

'Ivan?'

Nothing.

'IVAN!'

Nothing. But then, a low groan.

'Ivan?!'

A burst of static as the phone is picked up again and Ivan says groggily, 'Glass . . . I walked into glass – a glass wall. My nose.'

Campbell breathes a sigh of relief. 'You're okay?' Ivan says he is. 'Good. Now feel your way along the glass wall. That's it – feel your way . . .'

'I thought I'd been attacked. The Sheriff of Nottingham . . .'

'You've seen the Sheriff of Nottingham?'

'No, but he must be here somewhere. I can feel him – it's an evil presence. I've reached the end of the glass wall . . . there's a space . . . I can feel the breeze of the forest. There's a wall . . .'

'Okay . . . Ivan, I want you stop there. I want you to feel the wall – yes, feel the wall.'

'But—'

'Just feel it! Feel for a light switch.'

'A . . . ?'

'Ivan, just find it!'

There's a pause. Campbell puts the phone in the crook of his neck and looks under papers and books for his lighter; the cigarette is already stuck firmly in his mouth. He growls impatiently to himself. If this goes on much longer he will chew the cigarette raw.

'I've found a light switch. Now what will I do?'

'Switch it on.'

'I can't, I'm scared.'

'Switch it on, Ivan.'

'I can't. What if I'm in hell?'

'You're not in hell, Ivan, you're in Nottingham. Now switch it on.'

There is a lengthy pause, some deep breathing, then the merest click.

'Oh,' Ivan says.

'Oh,' repeats Campbell. 'Now where are we?'

'Well . . .' Ivan says.

'Are we in a forest?'

'Sort of.'

'Ivan!'

'I have to go.'

'What? Ivan . . .'

'I'll call you tomorrow.'

The line goes dead.

By the time Ivan gets back to the hotel, Donna has checked out. It is a little after 8 a.m. He is at death's door.

His skin is translucent. He tries asking various members of the staff if they have any idea where she has gone, but they don't understand what he's saying. He collects his bag and he checks out. He tramps the streets. If he doesn't eat soon he really will die. He stops at a café and eats half a bacon sandwich, then throws up outside. He re-enters the café and eats the other half. He feels slightly better, and tramps on. Eventually he reaches the train station, and finds Donna sitting with her bag. She stares ahead, stony-faced, as he approaches. When he stands in front of her she looks straight through him. When he kneels down so that his face is in line with hers, she turns in a different direction.

'I'm really, really sorry,' Ivan says. She ignores him. He moves round so they're level again. 'Really, really, really sorry.'

She looks away again.

'I don't know what got into me. Nerves. Panic. Don't be angry with me. I have a disease. My name is Ivan and I'm an alcoholic.'

She continues to look away, but says, 'You're not an alcoholic, Ivan, you're a drunk, and that's something completely different.'

'No, really, I'm an alcoholic. I've been assessed. I've been to classes. Fourteen step programmes.'

'No. What you are, Ivan, is a self-regarding, egotistical, vain, selfish child.'

'Yes, all of those as well.'

'But you are not an alcoholic. An alcoholic can't help it. I *know* alcoholics. You're just a social drinker on a very long weekend. You don't drink because you have to, you drink because you think it's great fun, and you're in a job where it doesn't matter that you have a hangover in the morning because you can choose to work when you bloody well like.'

'Okay. You're completely right. I'm still sorry.'

'You left me alone up there.'

'I know. It was reprehensible of me.'

She continues to stare icily away from him. He moves into the seat beside her. 'Where are you going?' he asks.

'Where do you think?'

'Well, Sheffield is the next stop on the tour.'

She lets out a sarcastic laugh. 'Yeah. Right.'

'Please.'

'Please, what?'

'Finish the tour. It won't happen again.'

She looks at him for the first time. 'You know, I was worried sick about you. You just disappeared, pissed, without a word. You could have been dead for all I knew. I was up all night.'

'I'm sorry.'

'I even called the police when you didn't come back to the hotel.'

'I'm sorry.'

'Where the fuck did you go?'

'*Tales of Robin Hood.*'

'What?'

'It's an interpretative centre dedicated to the legend of Robin Hood. There's a re-creation of Sherwood Forest and animatronic robots of Robin, Maid Marian and the rest of his merry band. They're very lifelike.'

'What the fuck were you doing there?'

'I have no idea. I do believe I broke in through a skylight.'

She can't help but give a short laugh, but she doesn't smile. 'You're a real menace to society, aren't you.'

'Yes. My brothers in the 'hood think so.' He sighs. 'I am sorry. Really. Please don't go home. We can make this work. Don't be put off by your first night; Nottingham audiences can be tough.'

'They weren't tough. They were lovely. They practically carried me on their shoulders back to the hotel.'

'Oh.'

'They loved April May. They loved the reading.'

'Oh. Well that's good, isn't it?'

'Yes, Ivan, the reading was fine. But the rest of it was arsey.'

'I know.'

'Bill tried to have his wicked way with me.'

'Bill?' She nods. 'Oh Christ.'

'He wasn't bad, a bit quick for my tastes.'

'You *didn't* . . .'

'Of course I didn't, you stupid prick.' She stares hard at him. 'This had better not happen again. Or I'm walking.'

'It won't, I promise.'

They sit quietly for several moments, her face back in stone mode.

'I, um, bought you a present,' he says.

'I don't want a fucking present – I want some support.'

He nods. He sits quietly.

'Okay,' she says, 'what did you buy me?'

'You said you didn't want it.'

'Ivan . . .' He smiles and reaches down to his bag. She

shakes her head. 'And if it's a model of Friar Tuck, I don't fucking want it.'

But instead he produces her book of poetry, and her face just melts. 'Oh *Ivan*,' she says. There are tears in her eyes. She holds the battered exercise book at arm's length, then presses it to her chest. As the first tear falls she looks at Ivan, smiles, then suddenly pulls him towards her and kisses him on the lips. It is a brief, moist peck of a thing. She pulls quickly away and wipes her sleeve across her face.

'I hope you don't think this makes up for you being a complete bastard,' she sniffs.

'Of course not,' he replies.

20

He is as good as gold, although of course the value of gold fluctuates.

On the train, she spends ages reading her recovered book of poetry, smiling happily up at him from time to time, and then groaning at the standard of her work. He tries to reassure her. She reads him stanzas and he nods thoughtfully, and makes all the right noises. He wants to put his head out of the window and scream, but he remains as good as gold.

They get to Sheffield and find that the hotel is of a marginally higher standard. They have adjoining rooms on the third floor and he's just relaxing on his bed for a kip, because the previous night's rest was limited to a few hours' uncomfortable sleep in the primitive forest dwellings of the Merry Men, when the dividing door is flung open and Donna dances in full of the joys of spring.

'C'mon, Ivan,' she says, 'let's do Sheffield.'

'I would rather not.'

'What are you going to do, sleep?'

'That was the general idea.'

'Plenty of time to do that when you're dead. You might never get to Sheffield again.'

'That will be a source of eternal regret. Nevertheless . . .'

'Oh Ivan, please, come with me. Show me Sheffield. Inspire me with Sheffield!'

'I spotted a *Woman's Own* in reception, have a read of that.'

She makes a pouty face. 'Honest to God, Ivan, you'd think you were about a hundred years old. You're like Whatshisname – Mr Chips.'

'Thank *you*.'

'Then come out and play.'

'No. Really.'

She blows air out of her cheeks, then shouts, 'Well, Goodbye Mr Chips!' as she disappears through the door again.

'Mr Chips is one of the best-loved characters in English Literature!' Ivan yells after her. And the book is a true classic, he acknowledges privately – short, well reviewed, and a best-seller.

A moment later her head pops around the door again. 'No,' Donna says. 'If you care to read it, you'll find he was actually a doddery old git with an unhealthy interest in young boys.'

'Oh, what a cynical age we do live in.'

'And *boring*. You're no fun.'

'I'm not boring. I'm tired. Now go away.'

She makes another face and says, 'All right, have it your

way.' She slams the door after her and he rolls over on the bed and tries to go to sleep, but instead he spends twenty minutes wondering why he didn't go with her, because annoying as she is, he has found he actually quite likes being with her.

Yawning, he phones Campbell and assures him that everything is back on track. Then, when Campbell has assured *him* that their plans are ticking along nicely, that he'll be able to transfer the first part of his advance in the next few days, and that Winfrey is all geared up for April May's London debut at the end of the week, Ivan puts the phone down and at last manages to get to sleep. There is a mini-bar in the room, but he hasn't touched it. He is never drinking again.

He wakes in late afternoon, to the sound of music coming from the next room. He shaves, showers, and then when he's dressed he knocks on the connecting door. Donna opens it in full April May uniform and gives a coy, eye-fluttering, 'Well, *hello*, Mr Chips.'

'You're supposed to be a serious author, not Marilyn Monroe.'

'Are we going to get off on the wrong foot again tonight?'

'No. Sorry. You look great.'

'April May looks great. I feel like a pig in a wig.'

'No really, you do look great. Relax.'

'I am relaxing. I've had a bottle of wine.'

'Donna . . .'

'April, please. I'm in April mode. I think our personalities are merging. Is that what happens to actresses? I bet it happened to Monroe.'

'Well, if it's any help, I think I'd rather have a drink with Donna Carbone than April May.'

'Why, Ivan, that's the nicest thing you've ever said to me.'

'I only mean that I'm jealous of April May's success, whereas I know what you really are.' Her smile drops and she turns wordlessly back into her room. She pours herself another glass of wine and turns the music up a notch. Ivan grimaces. 'What are you listening to?' he asks.

'I don't know, but rather it than you.'

'You take me too seriously.'

'Well, at least somebody does.'

He smiles. 'Touché. Sorry. Share a drink with an old man?'

She looks at him, shakes her head, but pours him one nevertheless. What he meant was, he's never drinking heavily again. He holds out his glass to clink, she hesitates, then clinks back.

'You know something, Ivan?'

'I know many things.'

'Yes, undoubtedly, but when I was in prison and you came to my cell, I saw you looking at my books, and I know that you were looking to see if I had any of yours.'

He shrugs. 'It's natural, and you didn't.'

'Yes, I did. I'd lent them out to some of the girls.'

'Because you didn't like them.'

'No, because I did like them. I do that – when I find something I love, I want to share it with other people.'

'Oh. Well. Thank you. Can I have that in writing?'

She smiles. 'Do you think I'd want to be taught by someone whose work I didn't approve of?'

'Well, you can always learn, even if you're just learning what you don't agree with.'

'I couldn't. I need to be inspired.'

'And I inspired you?'

'Your words, yes, a lot. But in the class? No, you didn't.'

'Oh. I see.'

'Most of the time you were condescending and patronising and bored.'

Ivan sighs.

'But occasionally, occasionally, you really lost yourself in it, you really got passionate when you were talking about some book or play or poem. It was as if we weren't there at all, as if it would have been pouring out of you whether you were standing in a prison workshop or at a bus stop or in the bath. It was amazing to see.'

'Well.'

'Unfortunately, it only seems to take up about one per cent of your being.'

'I can't go round being passionate about books *all* the time, I'd be locked up.'

'But you could be passionate about *life*. It *is* in you, I've seen it. It just needs teasing out.'

'If I'd known I was coming on tour with Oprah Winfrey I'd have,' and he can't for the moment think of the correct allusion, so he stumbles on with, 'baked a cake.'

She takes another sip of her wine. 'I can see,' she says, 'that I'm working with a rough diamond indeed. Not even a diamond – diamanté. But I can make you a better man, Ivan, if you give me half the chance.'

He blinks at her. It's not just the diamanté, it's the passion that she has, the commitment in her eyes, the challenge. 'Well,' he says, 'life lessons from a lifer, whatever next.'

'You can run me down as much as you want, Ivan, but I'm not going to change. Life is like a poem, it—'

'Yes, dear,' Ivan says, 'it is generally incomprehensible and invariably much, much too long. Now, don't we have a reading to go to?'

He smiles and turns for the door, clutching his glass. There is something about her that scares him quite a lot, and it's not just the thought of a kitchen knife in the kidneys.

The evening reading in Micawber Books attracts one hundred and thirty-nine fans of April May's hype. The shop scarcely has room for more than fifty, so they really are crushed in. Ivan and April wait in a back office with the owner, an affable bloke called Sid who seems to have extremely good taste in literature – there is a healthy selection of Ivan's novels on the shelves. April has three or four glasses of wine. Ivan is taking it easy. He drinks wine, but watered down with lemonade. Sid says his shop has very loyal customers, and Ivan stifles a yawn. April sits on a desk going over her lines, sipping her wine. From time to time she looks up and asks Ivan a question about intonation and presentation and when he responds she seems satisfied with his advice. When she goes to fix her face before starting the reading, Sid says, 'You seem to have a very close relationship.'

Ivan shrugs.

'We get writers and their agents in here, they hate each other's guts. We get writers who don't even recognise their agents. And vice versa. But you two seem to get on.'

'Well, what's not to get on with?'

'I know, she is lovely,' Sid says, and Ivan nods, though actually he was talking about himself. He sees himself as an easygoing kind of a chap, not as others see him.

April returns from the toilets. 'Okay,' she says, 'let's rock Sheffield.'

Sid leads her out of the office and Ivan hangs back.

He watches her from the wings. She's really very good. The audience loves her. Even when she stumbles over words, they love her. She says, 'Sorry, I didn't write this shit,' and they roar and she glances slyly back at Ivan who rolls his eyes in fake exasperation.

'Where do you get your ideas from?' a middle-aged woman asks from the floor after the reading.

'A small shop in Covent Garden,' April replies.

'How much money have you made?' a student asks.

'If I'd half as much as people think, then I'd have twice as much as I actually have.'

She's good. She could be on *Parkinson*. She'd give bloody Francesca Brady a run for her money, that's for sure.

Afterwards, Sid and his wife Cathy insist on taking them out for something to eat. There's a Chinese restaurant around the corner. It's a nice, pleasant evening's entertainment. Sid waxes lyrical about the state of British publishing and Ivan replies from the perspective of an extremely author-friendly agent. Cathy talks about their kids and how dangerous Sheffield can be and how so many of the kids she grew up with – she's only in her thirties – have ended up in prison, which launches Donna into a spirited attack on the dehumanising prison system which she successfully covers towards the end by saying she's been researching a novel set in a women's prison.

'Lesbians, then,' Sid says.

Cathy sighs and says, 'Men. First thing that comes into their minds.'

Donna glances at Ivan and laughs.

Sid and Cathy leave before midnight, blaming a baby-sitter. Ivan and Donna sit on, and at first they don't quite know what to say to each other, now that they're alone; but then she knocks her red wine over by accident and in reaching to help he knocks his over too, then the staff are fussing around them and they're soon laughing so hard that they don't really need to talk.

When they're walking back to the hotel, Donna slips her arm through Ivan's. 'I can't wait to get this bloody wig off,' she says.

'Same here.' They giggle. Then Donna does pull her wig off. 'Maybe you shouldn't do that in public.'

'Okay. What about this?' She goes up on her toes, and kisses him on the lips. She giggles again as she pulls away.

'Donna . . .'

But then she's back, and this time it's steamy and passionate and he's returning it with complete abandon when she breaks off suddenly and hiccups and then they both laugh. She takes him by the hand and leads him back to the hotel. They go up in the lift, she with a smile on her face, he frozen-faced with shock and his mind racing.

He breathes a sigh of relief when she lets go of his hand and goes to her own door. 'Good night, Ivan,' she says without looking at him and enters her room. She closes and locks the door. He stands in the corridor for several long moments, aware not only that this is very confusing but also that there is movement in his trousers. He rubs his hand across his brow and blows air out of his cheeks. He's old enough to be her big brother, if their shared mother had fallen pregnant long after her first brood of children had started attending an expensive private college. He shakes himself into the present and decides it is a good time to visit the mini-bar, except when he enters his room he finds that the connecting door is already open and Donna is lying on the bed, propped up on one elbow. She is not completely naked. She is wearing a smile.

'Hello, Mr Chips,' she says.

21

Ivan is dragged reluctantly from his slumber by the sound of a phone. As he staggers towards consciousness he is perplexed by the fact that his mother isn't answering it; then he feels a warm knee brush lightly against his spine and he's suddenly back on earth and his mind is racing again. He sits bolt upright.

Donna.

Bed.

Sex.

Phone.

Head.

Phone.

Sex.

God.

'What?' he snaps into the phone.

'Ivan, good morning.' It's Campbell.

'Good morning,' Ivan says.

'How's it going?'

'Fine.'

'Reading go well?'

'Yes.'

'No problems?'

'No.'

'Do you, by any chance, have a hangover?'

'Yes.'

'You don't want to talk, do you?'

'No.'

'I'll call you later.'

'Okay.' He puts the phone down, thinking, Christ, what have I done?

Fatal Attraction.

Basic Instinct.

He cautiously moves himself to the edge of the bed, leans out, then checks underneath for sharp knives. When he finds nothing, he lies back and sighs. Donna, hair tousled, smiling sleepily, emerges from under the covers.

'What're you looking for?' she asks. 'You know they don't keep po's under the bed any more.' She yawns. 'You have to go all the way to the bathroom. It's a scandal.'

'I know.' Ivan, pulling the covers back up over his chest, blinks at her. 'What have we done?' he whispers.

Donna stretches. 'I don't know,' she says wearily, 'but would you mind doing it again?' She smiles cheekily, then curls up again.

What the hell was he thinking of? Yes – okay – she's lovely and attractive and presented herself in such a way that he couldn't possibly have said no. But what the hell was he thinking of? He has no idea where she has been.

She's been in prison. He didn't wear a condom. *My God, she could have Aids!* She could be a junkie. Or a lesbian. Or a junkie lesbian. Wasn't her boyfriend a junkie? God. They probably shared needles! Ivan is suddenly terrified. He jumps out of bed and pulls on his pants and trousers. She rolls over and says, 'What are you doing?'

'Getting up.'

She throws the covers back and says, 'I thought you were going to make love to me again?'

'Okay,' Ivan says, and removes his trousers.

Over breakfast, downstairs – she wanted it in the room, but he thought it was better in public where she'd be less inclined to react violently, and at least there might be someone around to save him, a big bouncer with a mallet or a waitress – he says, 'This isn't such a good idea.'

'I know. We should have stayed in bed.'

'No, I don't mean that.'

'I know. We have to get to Coventry.'

'No, I don't mean that either.'

'I know, Ivan. You're thinking all kinds of weird thoughts. I can see your eyeballs shooting around in their sockets. It's a sure sign you're thinking too much. I've come to know that look. Just relax and go with the flow.'

'I can't do that.'

She shrugs, and butters toast. 'Did you enjoy last night?' she asks.

'The reading was wonderful.' She gives him a look and he says, 'Yes. Clearly. But in retrospect—'

'Bugger retrospect, Ivan, retrospect is for historians. I prefer to live in the here and now.'

'Here and now we have a big problem.' He has his full cooked breakfast before him, but he hasn't touched it. He's looking at her and thinking that he has just made love to a beautiful young woman, twice, and she's happy and he should be happy but he is in fact, not.

'Donna, listen to me, you were very drunk last night.'

'*You* were very drunk last night.'

'No, I wasn't.'

'Yes, you were, Ivan. We both were.' She bites into her toast and speaks with her mouth full. 'It's nothing to be ashamed of, you know. We got pissed, we went to bed. *I* enjoyed it. It's always the most awkward part of a relationship, isn't it, the first time you go to bed?' She swallows, then licks at the crumbs left on her lips. 'I mean, how many boyfriends have I had, four or five, and I've never gone to bed with any of them for the first time unless we were both drunk. Don't you find that?'

Ivan looks at her, then shrugs. 'It doesn't matter, Donna. This isn't right.'

'Why?' she says, buttering another slice, her voice quite light enough to suggest she is taking none of this seriously.

'Because . . .'

'Because why?'

He sighs. 'Look, Donna. We're in a business relationship here, and it's important that we don't do anything to jeopardise it.'

'Oh, bollocks,' she says, which rather stops him short.

He lifts his knife and fork, then puts them down again. 'Okay. Look. I – love – but I mean, if you're . . . how can I . . . ?'

248

She laughs. 'For a man of letters, your words are all over the place.'

'I know. I – Donna, we . . .'

'I think we're two lost souls.'

'I'm old enough to be your fa—'

'Thrown together by fate and fortune.'

'I think we made an understandable mist—'

'It's symbiosis – two organisms become attached with beneficial results.'

'I just think that if we agree to forget . . .'

'I just think it's really sweet. I mean, I want to live for the love and beauty . . .'

'. . . what happened and go back to . . .'

'. . . that poetry makes us strive for . . .'

'For fuck's sake, Donna! It's not about poetry!'

The other diners, mostly businessmen sitting by themselves, look up at his sudden outburst. Ivan lowers his head. Donna glares across at him. He notices how she retains the butter-knife in her hand. He puts a hand on his fork. She jabs the knife lightly towards him, making a point. He moves back several inches, but refrains from dashing for the emergency exit.

'But it *can* be about poetry, Ivan, don't you see that?'

'No, I don't,' he says flatly. Then: 'Oh Donna. Life isn't like that.'

'Yes, it is! If you feel something, feel it. If you love something, love it.'

'Oh get a grip!' He leans forward across the table, growing angry, forgetting her knife. 'Life – it's electric bills! Exhaust pipes! Builders! Ingrowing toenails! That's life, Donna, not poetry!'

She shakes her head. 'Oh you sad, cynical man. You think you can teach me about life, sitting in your little room typing? You should try prison, Ivan. That's life.'

'What do you want, a medal? Donna, I was there, it was like a fucking holiday camp.'

'That's right, Ivan, you were there for about twenty minutes. That's like saying you can relate to a round-the-world yachtsman because you have the occasional bath.'

There's a brief respite as a waitress gives them a coffee refill. When she leaves, Donna keeps her eyes down. She lifts another slice of toast and begins to butter it; she has two others buttered and waiting. Ivan reaches across and stills her buttering hand. She looks up at him and her eyes are wet.

'Donna,' he says softly, 'please. You don't understand. Look, I know you've had a hard time of it, and maybe that's why the love and romance and symbolism of poetry appeals to you. You see it all around you. You see it in us. But I'm a married man, I have children, this . . . well, you've lived out a little fantasy, you've slept with your teacher, you've slept with a real writer. But that's it, Donna. It was lovely. But that has to be it.'

She pulls her hand away. She sets the knife down. She clasps her hands together so tightly that her knuckles turn white. She leans towards him. 'Fantasy?' she says. 'Fantasy?'

'Well, perhaps—'

'You have the nerve to tell me about fantasy? You *are not* a married man. You are divorced, and you live with your mummy. You're middle-aged, you're out of shape, you look like a tramp, you can only get your work published under a woman's name and I bet you can't remember the last time you had any sort of a fucking shag, drunken or not. So which one of us is living in a fantasy, Ivan?'

'Now,' he says, 'that you put it like that . . .'

'What exactly are you scared of?'

He clears his throat. 'It's difficult to be precise.'

'If you ask me, you're scared of your own fucking shadow,' and when he opens his mouth, she snaps: 'Oh shut up, Ivan, and eat your breakfast.'

He obediently lifts his knife and fork, but she isn't finished. She leans closer and speaks with an intensity that would thrill him if she hadn't done time. 'You said things to me last night, you opened your heart, and I don't think you've done that for years. It meant something to me, and it meant something to you, and the problem is you were so drunk you can't remember what you said, and I think that's pretty fucking sad. Because for a while there, in bed, at dinner, walking home, you were in danger of turning into a really nice guy. And it's doubly fucking sad that someone can say that you're nicer drunk than sober, but it's the fucking truth.'

There are tears rolling down her cheeks now. She grabs her napkin, dabs at her face. Then she pushes her chair back and stands.

'Where are you going?' Ivan asks weakly.

'Coventry,' Donna says. 'And so are you. In both senses of the word.'

And then she's away across the breakfast room. Ivan sits, mesmerised, watching her go. Across the aisle from him a florid-faced businessman clears his throat, and catches Ivan's eye.

'If you don't mind me saying,' he says, 'you didn't handle that very well.'

Ivan is so taken aback that he can only fumble a, 'Well, I don't really . . .'

'I know I'm speaking out of turn,' the man with the red tie and face says, the man with the expansive girth and the three chins, 'but we appear to be of a similar age. Not so long ago, I had the chance of love with a younger woman, and I worried it away. Now look at me. I'm a sad, lonely bastard selling support tights to a health service which *does not want them.*'

Ivan wipes his mouth on his napkin and stands. 'We are not of a *remotely* similar age,' he says, throwing the napkin down and striding away across the breakfast room.

She spoke the truth. Coventry, in both senses of the word. They travel by train, they sit together, but they do not speak, or when they do there are not enough words to constitute a sentence. There are yeses, nos, shrugs, grunts and much rolling of eyes. They check into their hotel, they share a taxi to the bookshop, she conducts her reading in her increasingly professional manner, the audience loves her, she answers the questions afterwards in a lively and humorous fashion, then leaves quickly afterwards. He follows her back to the hotel, a dozen paces behind, like a bad dog. He asks her if she wants to join him for dinner, but she chooses room service. He phones her room and asks her if she wants to come down to the bar for a drink. He makes a joke of it. He thinks she might appreciate the lightness, that she might crack after so much bad humour all day, but she says no and puts the phone down. He has several drinks anyway. He convinces himself that everything is okay, that it doesn't matter if they don't get on any more, it's much better that they don't complicate an already complicated business. Make some money. Expose the publishing establishment. Exploit the situation for all it's worth, then they'll go their own way. She's so young. She's been in jail. They have nothing in common. He has done the right thing. He could have handled it better, but it's still the right thing. Except, after another couple of drinks, he's thinking about how they were in bed together and how fantastic it was to feel like that again, and then he's thinking about her body, and then he's thinking about how much they were laughing in bed together. He tries to remember what he said to her, how he opened his heart, but it's gone.

He's quite drunk by the time he goes upstairs. He stands outside her room. He knocks on the door. He will apologise and tell her what a fool he is and is there any chance that they could sleep together, but she doesn't answer.

His room is three doors along. He goes there and phones her, but she doesn't respond. He walks back along the corridor and knocks again. There's no response. He knocks again and says if she doesn't answer he will start to sing, and then she'll be putty in his hands.

So he begins to sing. 'You'll Never Walk Alone.' 'Maggie May.' He's just started into 'If You Want My Body, and You Think I'm Sexy' when the Assistant Manager advises him to stop making such a fool of himself and directs him back to his room.

Ivan asks if the Residents' Bar is open, and the Assistant Manager lies that it's closed.

Ivan flops down on his bed and imagines Donna without clothes.

The phone rings. He lifts it on the second ring and says, 'I knew you couldn't resist me.'

'How did you know it was me?'

But the woman's voice at the other end is not Donna's, and for several long moments he struggles to place it.

'I just knew,' he says, less confidently.

'That's nice,' she says. 'I hope you don't mind me calling so late.'

'No, God, of course not . . . Avril,' remembering finally that it's his wife. 'How did you know where I was?'

'I phoned Campbell.'

'Oh. Right.' And then he sits up, straight and panicked. 'The kids – are they okay?'

'The kids are fine.'

'Oh. Right. Great. So . . .'

'Just wanted to call for a natter.'

'It's one in the morning.'

'I know. Do you mind?'

'No, of course not.'

'I always loved you, Ivan. Maybe we didn't try hard enough.'

'Have you been drinking?'

She laughs. 'No, I haven't.'

'Has Alfred the Great left you – is that what this is about?'

'No, Ivan, he's here. Next room.'

'Oh.'

254

'I'm dying, Ivan.'

'You're dying. *I'm* dying. You should have seen me ten minutes ago, singing my head off like a fool.'

'Ivan, I'm serious.'

'So am I. You know I haven't a note in my body.' He waits for her to respond, but there is nothing, just her breathing. 'Where were we?' he asks.

'I said, I'm dying. I'm in hospital. I wanted to call you before—'

'What're you talking about?'

'Ivan, I'm dying. Death's door, all that.'

'You're not dying. You're the healthiest person I know.'

'Well, you should get out more then, because this is it.'

'Avril, don't be daft. What's wrong? Have you two had a row? You know swallowing a handful of Junior Disprin isn't going to do it. Worst you'll get is a bad cramp and an aversion to school in the morning.'

'Ivan, will you shut up and listen to me. I *am* dying. I have cancer.'

'Sure. What is it, one of those *Love Story* cancers where you look great, sound great until five seconds from the end?'

'No, I look pretty rough.'

'Yeah, sure. You never looked rough in your life.'

'Well, thank you, but I do now.'

'You're talking nonsense, Avril.'

'I'm not talking nonsense, I—'

'Put Alfred on then, if you're so sick.'

'Ivan, will you just—'

'See, there's nothing wrong with you.'

She sighs, then he hears her shouting, 'Alfred!'

A moment later she passes him the phone and Alfred says, 'Hello, Ivan.'

'Alf – what's the big joke?'

'No joke, Ivan.'

'Then what the fuck is she talking about?'

'It's like she says, Ivan, she's dying.'

'What do you mean, dying?'

'Dying, Ivan.'

'Seriously?'

Alfred clears his throat. 'Is there any other way? I'd—' And then Alfred loses his voice, and lets go with a sob, and Ivan holds the phone away from his mouth for a moment, appalled.

'Ivan?' Avril says.

'I'm here.'

'Now do you believe me?'

'Yes. And it's bloody typical.'

'*What* is?'

'Telling him before telling me. Honestly.'

He can tell that she's smiling, but she can't tell that there are tears rolling down his cheeks.

'I'm sorry, Ivan.'

'So you should be. Do you want me to tell the kids?'

'I've already told them.'

'Oh.'

'I told people in the order that I thought they could best deal with it. I'm afraid you're at the bottom of the list.'

'But, Jesus, Avril – they're six and nine, for God's sake, how can you say—'

'They're seven and eleven, Ivan. That's how.'

'Well, thanks a bunch. Except I couldn't be right at the bottom of your bloody list, because you're forgetting my mother.'

'No, I told your mother yesterday.'

'Christ, Avril, you must have a really low opinion of me.'

'Well, that goes without saying.'

They are silent for several long moments.

'You're not really dying, are you?'

'Yes I am, Ivan.'

'But I mean . . . how long?'

'A few days.'

He laughs. 'Be serious.'

'I am. I just . . . well, I wanted to say goodbye.'

'Don't be ridiculous.'

'And ask you to look after the kids. I know money's a bit tight, but I'm insured, that'll help.'

'Avril . . .'

'They do love you, but you really need to get your act together.'

'Avril . . .'

'And I loved you, and you made me very happy, and it's a pity we couldn't make it work.'

Silence. And tears.

Avril.

'I'm going now,' she says. 'Not *going* going, but I'm tired and I need to talk to Alfred and then I have to do my Ali MacGraw thing and that will be that.'

'Avril . . .'

'Don't worry, be happy.' She laughs quietly. 'You'd be really pissed off if those were my final words, wouldn't

you? My little writer. You'll be wanting something profound – comedy is easy, dying is hard. What about *Sod
off*? That'd be appropriate, don't you think, considering
where I'm going? Sod *on*, in fact.'

'Don't, Avril, please.'

She laughs again. And he does too. 'Bye,' she whispers.

'Bye,' he whispers back.

As he's putting the receiver down he hears her say
suddenly, 'Ivan?'

'What?'

'Missing you already.' And she giggles again and finally
does put it down.

Ivan sits on the side of the bed, rocking. He is very
drunk. He's not sure that he spoke to his wife at all. It
might have been a wrong number.

22

He wonders how he can use this in a book: ex-wife dies, but confesses true love for husband on deathbed.

A heartbroken writer struggles to immortalise his wife in a novel, and in so doing rebuilds his own fractured life.

Husband struggles to bring up kids by himself while trying to immortalise wife.

Motherless kids become withdrawn/stroppy/bullies/killers/vegetarians.

Ex-wife dies, boyfriend tries to win custody of the kids. The kids decide to stay with boyfriend.

Boyfriend and ex-husband fall in love. And the Government takes the kids away from them.

She said to him once, 'Is there nothing of ours that you won't use in a book?'

'Sorry, say that a bit slower until I get it down.' She threw a book at him then, and he protested that all writers are magpies.

'You're not a magpie, Ivan, you're a rapist. You rape people's lives, and they can't do a thing about it.'

'I change names and add moustaches. Although only to the women.'

He does not sleep that night, and he does not drink any more. He phones his mother and she breaks down. He sits by the window watching what little traffic there is. Kids are spilling out of a nightclub and waiting for taxis. There are several couples snogging in shop doorways. A kebab shop is doing a roaring trade. His wife is dying while people thoughtlessly consume kebabs. She's lying in a hospital bed and she's thinking to herself: I'm dying, I'm dying, I'm dying. In a few days or hours or minutes I will be no more. I will not be able to think or breathe or shop or kiss or read or laugh or cry – and she will weep again. She will think about heaven and hell and know that neither of them exists, that the end is the end and that there is nothing, but she will pray nevertheless. She will look at her children and think she has done the right thing by telling them, treating them like adults, but they still won't understand, not really. Her son will bring her his favourite book for 'the journey' and her daughter will ask who will do her hair and make her packed lunch for school if her mum isn't there. And Avril will try not to cry in front of them but she won't be able to stop herself and Alfred will usher the kids out but she won't let them go because she will never, ever, never, ever, never ever see them again. She will not know how they turn out. She will not be able to protect them or shout at them or laugh with them. They will not look after her in her old age because she will have no old age. *For all the things I've done for you – no charge.* In fact it is not only Avril who is dying: her whole family is dying, everyone in London, everyone in the world, the whole world, because the moment she closes her eyes for the final time, it will cease to exist. There will be no more children and no more television and no more laughter because it will all stop the moment she stops. She is not only dying, but she is massacring her family. Every memory will go, every moment of her life will have gone, every moment of her children's life will cease in that instant.

Is she in pain? Is she screaming through the night for release? Is she doped up on morphine? She might be feeling *great.*

How much pain is there? Can she describe it? Can she tell someone? Is it like a really bad hangover? Are there daggers jagging into her body? Has she wasted away to nothing? Have they operated? Have they *removed*? Is she in full make-up, like a painted doll, trying to cover up the emaciation? Is she bloated from the drugs she's had to take? Is she bald from chemotherapy?

Is there a mortgage on her house? Exactly how much insurance is there? Will there be a fight over it because she's divorced? Will it go to the kids? Will it be put in trust until they're twenty-one? Will Alfred fight him through the courts? Will he ever get the books back from her he never took with him when they parted? Burial or cremation? Wooden coffin or cardboard? Scatter the ashes or keep them above the hearth? Would she be dying if they had stayed together? Does the break-up of a marriage kick-start some physiological reaction that leads directly to cancer and death? Is it his fault? Is there a decent interval to wait before starting the book? Should he videotape her final moments? Will he fight with Alfred for the closest seat to her deathbed? Should he go to her at all? Should he teach her one final lesson for messing with his life?

He's the first into the dining room in the morning. He orders a full English breakfast and eats it down quickly because he can. He has toast and coffee and reads the free newspaper because he can. He is not dying in a bed. He reads features about soap stars and fighting in Macedonia and who has scored a hat-trick, and finds it completely fascinating because he doesn't have to think to himself that in an hour all of it will cease to be. He knows he will be here or there tomorrow and the day after.

There are four or five other people in the dining room when Donna comes in. There are other tables available, and for a moment it looks as if she's going to take one of them, but then she sighs to herself and sits down opposite him.

For a little while they don't speak. Ivan continues to study his paper, Donna accepts coffee from the waitress and orders breakfast. Ivan turns a page. Donna unfolds her napkin. She adds milk and sugar and stirs the coffee for a long time. She sucks on one of her lips then, decision made, ventures a conciliatory, 'Hangover?'

Ivan lowers the paper and shakes his head.

'I didn't realise you had such a good singing voice,' she says, and gives him a small smile with it.

He doesn't smile back. Instead he folds the paper, places

it carefully on the table. 'Listen, Donna, I'm going back to London after tonight's reading.'

'What?'

'I'm going back tonight. I can get a train from Leicester. I've spoken to Campbell and he's going to come up and look after you until the end of the tour. You've only a few nights left.'

She's looking at him in disbelief. 'Oh that's just brilliant,' she says.

'I'm sorry.'

'Yeah, I'm sure you are.'

'Really.'

'That's pathetic, Ivan.'

'I—'

'You know, that really makes me sick. You sleep with someone, you feel guilty, so you come on like an arsehole to frighten her off, and when that doesn't work, you run away. Run Away. I mean, what are you, Ivan – a man or a mouse? Do you have a back-bone at all? What animal is it that doesn't have a back-bone? Oh yes. A snake. That's what you are. That's what you fucking are. Sitting there being all cool saying "Oh I have to go back to London," when the truth is you can't make your mind up whether you want to be with me or not. You weren't going home last night, were you? You were phoning my room, you were banging on the door, singing your head off because the drink was in and you fancied a shag. Suddenly you were a fucking Argos catalogue Lothario. And just because I stand my ground and you have to go to bed shagless, now you're the cool fucking Ice King again, now you're crawling back to London like a spoiled bloody kid. You really make me sick.'

'My wife is dying.'

'You're divorced.'

'Okay,' he says, 'my ex-wife is dying. The mother of my children is dying. Is that good enough for you?'

She looks at him, trying to detect a flicker of deceit. 'What, she's suddenly dying between last night and this morning?'

'It looks that way, yes.'

'You're full of shit.'

'That may be. But I'm going.' He wipes his mouth on his napkin, then nods as he stands. 'Check out in about an hour, will we?'

As he turns away she quickly says: 'Are you messing me around?'

'No.'

'Swear to God.'

'Donna, I don't have to swear to God.'

'It's just . . . very convenient, isn't it?'

He fixes her with a look of extreme disappointment. 'Yes, Donna, that's it. It's very convenient. I'll give her a good telling-off when I see her.'

He turns and strides away across the dining room. Donna's mouth drops a little and she says a stunned, 'Oh my God,' to herself, and then she jumps up out of her seat just as the waitress is setting her breakfast down over her left shoulder. It goes flying, mostly on to the floor but she manages to get a strip of fried bacon to land on her shoulder. She lifts it off between two pinched fingers, suddenly squeamish, and bellows at the waitress,

'Why can't you watch what you're doing?' The waitress apologises profusely even though it clearly wasn't her fault; Donna waves her away and hurries after Ivan. She misses the lift and instead pounds up the stairs just in time to see him enter his room and close the door. She runs down the hall and bangs on it. He opens it, his face pale, his eyes dark, his attitude cold.

'I'm sorry,' she says.

'Thank you.'

'Is there anything I can do?'

'No. I don't think so. Let's just go to Leicester.' He begins to close the door. She puts her hand out to stop it.

'Ivan, please.'

He hesitates. 'It's not your fault,' he says quietly.

'Do you want me to give you a hug?'

He smiles. 'No, it's okay.'

She nods and turns for her room. She hears his door close behind her. When she's in her room she paces back and forth, unable to settle. Then she goes back down the hall and knocks on his door again and when he opens it she hands him her book of poetry.

'I want you to have it.'

'Oh. Well. Thank you. But really . . .' He's trying to give it back.

'No. Really. You might get something from it.'

'I don't think so, Donna.'

And he hands it back to her. He quite likes the gutted look on Donna's face. He likes having that power. He's not trying to be cruel, because she has been selfish and obnoxious and he is the grieving widower-in-waiting and he has to be cold because tradition demands it and it is exactly how the leading characters in his books would behave, but still he likes it that she cares enough to be hurt by his being cruel. He would indeed have liked a hug. But he can't help but feel that it would only have made matters worse if he'd accepted the hug in the spirit in which it was intended – grieving widower-in-waiting accepting sympathy – and then tried to unbutton her trousers. Because despite everything death doesn't stop him thinking about sex or novels, but instead *inspires* him to think about sex or novels. Tea and sympathy be damned. And poetry doubly so.

He closes the door.

23

He does get a hug, eventually, but it's from his mother. He's coming up the drive with his bag in hand when the door opens and she hurries out and throws her arms around him and sniffles back tears and says, 'Isn't it awful.'

Ivan kisses the top of her head and says, 'But you hate her.'

'No, I don't. No, I don't,' Mother says. 'I was huffing.'

'You've been huffing for seven years.'

She lets him go and wipes at her damp cheeks and says, 'We Connors always did know how to keep a grudge. But we've made up now.'

The kids come running down now and they hug him too. They seem as bright and bushy-tailed as ever. They don't pause long enough to say much. They're off chasing each other around the garden, laughing happily.

She leads him into the house, carrying his bag. 'She wanted to talk to me about how to tell the kids, so I went to see her in the hospital.'

'How is she?' Ivan asks. Mother looks like she's going to cry again. 'I'll get you a sherry,' he says, but what he means is he'll get himself a whisky. He was good last night, and he was good this morning and when Campbell met him at the station he was impressed at how sober and serious Ivan was; but it is an act, it is not really how he feels inside. He is behaving as he is expected to behave, but inside he's thinking the usual things. Career, critics, the fickleness of publishers, the greatness of Irish literature, sex, coffee, drink, the pretty girl walking past.

He gives Mother her drink and she sits down. He's only been away a few days, yet she somehow looks older. Smaller. He has a sudden vision of her own funeral and he wonders what she's put in her will. She hasn't any other children, so the house will probably come to him, but she's a strange old bird at times and it's not impossible that she'll leave everything to the East Grinstead Salsa Society or wherever the hell it is she goes to dance like a moron every week.

'She's being so brave,' Mother says.

'Well, she hasn't much choice.'

'Of course she has. When I go I'll be screaming and fighting, but she seems very calm.'

'She's drugged.'

'Well, yes of course.'

Mother nods thoughtfully. Ivan swirls his drink in his glass. He can hear the *Scooby Doo* theme tune coming from the next room. He grew up watching *Scooby Doo* in the afternoons on TV after school with a plate of bread and jam on his lap. He wonders how he ever went from loving

Scooby Doo to James Joyce. How *Inspector Gadget* morphed into *An Inspector Calls*. How contented he was as a child, how discontented as an adult. Puberty, probably, the birth of frustrated ambition, and ambitious frustration.

'Are you going to see her right away?' Mother asks.

'No. We said goodbye on the phone.'

'Ivan, you can't leave it like that.'

'It's what she wants, Mother.'

'Perhaps it's what she says she wants. But deep down . . .'

'I'd pretty well say that deep down, things aren't so deep down any more. She wants to be alone with Alfred at the end.'

'Well, if you ask me, it's not right.'

'The point is, she's *not* asking you.' He pours himself another drink – she's still sipping hers – and says, 'So what did you really talk about – me?'

'I told her one child in the house was more than enough.'

'Mother, you can't split them up.'

'I'm not talking about splitting them up, Ivan, I'm talking about *you*. I'm seventy-one years old, I don't need two children racing around here as well. You're difficult enough.'

'But they're your grandchildren!'

'Yes, and all very nice for weekends, but they're your children, Ivan – it's up to you.'

'But I live *here*.'

'Well, it's time you got your own place again. Somewhere you can be a family.'

'We *are* a family.'

'Not under this roof, you're not.'

'You're my mother, I can't believe you're saying this. You're supposed to look after me.'

'Ivan, we're getting to the point where you start looking after me.'

'Yeah, sure, that'll be the day, Salsa Queen.'

She chuckles indulgently, then wags a finger at him. 'Ivan, sooner or later you're going to have to dock with Planet Earth again. I'm getting old, your children need a father, and you need a job.'

'I don't need a job. You forget April May.'

She gives him a look.

'April May is going to make me rich.'

'Well,' she says, 'she's going to make somebody rich. I've seen Campbell's car. I've seen his woman friend. She was wearing jewellery.'

'You have a real problem with trusting people, don't you?'

'I've always been a good judge of character.'

Ivan sighs. He knocks back his drink. 'This isn't getting us anywhere. The simplest thing is, keep everything as it is, and we have the kids adopted. Or fostered. Or whatever it is you do with unwanted strays.'

He winks at her. 'Another drink?'

'Perhaps a little nip.'

He naps in his room for several hours, then lies thinking until dusk. He glances at his watch: Donna will be into her reading now in Leeds. He wonders how she's getting on with Campbell. Whether she's told him they have slept together. Whether she's complained about his brusque and boorish behaviour. Whether she's confessed

270

undying love for him. The reading last night in Leicester was again well attended and the audience was certainly appreciative, although Donna was more subdued than at the previous events. He told her afterwards that she'd done well. They walked back to the hotel together to collect his bag, and she insisted on walking him to the station, but when they got to the desk there was a message from Campbell saying he'd been delayed and couldn't make it up until the following morning, and that was kind of embarrassing because they'd said their fare-wells already. They were left with an awkward evening together. They ate dinner and chatted but neither of them quite engaged.

'It's been a bit of an adventure, this tour.'

He shrugged and told her again how well she was doing.

'It's not me. It's April May.'

'You should act, you're a natural.'

'I'm a poet.'

'You could stop being a poet and start being an actress.'

'Would you tell Seamus Heaney to stop being a poet and start being a juggler, if he showed some flair for it?'

'You're not Seamus Heaney.'

That hurt her, a little – but what did she expect? Nobody had ever compared him to Shakespeare or Joyce or Hardy (Thomas as opposed to Oliver), and he didn't get annoyed about it. Although, of course, it was early days yet. There was plenty of time for him to enter the pantheon of literary greats. He was just embarking on what would surely be the most productive period of his career – nothing like a setback and a little death to

271

get the creative juices flowing. He no longer had much stomach for either his historical novels or that account of his turbulent youth he'd been toying with. No, once this April May thing was out of the way, and he was nestling comfortably in his new house, with his new children, and a nice tidy sum in the bank, he would at last be free of the burden of having to make a living, of having to satisfy anachronistic publishers or somnambulatory literary critics; he would allow his mind to wander into those inaccessible caves of semi-consciousness which had already yielded the instant classic that was *Kissing Cousins*. If he could create something as universally lauded as that by accident, who could tell what he might come up with if he really tried?

Mother shouts up from the kitchen that his dinner is ready and he rolls out of bed and down the stairs. Mother returns to the kitchen doorway and calls down the hall for the kids to come for theirs. Ivan is dreading this. It's the first time he'll have sat down with them properly since they were told about their mother's imminent death and he's scared stiff they will ask him things he cannot answer. About God and heaven and *why*? As he waits for them to arrive he keeps telling himself to be as honest as he can with them, and to try not to be too sarcastic.

But there's no sign of them and Mother looks in danger of blowing her top so he gets up from the table and goes along to the TV room to gee them up. The cartoons are still blasting away but there's no sign of the kids. So he goes through the house room by room, shouting for them and getting progressively angrier. He does a circuit of the front and back gardens, his jumper pulled up against the rain, but they're nowhere to be found.

'The little buggers,' Ivan says as he comes back into the house, but there's Mother running down the hall as fast as her salsa hips can carry her, waving a piece of paper with the urgency of peace declared but a dread look that says war is coming.

'They've run away!' she bellows.

Ivan takes the note from her and examines it.

Dear Daddy, Ivan reads, *we don't want to be adapted, or to live with forster parents, so we are running away. Love, your children. And we hate you.*

'Oh dear,' says Mother.

'Christ,' Ivan says. 'This is all I need.' He sighs. 'Okay. They can't have gone far.'

'Oh dear,' Mother says. Usually she's very practical in situations like this – they have run away before – but now she seems rooted to the spot.

Ivan puts his hands on her shoulders. 'You make sure the dinner doesn't burn, Mother, I'll go and get them.' He turns her gently and directs her back to the kitchen.

Then he goes back outside and hurries down the drive. When he was lying in bed he definitely heard their voices from downstairs, so they can't have been gone for more than half an hour. But that's a long time in London. It's dark and it's wet and there's no sign of them on the road. He runs to the corner, then back past the house to the opposite corner. The traffic is heavy, a thousand windscreen-wipers conducting the rain. He says, 'Shit,' a lot as he runs back to the house for the car. He drives to Avril's house, which is less than a mile away, in case they've gone home, although he's sure they don't have a key. He hopes to find them damp and sorry in their wooden playhouse in the garden, but no, the house is in darkness, the playhouse dank and forlorn. He curses. He thumps the steering wheel.

He checks a McDonald's and a Burger King and a KFC. Yet he knows, really, he's just been putting it off.

The hospital.

He doesn't want to go near the hospital. The smell of disinfectant. Sick people. Dying people. Dying ex-wife.

What will he say? How will he explain it? *You're dying, and they hate me.* That'll smooth her passage. Better not to go in at all, but loiter outside and deal with Alfred when he comes out to take them home.

Alfred, *fuck.*

Alfred will know how to deal with runaway kids. Spoiled little brats and clip them around the ears. He'll get on his reinforced soap box and shout and yell: 'Your darlin' angel of a mother is lyin' dyin' here . . .' Inexplicably he will have become stage Irish, 'and all you can think to do is run away – what sort of evil little divils are youse, eh? I've a good mind to put youse on a slave ship to Africa! And as for you, Ivan Connor . . .'

And Ivan will search his soul for something Wildean to put him down with, but his temper will get the better of him and he'll shout, 'Ah, shut your hole, you big fat bastard!' and he'll grab the kids and run for his life.

An ambulance flashes past and Ivan shudders involuntarily. What if they've been snapped up by some pervert? What if they've been knocked down by a bus? Or what if he enters the ward of death, and they're not even there.

'My . . . children,' Avril will manage to croak.

'Sorry, love, no idea, but don't worry yourself, I'm sure they'll turn up.' And she'll pass suddenly into the next world never knowing whether her children are safe or not. A recipe for a haunting.

Ghosts. Jesus, he hasn't thought about ghosts yet. What if she comes back to haunt him? What if she hurls plates at him? What if she switches his computer off before he can save his latest chapter?

He just manages to stop at a red light. But it's a good thing; he glances right and sees his children emerge from behind a parked truck, heads down, walking into the rain in the direction of the hospital. They're still a couple of miles short of it, but moving at a determined pace. At least, he presumes it's them; what he actually sees is Michael's trademark anorak. He waits until the lights change, then drives ahead of them about a hundred yards and draws into the kerb until he can get a good look at their faces – he has no wish to spend another night down at the police station. But it's them okay, pink-faced, soaked to the skin. He swings the passenger door open and shouts.

They start running.

He's out of the car and splashing after them. They're small and fast, he's big and slow, but he gains on them.

He stretches and grabs Michael by the hood, but then stumbles over a cracked paving stone and falls forward on top of his son, knocking him to the ground and then falling on top of him. Michael lets out a squeak as the wind is knocked out of him while Anna, having let go of her brother's hand, keeps on running, at least for a

275

dozen yards. Then she stops and turns and screams: 'What do you want! Leave us alone!' with enough malevolence and volume for the owner of a Chinese restaurant to dart out and demand to know what's going on. Ivan tells him to mind his own business and the Chinese restaurant owner raises his hands in a manner which reminds Ivan of a scene in Ang Lee's seminal *Crouching Tiger, Hidden Dragon*.

Ivan immediately appeals for calm. Anna kicks Ivan in the shins and calls him a bastard. The restaurant owner hurries back inside to call the police.

Ivan takes Anna by the ear and trails her into the restaurant in pursuit of the owner. Ivan orders Anna to tell the Chinese restaurant owner that he's her father or he will tell all of her friends about the night last month she wet the bed.

Anna immediately changes her story. The Chinese restaurant owner hesitates, still holding the receiver.

Ivan orders Chicken Fried Rice with Curry Sauce.

They eat in the car, the windows steamed up, hot air blowing out of the heater, the Rolling Stones playing on tape. Michael says, 'Would you really have us adapted?'

'No, of course not.'

'Or forrested?'

'No, of course not.'

'I still want to see Mummy,' Anna says.

'Let's take her some supper,' Michael adds.

'It's very late,' Ivan says. 'She'll be sleeping.' Tears begin to form up in Anna's eyes. 'Okay,' he says quickly, starting the engine, 'we'll go – just don't start burbling.'

They go, and Avril is pleased to see them, and Alfred stays out of the room, and they hug as much as they can with the tubes and it's all very Ali MacGraw until Avril spoils it rather by making the kids go out of the room while she's sick in a disposable cardboard bowl. They come back in and talk about school and cartoons. Avril smiles a lot, and hugs her children, and hugs her ex-husband and even manages to squeeze him tight.

She dies in the night, with Alfred holding her hand and a copy of Ivan's first novel under her pillow.

Alfred tells him this on the phone and Ivan says it isn't his best book, but he fears he's destined to be remembered for it.

24

Julia *Winfrey*.

Julia quite likes the sound of that.

She finds herself dreaming about it recently. Not that she's had a lot of time for day dreaming – she's been so keen to keep a tight grip on the April May campaign that she's seconded herself to the Marketing Department and is now personally managing every aspect of her prize discovery's publicity campaign. It is the day of April May's London debut, the perfect start to the publicity blitz which will culminate in the publication of *Kissing Cousins* four weeks from now. A small, intimate event in the small, intimate Pages bookshop, it's not quite Harrods, but perfect for their purposes; it can hold a maximum of seventy-five people, so naturally she has sent out six hundred invitations.

Carson has promised to leave his wife. He has said it before, but he said it again last night in bed.

Well, not in bed, on the office couch, but it's the

closest they get these days, what with *Kissing Cousins* on the horizon and his wife up from the country for the sales. He stroked her hair and told her how much he loved her work. She stroked his hair and told him how much she loved him. He kissed the nape of her neck and said she'd worked wonders with April May. She kissed his ears and asked if he'd ever thought about them having children. He said he had children, thousands of them. Hardback, paperback, instruction manuals, glossy coffee-table books, they were all his kids, as much his progeny as mere flesh and blood. 'My children will live forever,' he whispered huskily as he nibbled at her neck. 'Well, one of them will,' she murmured, bringing it full circle back to April May.

A wonderful, wonderful girl, April. Enigmatic, mysterious, writes like an angel – looks like an angel. Julia spends the morning with her doing a series of local radio interviews plugging that night's event. April is cool and charming and funny and the interviewers invariably keep her on air for longer than scheduled, which is practically unheard of. She poses for photos outside Winfrey Books. Passers-by stop and ask her for autographs. Julia thinks this is amazing. She can only recall a handful of other authors who would be recognised by the general public, and then invariably for reasons other than their writing: Salman, Jeffrey, Naomi. Francesca Brady might turn heads on a bus, but so would any beautiful, rich woman slumming it on public transport.

In the early afternoon April says she needs a few hours to herself, to get her head together. Julia is a little disappointed because she's set up a couple of interviews, but April insists with such charm that Julia says, sure, blow them off, they're not going anywhere. She can do them after the reading. April goes directly to a branch of Principles ostensibly to try on a dress; but she exits as Donna Carbone.

Campbell is downstairs, mixing drinks. Mother, in her black dress, is sitting in the lounge, cradling a sherry. The kids are in the garden looking for hibernating hedgehogs. Ivan's upstairs in his study. He can't rouse himself. He should be enjoying this. It's his moment in the spotlight. He should have his routine worked out in advance, but he sits behind his desk thinking of everything but his upcoming performance. Model aeroplanes as a kid, holidays in New York, the back row in the movies with various girlfriends, he thinks of everything but Avril's funeral. He needs to focus, because attention will be focused on him. A funeral isn't so much about burying a body as watching the bereaved, and in particular the husband/father/daughter of the deceased to see how they cope, how they react. For most people, apart from their wedding, it's the most public thing they have to do in their lives. It's a shaking-hands day and listening to a hundred people say, 'I'm very sorry.' It can either be about holding oneself together, showing the stiff upper lip, or it can be about falling apart, throwing oneself on the coffin and pounding it with one's fists, beseeching her/him not to go.

There's a tap on his door and Campbell is standing there in a smart black suit, a drink in each hand.

'I took the liberty,' he says, holding one of the glasses out to Ivan.

Ivan takes it. 'Nice suit,' he says.

'Armani,' Campbell says.

'Mmmm,' Ivan replies, 'whatever happened to *armani*?'

Campbell smiles weakly, and appropriately. 'Your money should be in the bank. Have you checked?'

Ivan shakes his head.

'Well, that's understandable.'

Ivan snorts. 'Why is it understandable?'

'Well – Avril. I'm sure you've had a lot of organising to do.'

'Alfred did the organising.'

'Oh right. But still. The kids . . .'

'Mother has sorted them out.'

'Still, I'm sure it's been very traumatic.'

'No, actually, it hasn't been traumatic at all.' Ivan takes a sip of his whisky. 'I had sex with her four nights ago.'

'With *Avril*? Christ.'

'No. With Donna. With April May.'

'Oh, thank God. I mean – you know what I mean. Donna. Yes. Well, can't blame you.'

'I shouldn't have.'

'Why not? You're both young, you're both single, you both have a conviction for GBH. Oh – sorry, that's only her.' He smiles. 'Don't beat yourself up about it, Ivan. I don't blame you. And she's fine about it.'

'Did she say?'

'No.'

'How do you know then?'

'Well, she wasn't visibly upset. Quite chipper, really.'

'So you don't know.'

'Ivan, this isn't really the time. Your wife . . .'

'My ex-wife.'

Campbell sighs. 'Let's forget it for now. Let's go and look after Avril.' He squeezes Ivan's shoulder, then leaves the room. When he goes downstairs he says to Ivan's mother, 'He's really cut up about it,' and she nods sadly.

Upstairs, Ivan begins a crossword.

It's cold, of course. A bitter wind slices across the tops of the gravestones and into their faces as the coffin is trundled across the cropped grass towards the hole. Ivan's quite pleased with the turn-out, and that most of the mourners have made the short journey from the warmth of the church to the chill of the graveyard. Usually most sneak off back to work after the actual funeral service; certainly he does.

Alfred has been a real brick. Bigger than that, even – a breeze block. Grey and heavy and plain but strong, efficient. He has organised, supervised, greeted, hugged. Christ, he knows more of her relatives than I do, thinks Ivan.

There are flowers on top of the coffin. Thankfully nobody has thought to send bouquets in the shape of a guitar or with Avril's name spelled out. Ivan has his arm around his mother; she's not steady on her feet at all and he can feel her shivering against him. The kids stand beside him. They are being very brave. Or are they like me? Ivan wonders. Are they thinking about PlayStations and *Star Wars*?

It came to him in the bath, finally, what he would do. Something simple, but in its own way dramatic: a statement, that despite what happened at the end to their relationship, it was *love*. Not true, of course, but who needs to know that? It will be a more affecting performance, in fact, than any of his readings. The audience here will be more familiar with the basic material. There won't be a dry eye in the cemetery.

He has a single red rose.

The undertakers are lowering the casket.

Ivan has to be on his toes, because he has a suspicion that Alfred might try to get in first. He must get there before him, because nobody remembers who comes second, only who wins.

The undertakers move back from the grave, and Ivan steps smartly forward. He hesitates for a moment, looks serious and contemplative, and then throws his single red rose into the hole.

Except the wind catches it, and it blows back out, landing at his feet.

It is Avril saying: *I don't want your acting, Ivan, I want your soul.*

He picks it up and throws it back into the grave.

Again, the wind catches it and throws it back, this time a few yards further along. Ivan shuffles along and bends to pick it up. Apart from the wind, there is complete silence. Everyone is embarrassed. He throws the rose in for a third time and for a third time it blows out again, this time onto the other side of the grave, and now the wind is really going to work, blowing it back and forth at the feet of the mourners. Ivan hurries after it, nearly bent double as he grabs at it, but it remains just out of his grasp while he charges around the grave like a wounded Spanish bull let loose on the streets, the mourners backing away, scared of its reckless charge, none of them brave enough to put it out of its misery.

Ivan finally falls upon the rose, his knees sinking into the churned-up mud. He holds it securely, then glances back to see Alfred step up and throw his own flower into the grave; Ivan watches despairingly as it floats lazily down and settles with perfect tranquillity on the lid of the coffin. Ivan cannot quite believe it. The other mourners wait for him to follow Alfred's lead, but he remains where he is; there are tears rolling down his cheeks. He thinks this is quite good and effective and is quickly rewarded with sympathetic whispers from all around. When he has milked them for long enough he begins to get to his feet. He intends to stagger across to the grave and throw his own flower in first time, just like Alfred. He is aware that he's very much in second place now, that his downfall was failing to take into account wind direction and strength in calculating the best position from which to throw the rose.

Then he has a sudden flash of inspiration. Perhaps all is not yet lost! He will throw the rose into the grave *and then* he will turn and extend his hand to Alfred, and *then* he will hug him, two lovers of a dead woman united in grief, but it will be his move, his big-of-heart gesture that will instantly trump Alfred's cheesy victory in the flower-throwing competition. As he wipes at his tears, Ivan feels quite pleased with himself. Not a bad result at all. Except that when he tries to get up he finds that he can't, that he has lost all the strength in his legs, as if it's been sucked out of them by the ground below. And his tears, they won't stop coming even though the act is finished; and then his body is suddenly shaking and he is convulsed by great, tired, swollen moans of despair which he can do nothing about.

He's crying like an idiot. He's hysterical, and he can't do a damn thing about it. He can hear his own children crying now, and he can't move to help them. His mother is pulling at him, trying to get him up, but he really can't move.

Campbell kneels down in the mud beside him, whispering reassurance, but he can hardly hear what he's saying for the roar of the wind – not in the graveyard, but in his head, a banshee howl racing through every chamber of his mind. Then he's rocking back and forth in Campbell's arms and people are looking at him and shaking their heads and moving away from the graveyard and back to the warmth of their cars and offices, thinking about that poor devastated man on the freezing hill who cannot cope with the death of his wife, and how he must really have loved her despite the divorce, and those poor children left standing looking lost at their poor father, and them without a mother.

They go back to Avril's house after the funeral. Ivan stops off at home to change out of his muddy trousers, then drives Mother around. Alfred has laid on a spread, which Ivan thinks is quite considerate, seeing as how this is *no longer Alfred's house.*

Thanks for the sandwiches, Alfred, but be out by Friday. No wait, I've reconsidered. Make it Thursday.

Ivan is confused. He is not used to his body acting

without express commands from his brain. Hangovers have their own logic, breakdowns at funerals do not. He was in control, and then he was not. His body made the decision for him.

Or perhaps he is schizophrenic. Did his other self make the decision for him, much as it made the decision to create *Kissing Cousins*? Is he, in fact, *Dr Jekyll and Mr Hyde*? (Short, popular, well reviewed, he notes.)

Those mourners who have come back to the house do their best to avoid him. His display at the cemetery has struck them dumb. What, after all, can they say? *Wonderful performance, Ivan! Bravo!*

Even Campbell seems lost for words.

Mother helps with the sandwiches; his daughter carries cups of tea through from the kitchen to the elderly relatives who have difficulty getting off their lazy arses; Michael plays around like Michael. At some point, Ivan fears, he will be called upon to act out the scene where he has a grown-up conversation with his two children, about getting through this together, about making this work, about it's what your mother would have wanted. Perhaps after the mourners have gone. Perhaps when they're about twenty. Maybe he should write something down for them? A letter, perhaps? *No.* A short story, with a message. A children's story, of course – wouldn't want to confuse them with something too Carver-esque.

The doorbell rings and he answers it only because he's the closest.

Donna stands on the doorstep, wearing a short black dress. She smiles uncertainly and says, 'I hope you don't mind. I didn't know whether . . .'

287

'No, I . . .'

'I didn't know her. But I know you. So I thought . . .'

'No, sure, glad you came. How did you hear about it?'

'Oh. Campbell phoned, to see how things were going for tonight.'

'Tonight?'

'Big London launch, all that.'

'Of course. I'm sorry. With everything . . .'

'Well,' she says. She half-nods at the door, and for a moment Ivan doesn't understand, then he shakes himself.

'Oh sorry,' and he stands back from the door and she starts to move into the house, but then he blocks her way again and says, 'Look, maybe it's not such a good idea.'

She stops instantly. 'No. I know. It was a stupid idea,' and starts to back out again.

'No, I mean, it's Death City in there. Maybe, I don't know, we could go for a walk.'

So they walk, and five minutes into it she takes his hand. They don't say much. When they get near to his mother's house, instead of taking her inside, he leads her across the road on to the green, and then on to the pond. The ducks, who haven't seen him in more than a week, quack around them.

'They're looking for bread,' Donna says.

'No, they're just saying hello.'

She sees that he's right. There's uneaten bread floating bloated on the pond. Ivan reaches down and strokes some feathers.

'They really do seem to know you,' Donna says.

'Yeah,' Ivan says, straightening again, and moving his feet deftly out of range. 'Doesn't mean they won't shit on a suede shoe.'

She smiles and says, 'I'm really sorry.'

'Don't worry. We were divorced.'

'You won't be feeling like coming tonight.'

He shrugs.

'I know. I understand.'

'Do you?' She nods. 'I don't understand anything,' he says. 'Death. Literature. Or ducks.'

'Well, maybe you don't have to. Understand. Maybe you just have to keep doing what you do.'

'And what is it that I do?'

'You piss people off, generally.'

'Ah right. I was wondering about that. And do you think that's a good job to have?'

'Well, someone has to do it. And you're one of the best. You should be proud of that.'

'Is that why you find me attractive? This God-given talent to piss people off?'

'I wouldn't say it's everything I'm looking for in a man. But it's a start.'

She smiles up at him. He puts a hand behind her head and pulls her close and kisses her. Then he takes her home and they make love in his mother's bed, while his mother is a mile away drinking sherry with her elderly relatives.

She has to go to her reading. He says he has to wait there for the kids to come, and then he will follow on. He wouldn't miss it for the world. They whisper and fondle and kiss and then she rushes happily away down the stairs and out of the front door. He stands at the window, naked, watching her go. Then he opens a bottle of wine and switches some music on.

He has no intention of going to the bookshop.

She's been stalking him, no doubt about it, and while it might be considered a mistake to sleep with your stalker (twice), it also makes good business sense to keep her interested. He has a readymade excuse for not going to the reading (dead wife, bereaved kids) so that'll keep her sweet, then he can just egg her along until the book comes out and the real money comes through.

25

The kids arrive home after seven, with their grand-
mother.

He has looked after them many times, but only in the
loosest sense of the word. Now they have little suitcases
at their feet and they stand rather formally in the hallway
looking about the big house as if it's the first time they've
visited. They look like the kids from *The Railway Children*
or *The Lion, the Witch and the Wardrobe* or any of those
books where children displaced by war, poverty, disease
or boredom are sent to stay with austere relatives and
have AN ADVENTURE. The only adventure they're going
to have here is *The Great Dishwashing Adventure* or *The
Great Tidy Your Bloody Room Adventure*. If he has his way
they will be miniature servants, although occasionally he
might throw a ball for them. They will not speak during
daylight hours while he is writing. Eventually, of course,
and once Alfred the Great gets on his bike, they will all
move together back to Avril's house and attempt to play

Happy Families there. But Ivan's in no rush for that. He's thinking of his mother. Travelling that mile every morning to make his breakfast wouldn't be good for her at her age.

'Well,' Ivan says as he comes down the stairs, 'no point standing on ceremony, don't you have homework to do?'

'We weren't at school today, Daddy.'

'Why not?'

'We were burying Mummy.'

He tuts. 'You always have an excuse.' But he winks, and they smile, so it's okay. Mother makes supper, then while they're getting ready for bed Ivan phones Campbell and asks him to tell Donna that he won't be able to make it to the reading. Family commitments.

'Shame,' Campbell says. 'This is when it all really starts to crank up.'

'Yeah. I know.'

'Have you two had another row?'

'No, of course not.'

'This is a grand adventure, isn't it, Ivan?'

'That's a matter of opinion.'

'And it isn't over yet. We're just entering Act Three.'

'Yeah. Whatever.'

'Ivan, cheer up, it's not the end of the world.'

'I've just been to a funeral, Campbell.'

'I know. But. We mustn't lose you to the dark side. Do you want a word with Dolly?'

'*No.*'

'It's no problem. She's right beside me.'

'No. I have to go. Call me later.'

He puts the phone down quickly, and is perplexed to

find that he has broken out in a yellow-chicken sweat like he hasn't suffered since he was avoiding betrayed girlfriends in his youth. He pours a glass of wine and goes to say good night to the kids, but they're having none of it.

'We have a story every night,' Anna says.

'Mummy always tells us a story,' Michael adds. 'Even in the hospital.'

'That may be true. But I don't have any children's books.'

'Make one up!' they chorus together.

'No . . . no, I don't think so.'

'Please!'

'No. Really. You'd have to speak to my agent.'

'Daddy!'

They've pushed two single beds together, and he's lying between them. He sighs. 'So what did Mummy tell you stories about?'

Anna looks at Michael. 'All sorts of things.'

'Specifically?'

'Adventures,' Anna says.

'With pirates,' adds Michael.

'On different planets.'

Ivan nods. 'Give me some more detail.'

'Well,' Anna hesitantly begins, 'there was this pirate. And he went to a planet.' She looks to Michael for help, but he just stares blankly at her. 'And he had an adventure.'

'Mummy didn't tell you stories at all, did she?' Anna shakes her head. 'What about Alfred? Did he not tell you stories?'

'Huh,' Anna says.

Ivan takes that as a no. He lies back on the bed. He sighs. They don't think they're going to get anything out of him at all until he suddenly asks: 'Did I ever tell you about when the world was young and completely covered in trees?'

Anna looks at him. 'Trees?'

'Apple trees.'

'Apple trees?' Michael asks, suddenly all wide-eyed.

Ivan puts an arm around each of them. 'Let me tell you,' he begins, not at all sure where he is going, 'let me tell you about . . . Ciderland.'

Ivan's quite pleased with his ramblings. Twenty-five minutes on the fantastical Ciderland and they were laughing all the way. He thinks there might be a book in it, one of those post-modernist efforts that appeals to kids on one level, and cynical adults on another. He asks his children if they'd buy a book about Ciderland.

'No!' Anna laughs.

'Why not?'

'Because nobody buys books any more!'

'Harry Potter seems to sell okay.'

'That is *so* yesterday. *Honestly*, Dad.'

'Make it a movie,' Michael shouts. 'Make it a film!'

'I don't think so, somehow,' Ivan says.

'Make it a movie!' Michael demands, now bouncing on the bed.

'Stop it, Michael,' Ivan gently admonishes, and is ignored.

'Make it a movie!' Anna shouts, joining in the bouncing.

'Don't be ridiculous,' Ivan says.

'A movie! We can eat popcorn and drink Coke and watch Daddy's movie.'

Ivan laughs. They settle down after a while. He tucks them into their beds. Anna says, 'But why can't you make a movie, Daddy?'

He sits on the side of her bed, kisses her forehead. 'Because movies are ridiculously expensive to make, and they appeal to the lowest common denominator.'

'What's that?' Michael asks. 'Locust what?'

'Lowest common denominator,' Anna repeats. 'It means everyone can enjoy something.'

Ivan clears his throat. 'Well, it's not quite that.'

'If you wrote a movie, Daddy, then everyone would like you. We'd like you, wouldn't we, Michael?'

'Certainly would.'

'Instead of sitting around being arsey all day,' Anna says, 'that's what Mummy said.'

'I'm not sure you should be saying arsey at your age.'

'Well then, write us a movie. About Ciderland.'

'Don't be silly.'

'But *why* not?'

'Because movie scripts are stupid and simple. A monkey could write one.'

'Well then,' Anna says, 'you wouldn't have much competition, would you?'

Ivan smiles. He kisses her again and says, 'I do believe you're going to be a motivational speaker when you grow up.'

'What's that, Daddy?'

'Well, basically it's someone who gives other people a kick up the arse.'

She smiles. Michael is already drifting off. As Ivan moves to get up Anna says, 'We haven't said our prayers.'

'Well,' Ivan says.

'We should say one for Mummy.'

He sighs, and sits down again. 'Okay. Quickly then.'

'Do you think you could sit down?' Mother says. 'I'm trying to watch *Inspector Morse*.'

'Sorry.' He sits. He stands up again.

'Honestly. You've got frogs in your pants.'

'I've been to a funeral. I have a new family. I'm *blocked*.'

'You don't look drunk.'

'I mean *writer's* block.'

'Oh. How long has it been?'

'Long enough.' He sits. He stands. He's been upstairs working on a paragraph for about half an hour and it won't flow. It's the weakest case of writer's block on record. 'That's a repeat,' he says, nodding at the telly. 'It was the teacher what done it.'

She sighs. 'I know. I just think John Thaw had such a nice way about him. Didn't his voice change after *The Sweeney*?'

'I'm not even going to answer that.'

She looks at him kindly. 'It's been a long day, Ivan. Why don't you just go to bed?'

'I can't.'

'Then go out.'

'Where would I go?'

'I think you know.'

'What are you talking about?'

'*Ivan*. April May – the reading. You've been itching to go all night.'

'No, I haven't.'

'*Yes*, you have.'

'They'll be perfectly fine without me.'

'Yes, they will.'

'I'd only get in the way.'

'You probably would.'

'There's absolutely no point in going.'

'No, there's not. And on a totally different subject, you weren't in my room this afternoon, were you? Were the kids jumping on the bed?'

'I will go,' Ivan says abruptly, 'just to make sure they don't fuck it up.'

'There's no need for language like that,' Mother says, but he's already half out of the door.

'Don't wait up!' Ivan shouts back.

As if.

He's there in *zip*.

He doesn't know why he's there at all, but his pulse is racing and his shirt is sticking to his back and it's not the exertion, although he has exerted, it's a crazy kind of excitement. It's money, sex, ambition, love and death. He hesitates at the corner, telling himself that if he rounds it there will be no turning back. He knows at the same time that that is *arse* because you can always turn back. But it will be difficult and hard and harrowing, and he's normally averse to all three.

He closes his eyes, takes a deep breath, then turns the corner.

Christ!

There are hundreds of people *outside* the shop, desperate to get in, *battling* to get in. He sees Julia and Campbell in the doorway, doing their best to sort the wheat from the chaff, but neither of them are built like bouncers and they're having a tough time of it. There are television crews cursing Julia up and down because they can't gain access without guaranteeing access of their own to a national audience. There are reporters banging on the shutters, which are half down. What little he can see of the shop window is steamed up by the hot crush of those lucky enough to be already inside. And still taxis are arriving, disgorging reporters, publishers, agents and mortals.

The hottest ticket in town.

He'll wait until it quietens down. There's a pub across the road. He hurries inside. He half hopes that he'll find Donna at the bar, but there's no sign of her. He buys a pint and sits by the window, keeping one eye on the shop. Before he's halfway through it there's an audible, communal groan from several hundred invited guests as the front door is finally closed, locking them out.

Ivan finishes his pint, then slips out of the pub and moves swiftly past the frustrated crowd. He reaches the end of the street, and then hurries along an alley behind the row of shops. He counts along until he comes to Pages' rear exit, and tries the metal door. It's locked. He hammers on it.

Nothing.

He steps back and looks up at a window high above, and barred. He curses. He returns his attentions to the door, and bangs for longer, and harder.

Eventually a nervous voice comes from within. 'Go away or I'll shoot!'

'Marcus! It's me – Ivan!'

The door opens a fraction and Marcus peers cautiously out. 'Ivan – Christ. Come in. What a nightmare.'

He hustles Ivan into the back room of the shop. Ivan's stomach lurches. He expects Donna to be there getting ready and he has no idea how to tell her he's not the slightest bit interested in her, but she's already gone through to the shop.

'Here,' Marcus says, pressing a drink into his hand, 'you'll need this. It's pandemonium out there.'

'Isn't that a good thing?'

'No. Christ. I'd no idea it would be like this. I made sandwiches, for God's sake. Last time I looked, somebody was standing on them. There's books all over the floor, I caught someone with his hand in the till, the wine lasted about three minutes and I've had to fight to hold onto this freakin' bottle and it's my own shop. Christ, Ivan, I've never had more than eight at a reading before. This is your genuine phenomenon.'

Ivan sighs.

'And sorry about Avril. She was lovely.'

'She hated me.'

'No, she didn't.' He pumps Ivan's arm, then nods towards the office door. 'Come on, fill your glass, we're missing the show.'

26

He's hidden off to one side, squeezed into a corner where she can't see him. She's already up before the microphone, blinking shyly against the barrage of flashguns. Ivan stares at the urgent pink adoring faces of those who have come to celebrate April May and he is pinged again by jealousy. He should be up there, drinking in the applause, smiling for the cameras, wowing them with his slinky vowels and immaculately constructed paragraphs. From the other side of the room somebody lets loose with a wolf whistle, and it's followed by raucous laughter, and it seems to break the spell which has transfixed Ivan.

They *aren't* here to hail a literary sensation, they are here to exploit an image. They're here to get a beaming blonde on the front page. Marcus was right, it has become a phenomenon. *Kissing Cousins* will sell five million without a doubt, lots of people will make lots of money, but four million will sit unread, on coffee-tables at first, then on bookshelves and finally piled high in second-hand bookshops, a moment in time frozen in yellowed pages, April May's face cracking, bent and stained on the front. This is the world he has longed to live in, in microcosm: books ignored on the sales tables, sandwiches tramped into the floor, the drink drunk and somebody with his hand in the till. All of a sudden he hates it, hates it with a passion, a venom. Why does he bother with it at all? Why write great dense novels when *nobody* is interested? Why propagate some archaic tradition that is clearly going the way of music hall? Why lock himself away in a room for years to satisfy three literary critics and five readers? He is forty years old and he might only have fifteen years left on the planet, so why waste his time? He wants to leave now, right this instant, and become a shepherd or a lumberjack or a park-keeper specialising in ducks. But he doesn't because April May has stepped back up to the microphone and he cannot drag himself away.

'Ahm – hiya all,' April says, smiling, waving *faux* shyly. 'I know you're all here to hear me read something from *Kissing Cousins* but, hell, why spoil the surprise. Wait until it comes out.'

There's an anxious murmur from the crowd. Ivan sees Julia's perplexed face glaring across from the front door, Carson Winfrey whispering anxiously in her ear. Campbell's gesticulating at the stage, but Donna is paying no attention.

'I thought, just for a change, I'd read you some of my poetry instead.'

There's an audible groan from the crowd. Carson is

shouting something in Julia's ear. Ivan rolls his eyes and says, 'Christ.'

'I've had the doors locked,' April tells them all, 'so don't even think about trying to leave.'

And this gets a laugh.

'This first one's called *My Old Man's a Waste Disposal Agent*.'

And they laugh even more. Somebody turns to Ivan and says, 'Christ, it's Pam Ayres with tits.'

Ivan laughs along with him, but drops it as soon as he turns away.

Don't do this to yourself, Donna. You're not a poet, you're an actress. You're not an actress, you're a jailbird. You're not just a jailbird, you're a killer.

And we're offering you a way out. Don't flush it down the toilet.

She starts to read her poem. There are a few pre-emptive chuckles, but they quickly die away as the audience settles into a queer kind of expectant calm; they're waiting, waiting for the laughs, but they're not coming, they're not *meant* to come. This poem is not about a dustman, it's about a monster, a father who beats his children until the blood runs, who destroys his wife; this is harrowing stuff and April May's voice is breaking and the room is completely silent and there are tears rolling down her cheeks and then there are tears rolling down *a reporter's* cheeks but there's nobody taking a photograph of *that*, there's nobody taking a photograph of anything – there's scarcely anyone *breathing*, for Christ's sake.

There are fifteen verses.

Fifteen verses of child abuse, spousal abuse, blood, hospitals, revenge and finally triumphant survival and – wait for it – *forgiveness*.

She finishes, and there's a sullen pause before she smiles weakly and says, 'Well, I hope that cheered you up.'

But they're still stunned. There are five seconds of just looking at her, and then someone on the other side, maybe even the wolf whistler, begins to applaud, and in moments it all erupts into a vast cheering mass.

She moves people.

With her own words, which make sense, not the drivel I have created by accident.

Her stupid fucking lyrics have moved this hard-bitten audience to tears and cheers. If Ivan had a gun, he would take it out and shoot himself, pausing only to shoot her. If they were married, she would be Judy Garland, he would be James Mason.

He hates her.

He loves her.

He drains the rest of his glass. He must go, he must go and hide somewhere. He *will* become a shepherd. In Patagonia.

But then she's back at the mike, asking for calm. 'Well then,' she says, 'you won't mind if I do another?' *Spontaneous* applause. She calms them with little more than a look. She says, 'I wrote this poem this afternoon, so it's as fresh as a cream cake, and just as bad for you – or me, at least. It's about a man I've fallen in love with – no, don't be sick, it's not like that – a man who can't be here tonight because, well, he's a bit of an eejit and he takes himself too seriously, and doesn't know when he's on to a good thing.'

Ivan begins scanning the crowd for this man who has usurped him in her affections.

'Ivan,' she begins, and he freezes, 'for Christ's sake get a life.' She continues:

'Ivan, change your pants and cut your hair,
and realise that all of life is not there, or there,
or there,
But here.'

He's not really even hearing this.

'Ivan, I know you will not listen, you never do,
Except to Joyce, James not Yootha,
Although you would do well to consider the latter,
As she's closer to you in style.
I joke, but it's hard to take,
as funny as lyrics are to poetry . . .'

He feels smaller. He feels like he's wearing a school uniform, a cap. His face is glowing. His wine is finished. He cannot escape from this shop.

'Ivan, I hardly know you, but sometimes you know
what's for you doesn't go by you.
Ivan, I will change you, and you will love me for it,
one day.
But in the meantime, for Christ's sake get a life.
Change your pants, and cut your hair

But for Christ's sake get a life.'

She finishes. They applaud. She does a little pirouette and says a cartoony, 'That's all, folks!'

He doesn't want a gun any more, he wants a bazooka; he'll blow her to fucking smithereens.

Beside him the same man says, 'Christ, what a lucky guy.'

Ivan grunts.

'Beautiful, funny, writes like an angel, I'll bet she's fantastic in bed.'

Ivan sighs.

'She's so fresh and different and irreverent, she's something new, isn't she? Something for the next generation of readers. She has real heart, don't you think? That's what she is – the heart of a generation. I'm going to use that in my review. I really am.'

The critic is beaming at the stage, barely aware that he's within an inch of losing his life.

But he's not the real problem.

It's April.

It's Donna.

You can't go around telling the world you love someone. You have to tell the someone first. You can't write irresponsible poems about someone, even if the poems are wildly popular.

There are ways to do things.

He's moving through the crowd. They don't part before him, exactly, but they're so relaxed and happy that they don't protest as he begins to force his way through.

He doesn't know what he's going to say. He might kill

her, or at the very least hug her. No one's ever written a poem for him before. Or declared love in such a public fashion. He actually feels quite warm now that he thinks about it.

She's answering shouted questions from the audience. She's being smart, she has them eating out of her hands. Julia is clapping her hands together happily, Carson nibbling at her ear – quite openly. Campbell is being interviewed and talking up his own role in the discovery of April May without providing any personal details about her whatsoever, and all the time Ivan is closing in.

She's in the middle of saying something when she spots him, and she trails off, and her mouth drops open, and her hand goes up to cover it, and there's an embarrassed, silent *Oh my God* and then she's stepping off the makeshift stage towards him and he's getting closer and closer and she's smiling and he can't help but smile back and he knows now without a shadow of a doubt that—

'You fucking bitch!'

Before she can even turn to the source, a hand reaches out and yanks the wig from her head; another hand arches across and slaps her hard across the face and she tumbles back into the audience. Screams erupt all around her.

'You fucking stupid cow!'

She's scrambling backwards as Jon Teckman steps out of his horrified surroundings and lunges after her, screaming, foaming, feet and arms flailing, the whole scene slowed down to a weird stop-go motion by the photographers' flash and the frozen reactions of the frightened but fascinated audience.

Ivan hurls himself forward, just gets close enough to grab Teckman's shoulder. He tugs it back, but as Teckman turns he comes with the free gift of a bunched fist which crunches into Ivan's nose and sends him staggering back with blood cascading down his face. Teckman turns to aim another blow at Donna, who's taken advantage of the interruption to dive into the audience.

'You fucking cunt!' Teckman screams and plunges in after her.

They make room.

Donna trips over a foot and goes sprawling and Teckman is just about to dive on her when Marcus steps out of the crowd and fells him with a copy of Francesca Brady's *Insanity Fair*. It's big enough and thick enough to knock him senseless and he flops down like a slaughtered cow. Immediately several men in the audience recover their manhood and rush to pin him where he falls. Marcus stands triumphantly over him, then darts for cover as Teckman shakes his head and tries to get up. But he's held firmly in place.

'I've called the police!' somebody shouts.

Donna is back on her feet now. She cautiously skirts Teckman and hurries up to Ivan, who's holding his head back to try and stop the blood flow. 'Are you okay?' she asks anxiously.

'What the fuck do you think?' he snaps back. 'Fucking love poems.'

She half laughs, half cries. She ignores the flashes going off all around her. Her wig is off, her make-up smeared.

'Yeah, take your fucking pictures!' Teckman yells, straining against his captors. 'She's not fucking April

May! She's on the run from prison! She's Donna Carbone!
Write that in your fucking papers!'

A reporter steps forward and says, 'Is that it?'

'No!' Teckman bellows. 'You're all cunts!'

The reporters are now turning on April May. *Is it true,
is it true, is it true?*

Campbell's round her, Julia's there, Carson's hyper-
ventilating.

They try to smuggle her through to the back office
and then out of the emergency exit, but the reporters
won't budge. Donna's upset and crying now and holding
on to Ivan for support. He's still bleeding, so she gets
half covered in blood, and what with her swollen eye
from Teckman's slap and her short hair and her ravaged
make-up, well, that makes a bloody great pic, especially
when they put it side by side with the beauty who took
the stage and had them eating out of her hands not five
minutes ago.

What a story!

What a carve up!

And then the police are there and they snap Teckman
into handcuffs, but the story is out that April May is
Donna Carbone and some sort of fugitive from justice. Before very many minutes have passed, despite
Campbell's impassioned implorings, April is also cuffed
and removed.

Those photographers, they're running out of film!

27

It is morning again, the sky is clear and bright with a winter sun. There are children playing in the garden. His children. He yawns, stretches, opens the bedroom window and shouts at them: 'Will you keep the bloody noise down!'

He is filled with dread.

His mother comes in with a tray, soft-boiled egg, tea, toast, the morning paper. He doesn't want to see the morning paper, and clearly his toast has not been cut into soldiers.

'Well,' Mother says, 'that was an eventful evening, by all accounts.'

Ivan sighs. 'Who have you been speaking to?'

'Well, I wasn't getting much sense out of you last night, so I phoned Campbell first thing. Dreadful state of affairs.'

He has the tray on his lap now.

'This is the last time, Ivan.'

'I enjoy a drink.'

'Not the drink, the tray. From now on you come down. You have children to think of.'

COLIN BATEMAN

'They don't want to talk to me in the morning. They have television.'

'Ivan, you're going to have to start setting an example. A different sort of example.'

He rolls his eyes. He wants to scream at her, *What's the fucking point? It's all over, the game's up, it's a fair cop, I'm going to prison.*

She lifts up the newspaper. 'Have you seen this?'

He averts his eyes. 'Yes, while I was sleeping.'

'There's no need for sarcasm.' She folds it again. 'Well. In your own time.'

He eats his breakfast, continuing to ignore the paper, then takes a long bath. When he is good and ready, as calm and collected as he can be, he goes to his study with the newspaper and sits down. He phones his bank. He asks how much money is in his account.

'Your account is three thousand and six pounds in the red, Mr Connor. You do seem to have been spending rather a lot in recent days.'

Ivan takes that on board with a huge sigh of relief.

'Is that all, Mr Connor?' the bank clerk asks.

'Ah yes. You're absolutely sure? Three thousand . . .'

'. . . and six pounds in the negative. Not a penny more, not a penny less. That's a novel by Jeffrey Archer.'

'There's no possibility of you having misread that? No possibility of it actually reading one million pounds, less this troublesome three thousand and—'

'No, Mr Connor. Why, is one expecting a windfall? Sales picking up, are they?'

'Something like that.'

Ivan puts the phone down. His hands are shaking. He has

312

about a minute of thinking that perhaps he'll be okay, that if there's no money in the bank, how can he be charged with fraud? But then he thinks – conspiracy, conspiracy to defraud. He'll be thrown into chokey without even the benefit of having received the money.

He stands by his study window and watches the ducks racing this way and that as several small children skim stones across the water at them. Ivan bangs on the glass, but they are too far away, there's too much passing traffic, for them to hear. But they're not intent on killing them, they're just kids, messing, and soon they drift on. As he continues to stare out, a police car cruises along the road and Ivan instinctively steps back. But it travels on past. Yet it is surely only a matter of time. He will go to prison for conspiracy to defraud Winfrey Books out of six million pounds. His mother will suffer a heart attack and his children will be sent to a children's home or fostered by Latvians. Ivan returns to his desk and calls Campbell.

'Campbell Foster & Associates, good morning.'

'It's Ivan. Put me through to Campbell.'

'Ivan who?'

'Just put me through!'

'Hold on, please.'

He comes on a moment later. 'Ivan, what a night! What a bloody night! Have you seen the papers?'

'No, I can't bear to.'

'But it's *fantastic*.'

'What is? I'm sitting here waiting for handcuffs.'

'Ivan, *relax*. We're home and clear. You know that song "Things Can Only Get Better"? Well, they just have. It worked a treat.'

'*What* worked a treat?'

'Inviting Donna's ex-boyfriend to the party.'

'You what?'

'It was a stroke of genius. I cooked it up with Julia. It was a gamble, but the press fell for it hook, line and sinker. I mean it, go out and get the papers, man, we're all over the front pages.'

'I have.' He unfolds his paper for the first time. There's April May, there's Donna. The huge headline reads *Best Cell-ar!* A strapline beneath: *Jailbird Donna writes steamy sensation behind bars – then breaks out to become literary outlaw April May!* 'Christ,' Ivan says.

'Don't you see? They were bound to get to the bottom of April May eventually, but this way they have a better story, and it's the truth. We'll sell twice as many copies!'

'But it's *not* the truth! She didn't write it!' Ivan objects.

'But nobody else knows that apart from me, you and her. It's perfect.'

'She's in prison!'

'But not for long. Ivan – the press have been on to me all morning. They've dredged up all kinds of shit about Teckman that didn't come out at Donna's trial. He's done time himself, he has a long psychiatric history and, get this – he's into self-mutilation in a big way.'

'I don't believe—'

'Ivan – Donna didn't stab him at all. It was like she said, he did it to himself. She didn't *do* anything. What a story. What a fucking story.'

Ivan sighs.

'We're going to get her out, Ivan. *Nothing* can keep her in. The public are mobilising behind her. Her only offence

314

was failing to return to prison, and she shouldn't have been there in the first place! She'll be out in a couple of weeks, tops, and then the sky's the limit. You thought she was big a few days ago? Christ, now she's mega, she's monster, she has all your money.'

It takes a moment to sink in. *What?*

'Ah. Ivan. Are you sitting down?'

'No.'

'Well, perhaps you should.'

'Campbell, talk to me. I've been up and down so often I'm fucking dizzy. One moment I'm going to prison, the next we're millionaires again. Now what are you talking about?'

'I . . . don't want you to worry, and we'll get it sorted out. It just might take a bit of time. She's a reasonable young woman, I'm sure—'

'Campbell!'

'Okay. All right. Have it your way. Ivan, you have no money. There, I said it. The money you are perfectly rightly entitled to – well, you're not entitled to it. I can't say it more clearly than that.'

'You better fucking had.'

There's a deep intake of breath. 'We have been friends for a long time, we've been together through thick and thin.'

'Mostly thin.'

'Granted.'

'And now it's time to reap my reward. So what the fuck are you talking about?'

'Ivan. Just listen to me.'

'I don't want to hear excuses. *You're* living like fucking Rockefeller . . .'

'Ivan, I swear to God, everything I've spent – the car, the office, the receptionist, the paintings – it's all come out of my commission. I haven't spent a penny I haven't been entitled to.' Campbell clears his throat. 'This is the situation. Clearly, we own April May, she is our – she is *your* – wonderful creation and you were, are fully entitled to all of the money. Anyway, unfortunately, when it came to signing the actual contract – and you'll remember what an eventful day that was – what with all the photographers and the questions and the car accident, of course, the long and the short of it is, Donna signed the contract in her own name. Not April May's. She signed it *Donna Carbone* and I can't pay you your money because it's her money. Nobody noticed in all the excitement, but that's it. What more can I say?' He clears his throat. 'Ivan?'

'I'm going to fucking kill you.'

'Look – we'll sort it out.'

'How the fuck are we going to do *that*?'

'Well, my solicitors are looking at the contract, to see what we can do. But if we start making a fuss about it, it could blow up in our faces. We just need to let it sit for a while.'

Ivan takes a breath that stretches to his toes. 'What you're telling me, my agent, my friend, is that despite the fact that I created April May and wrote *Kissing Cousins*, I have as little money now as when I started, and it's all been a colossal waste of time.'

'Well,' Campbell says, 'I wouldn't say that. You did get to sleep with a famous author.'

Ivan puts the phone down.

28

Ivan knows that at the end of these stories there's always a scene where the boy and girl meet for what might be the last time. The audience is on tenterhooks: will they go their separate ways, or get over their differences and be united for ever? He or she will be doing something innocuous – the garden, the shopping, or perhaps teaching a creative-writing class in prison – when she or he appears unexpectedly, perhaps released from that very same prison due to overwhelming public demand while the other he/she is forced into a menial job like teaching in a prison because he/she hasn't a penny to his/her name. Nearly always, there are other people watching so that they can erupt into cheers whenever the pair declare their love for each other, or floods of tears as two broken hearts kiss and then depart, never to meet again. The scene will almost exactly mirror a similar scene from the start of the film . . .

Film?

Yes, film.

He finds himself thinking increasingly these days in terms of films, and lowest common denominators.

If, for example, the man is the teacher, he'll be in the middle of showing how poetry relates to real life, why it is so important, and he will ask his class if they think they could express their feelings of love for someone in a poem, and they'll all act shy, and he will show them how it can be done by starting to read the poem his lover wrote about him. But halfway through, another voice will take over and it'll be his lover, standing in the doorway, finishing it for him. Neither of them will fall into each other's arms – at first. He'll look at her, and she'll look at him, and he'll say, 'So, you're getting released,' and she'll say, 'Yeah.'

'Looks like everything's turned out all right in the end.'

'Yeah. Looks that way. I couldn't have done it without you.'

'Yes, you could. You always had it in you.'

Except, of course, in Ivan's version he'd say: 'Of course you couldn't, are you brain dead or something? You didn't write a word of it.'

'I wrote the poetry.'

'Poetry, shmoetry, the book's the thing, and that's all mine.'

'Well, the money's all mine.'

And then they'd have a knock-down fight about it, featuring hair-pulling and eye-gouging.

In actual fact, Ivan hears that Donna's getting out on a Friday, which thanks to a timely piece of public relations work by the Prison Service – Donna promises to be a regular guest speaker at the creative-writing class – is the publication day of *Kissing Cousins*. The book is now into its eleventh print run before a single copy has appeared in the shops.

She has a full pardon, she will be paid compensation for this gross miscarriage of justice and Jon Teckman has been put away for assault. She will host a press conference at the prison gates, and will then be taken by limo to a launch party at Winfrey.

Ivan hears all this, and immediately borrows some money from Mother and takes the kids to EuroDisney. He has been curiously calm over the past few weeks, and he surprises himself by having fun. He hardly drinks at all. He's up early, he's in bed early. He goes for a jog – no well, let's not get carried away. He does a press-up one morning, he manages not to spill ash on the carpet as he's doing it, and that's quite enough of that, thank you.

The launch goes well. Donna is mobbed, the book comes out, the reviews are uniformly excellent. She is immediately whipped away on a promotional tour which not only takes her to all parts of the UK and Ireland, but then across Europe, to Australia, and finally to the United States. She spends three months criss-crossing the States, talking up the book, though truthfully it doesn't really need it. It is number one on both sides of the Atlantic. She gets to meet Oprah Winfrey. They have a great laugh about Winfrey being the name of her British publisher. Oh, how they laugh.

And one day, six months later, Ivan's in the back garden – not gardening, you understand, because when

it comes to gardening he's a great believer in Tarmacadam
– drinking a cool beer, with the kids playing Twister and
Mother filleting a fish in the kitchen, when the side gate
opens and he turns to find Donna standing there.

She says, 'I hope you don't mind – nobody answered
the front.'

'That's Mother – deaf as a post.'

The kids stop playing Twister and Mother opens the
kitchen window as she sees the beautiful blonde woman
who looks remarkably like April May walk across the
patio and down onto the lawn.

She stops in front of Ivan and says, 'You're looking
well.'

'So are you. You've grown your hair.'

'Dyed it as well. Do you think it's too tarty?'

'Can you be too tarty?'

She smiles. The kids come over and shyly say hello,
and then they realise it's only Donna with a lot of
make-up on, so they laugh and joke with her for a few
minutes as if they're old friends, though really they've
only met a few times. Then they catch a look from
their father and they go inside to watch out of a window as their father squirms with embarrassment and
confusion.

'So. Good tour?'

'Yeah. Great.'

'I hear America loves you.'

'Yeah. What about you?'

'No, America doesn't love me at all. Never did.'

'That's not what I meant.'

'I know. Have a seat.'

She sits on the spare sun-lounger. 'I left a dozen messages for you.'

He nods. 'When did you get back?'

'About two weeks ago.'

He nods some more.

'Ivan, I didn't know about the money. I didn't know you'd had a falling out with Campbell. Not until I got back.'

Ivan shrugs. 'He seems to think that because I can't prove that I wrote *Kissing Cousins* – and he's right, I can't – that I wouldn't have a leg to stand on if I tried to sue him – or you, for that matter – for the money. I suppose money changes people.'

'It hasn't changed me.'

'Yeah, new hair, new teeth.'

'Ivan, I'm still me, I can't help what's happened to me. I'll give you whatever money you want. All of it.' She looks intensely at him, and he looks intensely back. She's the first to blink. 'Well, not all of it, obviously. But a fair share.'

'I don't want the money.'

'Yes, you do.'

'Okay – yes, I do. Is that why you came to see me, your good deed for the day?'

'Ivan – Christ, you're such a pain sometimes.'

He shrugs again.

'No. That's not why I came.' He raises an impatient eyebrow. 'I wanted to show you this.' She reaches into her Prada handbag and produces an envelope. She carefully withdraws a letter from within and hands it to him.

He scans it quickly. 'So. You've been shortlisted for the Booker Prize.'

'Yes.'

'Fan-fucking-tastic.'

'I don't want it.'

'You haven't got it.'

'I will. *You* will and that's why I don't want it. It's yours. I've been selling myself for months and I feel tired and dirty and such an awful liar. It's time to finish this. I want to come clean.'

Ivan shakes his head. 'You'll be thrown back in the pokey.'

'No, I won't.'

'You will. People will feel cheated. April May into Donna Carbone was one thing. Donna Carbone into washed-up Ivan Connor is something else entirely. You're the heart of a generation. People adore you. They'll hate you and want their money back. You can't do it – simple as that. Besides, you're on to a good thing. Sit back and count the money, Donna, and toss me a few pounds when nobody's looking.'

'Ivan, for Christ's sake, it's the Booker Prize! It's all you've ever dreamed about.'

'I've *never* dreamed about it. A few nightmares, maybe.'

'Ivan, that first night we slept together, that's one of the things you talked about. How much it meant to earn the respect of your peers.'

'I can have that without getting a prize from some dodgy sugar merchants, thank you very much.'

'I don't believe you for one moment.'

He shrugs.

'If I win it, I'm going to tell them that you wrote it. Honestly, I will.'

'Don't be stupid, Donna.'

'I'm not stupid.' He takes another sip of his beer. 'What about us, Ivan?'

'What about us?'

'What are we going to do?'

'Do?'

'Ivan, I love you. You know that.'

'Yes, well, there's no accounting for taste.'

She smiles. She kneels beside him and puts a hand on his leg. 'Please, take me seriously, for once.'

'I can't, Donna. I know too much about you.'

She glares at him for a moment, then stands and hurries away across the garden.

He lifts his beer and takes another drink. He calls the kids out to play Twister. He's something of an expert at it.

29

Ivan is just ordering his third pint when he sees Campbell come through the door and look about the gloomy interior of the White Hart. Campbell spots him immediately and slips onto the next bar stool and says, 'Let me get that.'

Ivan shrugs.

'And one for me,' Campbell tells the barman.

The barman brings the pints. Ivan lifts his. 'Thanks for the drink,' he says, then climbs off his stool and walks to the other side of the pub. Campbell watches him go, then tuts. Ivan sits at a table which gives him a view across the busy road to the property formerly known as Pages. It is shuttered, and a sign attached to the side of the shop reads *Acquired for Dunkin' Donuts*.

'Terrible,' Campbell says, nodding at the sign. He stands expectantly beside the table, but Ivan doesn't acknowledge him. He sits down anyway. 'Dreadful,' he adds. 'So what's Marcus up to?'

Ivan doesn't look at him, but he hisses through gritted teeth: 'Writing a novel, I hear. I warned him against it. That way doth darkness and betrayal lie.'

Campbell sighs. 'Ivan, I'm sorry. I was angry. I was doing my best for you.'

'Yeah, sure.'

'She's left me, you know.'

'Who, your sweet little receptionist?'

'Donna.'

'What do you mean, left you?'

'She's found another agent.' Ivan starts laughing. 'It's not funny.'

'Yes, it fucking is.'

'She's signed another big deal with Winfrey. Even bigger. But wait until Julia gets a look at book two. The world will soon know how crap a writer she really is.'

'She's not crap,' Ivan says.

'Whatever. She's done well out of it. She's rolling in it.'

Ivan glares at him. 'Don't go there, Campbell.'

'I did my best for you, you know. I really did. You two shouldn't have fallen out. I was trying to get your money out of her, but she's really taken against you, and her lawyers are bigger than mine.'

'My heart bleeds for you.'

'So it should. I'm down to my last couple of thousand.'

'Aw no, don't start that. You were on ten per cent. That's a fucking big whack of—'

'It's gone. I went a bit mad. Gambled. Crappy shares. And my sweet little receptionist has fleeced me out of the rest of it. I always was a stupid bugger when it came to money. And women.'

'Are you serious?'

'Would I joke about this? We're back where we fucking started.'

Ivan sighs. He finishes his pint. He looks at Campbell. 'Do you want another?'

Campbell shakes his head. 'No thanks. I've got to get back to the office, move as much stuff out before the repossession mob arrive. I just wanted to give you this.'

He delves into his jacket and puts something down on the table. Ivan picks it up.

'It's an invite to the Booker Prize,' Campbell says. 'It's on tonight. Not much point in me going now. Thought it might be of some use. Every agent in town will be there, every publisher. It's the best time to approach them, when they're pissed. I don't know. You might get something out of it.'

Ivan shakes his head. 'I'm not interested. I'm finished with all that.'

'Whatever. Stick it in the bin then.'

Campbell smiles, squeezes Ivan's shoulder, and turns for the door. As he reaches it Ivan says, 'Campbell,' and he stops. 'Do you think we'll win tonight?'

Campbell weighs it up for a very short moment, and then nods.

'She told me a few weeks ago she was going to confess all if she won the Booker,' Ivan says.

'Why the hell would she do that?'

'Because she loves me.'

Campbell laughs bitterly. 'Yeah. That's what they all say.'

The very thought of going makes him sick. He retrieves the invitation three times from three different bins. One in the pub, one outside on his way home, and one in his back garden. He stares at the gold embossed card. Once he would have given everything to be there, to be in with a chance of going up on that stage. He even has an acceptance speech hidden away in a drawer somewhere, when the early word on one of his novels was good enough for him to dare to dream the dream. Of course, it fizzled out, like everything else in his life.

No, he doesn't need to be there.

But there's something gnawing at him. He wonders what it would be like to go and mingle without any pressure on him at all, to confirm how poisonous it all really is, to feel the jealousy, the rivalry, the naked ambition, the bitter disappointment and know for once and for all that it is no longer a part of him, that he has moved past it, grown, become a better person.

But of course, he is not a better person.

He's exactly the same.

He just has the satisfaction that comes from writing a screenplay called *Ciderworld* which has attracted the attention of a major Hollywood studio.

He has a new agent called Chester who phoned him out of the blue when he heard he was agentless and said he reckoned he'd got a raw deal with his publisher and that he really loved his books and would really love to work with him – the usual bullshit. Ivan tried to fob him off by saying he wasn't writing any more and Chester said, 'Not at all?' with such disappointment that Ivan reluctantly admitted that he was writing a children's film just for fun and Chester said, 'Well, let me have a look.'

'You'll laugh.'

'I certainly hope so. That's the name of the game these days.' Chester read the first thirty pages – that's all there was – and loved it. 'Let me send it to my people in the States.'

Ivan has never met an agent who had people in the States.

One night, late, he gets a call from Dustin Hoffman. 'Yeah, *sure*,' Ivan says, and puts the phone down. Dustin phones again. 'Fuck off, Tootsie,' Ivan says and puts the phone down again.

Chester rings him almost immediately. 'Dustin says you just told him to fuck off. He's *very* impressed. You really know how to play the game, Ivan. He's just increased his offer.'

'His offer?'

'He has a deal at Columbia.'

'Oh. Right,' Ivan says, and next time he's much more cordial when Dustin phones and says, 'I want to play The Worm in *Ciderland*.'

'You're exactly who I had in mind,' Ivan says.

And now he's holding an invitation to the Booker Prize announcement in his hands knowing that he will never, ever be invited there in his own right and that it doesn't matter, but what does matter is that somebody he once slept with is going to receive the biggest literary prize in the land tonight, and although she may accept it with good grace, there is also a slight possibility that she will do what she threatened to do, declare Ivan to be the true author of *Kissing Cousins*. She will lose all of her money, her respect, her fans; they will turn on her like a pack of dogs – but never mind her. His life will be thrown into turmoil. He will become the focus of world press attention. And he doesn't want it. He wants to be left alone with his children, and to conquer Hollywood in his own way, not on the back of a book of gibberish.

He decides suddenly that he must go, after all; he must seek her out and convince her not to reveal their secret.

He hires a dinner jacket. He no longer fits his old one. He has lost weight, but in a good way. He has tidied himself up, and in trying to impress nobody but himself, has impressed everybody but himself. Mother grooms him for the evening, and the kids get permission to stay up late to watch it on television.

Ivan slips a medicinal flask of brandy into his dinner jacket's inside pocket, and takes the underground to the Natural History Museum where the event, appropriately enough, is being held.

She is seated at a table with Vincent Cranby, her new literary agent, Julia, Carson and various other members of staff at Winfrey Books.

Julia is *glowing*. She has just spent a long weekend in New York with Carson, where he told her he was definitely going to leave his wife after Christmas, probably after the New Year sales were over and she was in good form. They went ice skating in Central Park. She is the most succesful editor in British publishing, authors are flocking to her stable, and Carson, bless him, has made her a shareholder. Just one share, mind, but then it's a family company and they are exceedingly hard to come by. But it's a start.

Carson is drunk and nibbling at Julia's ear, but he's actually watching Donna Carbone. He's taken more of a hands-on approach with Donna than he has with any other Winfrey authors, and everyone but Julia has noticed. Carson is indeed planning to leave his wife after the sales, but he's thinking of moving in with Donna. Donna doesn't know this, of course, and has no idea of his interest in her, but how could she possibly resist? It will be a match made in heaven. He will promote Julia sideways into the New York office – they've just bought out Knopf publishers in the States on the strength of *Kissing Cousins*'s sales alone. If she doesn't like it, she can go. She's only an editor, for God's sake.

Donna sits with her fifth glass of champagne. Vincent Cranby is talking about market share and film rights and Spielberg this and Hanks that and she isn't paying a damn bit of attention. She's churning up inside. She looks across at sleazy Carson Winfrey and wonders how he'll react when he discovers who really wrote *Kissing Cousins*. Because she has every intention of confessing all.

What else is a girl to do? She's young, and she's in love.

She has tried every which way to bring Ivan back to her. Declaring her love. Declaring her hate. Offering him money. Cutting off his money.

But no. He is stubborn. Obstinate. Cold.

But she *knows* that he loves her. It is only a matter of

331

forcing him into the open. Like beating the heather for grouse. Or whatever they do.

Ivan is the writer, and deserves recognition. She has become a celebrity on the back of . . . nothing. He must be acclaimed.

She is a poet, but if she publishes her poetry now it won't matter a damn, because if she has learned one thing it is that nobody cares about the writing, they care about the image and the packaging and the marketing. People are told what is good and they accept it. They buy into it. They must have it. She could publish the telephone directory under her name and even though the sheer number of characters might confuse some people, and the plot might leave a little to be desired, it would still be a huge success.

She must stop this.

She writes her poetry for herself, and perhaps a few others. It is an expression of *her* and she will decide who gets to hear it.

Donna has decided all of this in the past half an hour. Of course it might be because she's pissed.

She pours more champagne and scans the vast hall, with its many dinosaurs. She picks out her fellow shortlisted authors. Mohammed Mahtoubi, the second-generation Egyptian out of Manchester, his novel *By the Light of the Silver'd Moon* is the second favourite. He sits quietly, studying a menu, his bodyguard by his side. Another table along, Victoria Cockburn, the 'Birmingham Brontë' according to the papers, an outsider with *The Fortuitous Missionary*, is smoking like a train, two puffs and into the toilets for repairs. Alec Rose, a Scot, is always in with a chance after being shortlisted on three previous occasions, but tabloid revelations about his private life – his fondness for women's clothing – haven't helped his chances this year, nor did the headline *Always the Bridesmaid, Never the Bride* do him any favours. And finally, sitting imperiously, but looking daggers in Donna's direction, is Francesca Brady, a surprise nomination with *Insanity Fair*. There's been a lot of money placed on *Insanity Fair*, and there's malicious gossip abroad that the judges might go for her just to prove that while they can be hip and trendy, they don't have to slavishly follow public opinion. Francesca Brady might be considered the lesser of two evils.

And then she sees him.

He is coming across the vast room towards her, and though she really, really wants to be with him, she doesn't want him here, not now. She wants to make her grand gesture on stage; she wants to show him, in front of the nation, in front of the world, what she is prepared to sacrifice for their love.

As he gets closer, she picks up her bottle of champagne and hurries off.

'Donna,' Vincent says, jumping to his feet. 'It's only a few minutes until—' But she keeps going.

Vincent sits down again. 'A lady must powder her face,' he says, smiling reassuringly at Julia, but tapping the side of his nose, suggesting that Donna's actually off for a cocaine top-up.

Carson watches her cross the floor with appreciation etched all over his face. He sees Ivan following. Who *is* that? The face is familiar, but he can't quite get the name.

*   *   *

333

If he was writing this for Hollywood, as he will, he would not yet have made it to the prize-giving. He would be delayed in traffic, he would only make it to the Museum as the result was about to be announced. He would be denied entrance by officious officials. He would hear it announced over the Museum's PA that Donna Carbone was this year's winner of the Booker Prize. He would punch the officious officials out of the way and finally enter the great hall just as Donna was approaching the microphone, the audience still giving a standing ovation; he would battle through them, determined to stop her sacrificing her career because of her love for him; he would yell at her, but be drowned out by the applause. She's not very tall, Donna, and she would reach up to lower the microphone, and in that instant Ivan would find himself standing beside TIM from Waterstones, who set up the chaotic wiring which electrified Ivan at the start of the film, and with sudden horror he would realise that TIM must have organised *tonight's* wiring and he would scream at Donna not to touch the micro—

But too late!

There would be a flash and Donna would fly across the room, dead before she hit the ground.

He would be the first on to the stage. He would cradle her in his arms and tell her how much he loved her, but too late, *too late*.

But Hollywood would demand a happier ending, and the new Ivan would acquiesce, because happy is good, sad is bad, and in the next draft she would not die. Her eyes would flutter and she would come back to life, and love, and they would all live happily ever after.

Or she would be whisked away backstage before he could get to her, and then Campbell would emerge from behind the curtains and announce that the great April May was dead. And there would be much wailing and gnashing of teeth. But this would be a trick ending worked up by Campbell: April May must die in order to give Donna her life back, and her romance with Ivan a chance in the bold, cruel world outside.

He catches her at the door to the Ladies toilets.

He says, 'Donna,' and she turns, feigning surprise. 'Oh. Ivan. How's it going?' She gives a little wave, forgetting for the moment that she has the bottle in her hand, realising only when it splashes out of the neck and onto her dress. 'Ooops,' she says, and giggles. 'Fancy meeting you here. Are you shortlisted as well? Oh sorry, silly me, of course you aren't.'

'Donna, please.'

'Please? *Please release me let me go*?' And she begins to sing, badly: *'For I don't love you any more . . .'*

He sighs. 'If you win,' he says, 'what are you going to do?'

'Have a party. Do you want to come?'

'Donna. I'm serious.'

'So am I. Everyone will be there.'

'Christ, this is a waste of time.'

He swings away, and Donna quickly says, 'Ivan.'

He stops and turns.

'I'm doing it for you, because you deserve it.'

He glances back at the gathering. 'What, *this*? I may deserve it, but I don't *want* it.'

'But I want to *give* it to you. It's within my power to give it to you.'

'Donna, what are you talking about? Who do you think you are?'

'I'm the heart of a generation. And now I'm going to be a heart donor. I'm going to give you the gift of life, Ivan. You will live for ever.'

He gives a disappointed shake of his head. She looks down. Tears are threatening to come. 'Oh Donna,' he says quietly.

He comes forward then. He takes the champagne out of her hands and sets it down on the floor. She doesn't protest. He lifts the tip of her chin gently until she can't help but look at him. Then he lets it go and gently places his hands on her shoulders. He gazes into her eyes. Her lips part just a fraction. She tilts her head slightly back.

Then he gives her a bloody good shake.

'Will you see sense, you fucking airhead?' he shouts. 'I don't want any of this shit! You're not doing me any favours, do you understand?'

'Ivan, I—'

'Shut *up*, Donna! You're going to ruin this for yourself, and you're going to fuck up my life.' He lets go of her shoulders and begins to pace back and forth before her. She's dizzy with the shaking, but it doesn't prevent her groggily reaching down for her bottle of champagne. He doesn't notice. He's kicked into gear. 'You were right – I wanted this my whole life, to be here.' He waves his hands around the Museum. 'I grew up adoring writers and what they achieved. But I've only realised now that what I loved wasn't what they wrote, but the lives they lived, the respect they had, the adventures they undertook. I thought a writer's life was one great drama and I was forever disappointed that even though I was publishing books that I knew were good, nothing seemed to happen to me, there was no excitement. Even when I went looking for it I was bored.'

'Ivan, I—'

'Shut *up*! I went on a safari and got malaria. I went to a bullfight and was ill. I climbed a mountain and had to be rescued. I got divorced because my marriage wasn't exciting enough. And then I was so bored I nearly killed myself! I've spent my whole life wanting to be something else, until right now, this moment in time, when I am at last completely and utterly happy with who I am and what I have achieved. Do you understand that?'

She says quietly, 'What have you achieved, Ivan?'

'Two beautiful children, and a first-look deal with Columbia Pictures.'

'And you think that's enough to make you happy?'

'Yes!' She casts her eyes down. He follows up quickly with, 'No!'

She looks up hopefully, and at last, after a hundred years, he softens. Her hair is cut short again and she's wearing black eye-liner and a choke-chain and every man in the room would kill to gaze at her and say: 'I also need the love of a good woman.'

'Why? Because your old one is dead?'

'No, because I'm lonely. And stupid.'

'Oh, right. I see. Do you have anyone in mind?'

'Yes.'

She swallows and says, 'Do I know her?'

He nods.

She comes at him, and kisses him.

He kisses back.

From somewhere in the background a magnified voice says, 'And now ladies and gentlemen, what you've all been waiting for.'

Donna steps back from him and says, 'Ivan Connor, you've been such a wanker for such a long period of time, a girl would need to have a screw loose to take any interest in you.'

'Well, I'm touched that you do. Perhaps you could write one of your limericks about me.'

There's a sharp intake of breath, then she hurries away back to her table.

Ivan stands near the back to watch. His head is reeling, with the champagne he has drunk too much of, with the intoxicating love of a good woman he has severely wronged, with a determination to get inside her dress within the hour, and with the realisation that in the morning he will wake up and want to run away and hide.

But she will find him.

And each time he runs, he won't run as far.

Headline hope you have enjoyed CHAPTER AND VERSE and invites you to sample another of Colin Bateman's highly entertaining novels, MURPHY'S LAW, out now from Headline.

PROLOGUE

Murphy hates this place.

Scotland Yard. Nobody says New Scotland Yard, like it says on the tin; they say, Scotland Yard. Scotland Yard. Like it's something out of a 1950s *Wizard* or a B movie. Worse, a British B movie. Like it's something special, not just a big building with paperwork. They like to think of it as the nerve centre. He likes to think of it as a Christopher Reeves kind of nerve centre, everything's there, but it doesn't quite work, but one day, one day there might be a revolutionary breakthrough, and then watch out, you, you dastardly criminals.

He comes here as little as possible, and more recently, never at all. He slumps in the back of the lift as they rise to the eighth floor, uniforms all around him. He's wearing his own uniform, of course, it's just a different one: black jeans, one knee gone to white, black T-shirt, bomber jacket, zips on the arms for the little pockets where you can hide things like squares of chocolate or

341

surface-to-air missiles. He ran a comb through his hair this morning, big sense of occasion and all, but all it really did was drag the mess to one side, making him look ever so slightly foppish. He soon fixed that.

He really hates this place.

Maybe he should have shaved, actually cut his hair, put on a nice suit. It's not like he's been working and has to stay shabby. Make the effort, Marty, make the effort. But no. He was up half the night writing a song; and as usual, when he came to look at the lyrics in the morning, his head thumping with Carlsberg, probably the worst hangover in the world, and a tiny, tiny amount of dope, right enough, they were shit, primary school lyrics. So he's feeling rough and sad and annoyed that he has to be here.

He sits there, Rebel Without An Ashtray.

Dr Coates arrives after a few minutes, full of apologies and the flu. She's quite cute but self-important. She has a pile of folders, and Murphy knows from past experience that his is the thickest, and growing. Fair enough.

She begins to fill in a form, then looks up at the sound of his lighter. She glances around theatrically at the sign behind her, then back to Murphy, who nods and removes the cigarette. She returns her eyes to the file, only to hear the lighter again and she looks up angrily to find Murphy now has two cigarettes in his mouth.

'Go on,' he says, 'give us a smile.'

There's no smile. Murphy removes the cigarettes.

'You've missed three out of your last five appointments, Martin,' she says. He nods. 'This is important. We're trying to help.'

'I'm feeling better,' Murphy says.

She nods, but is not convinced. 'Martin, the death of a child—'

'It's none of your business.'

They lock eyes. She doesn't blink. How does she do that? Perhaps Scotland Yard has developed an android. Perhaps there are so many crash and burns victims the regular psychobabblers all imploded. Or exploded. Covering the walls in gore and meaningful notes. Perhaps . . . Murphy blinks first.

'Yes it is,' she says, stern, but still trying to be family. 'Let's be frank here. If it wasn't for your history, you would have been retired on medical grounds months ago, but the fact is certain people don't want to lose you. That doesn't mean we can just ignore . . .'

He's laughing inside, really. Your history, your medical grounds. Like he's Mel Gibson in *Lethal Weapon* or Clint Eastwood in . . . anything when he had big hair. Clichés aren't clichés for nothing, missus. Maybe he should act all manic like Mel. Maybe they'll assign him a partner to help see him through this difficult time, and by the by solve the big case. A buddy. They'll be total opposites of course, they'll fight from beginning to just before the end, but they'll learn to love one another along the way, and then one of them will die. And it won't be Murphy, because he never dies.

He sits forward. 'I'm OK. I just need to go back to work. Look at me, you're trained, you can read me like a book, you can see I'm ready.'

'It's not as easy as that, Martin.'

'Yes it is. Just read me.'

'Martin, psychiatry—'

'I can read you.'

'What?'

'I'll do you a deal. If I can get you off like . . .' and he clicks his fingers, 'then you put me back on active. What do you say?'

'This isn't a game, Martin. I really don't think—'

'You're in the process of splitting up with your husband.'

'What?'

'You're in the process of splitting up with your husband.' He isn't even looking at her. He lights his cigarette and takes a drag. She ignores it. 'You've been on holiday with him to try and patch things up, but it didn't work out. You're at that can't live with him, can't live without him stage. You tried to talk things through with him last night, but you had too much to drink and you slept together.' He takes another drag. 'How am I doing?'

Dr Coates looks pale and annoyed. 'You can stop this right now.'

He doesn't, of course. In for the kill. 'You're like most freckled women who go away to the sun. You sit on the beach for two weeks but you don't quite get a tan, you just look a little bit dirty. That said, I can see by that band of pale skin that you wore your wedding ring while you were away, but no longer. You've had stale drink on your breath since you walked in—'

'I said stop it.'

'Now look at your nails – they're not false, are they?'

'No, I . . . Martin, this is getting—'

'Then consider your forehead.'

'I—'

'There's the remains of quite a hefty spot there. You've covered most of it with make-up, but I can tell by the skin around it that it didn't die of its own accord, it's been squeezed to death.' Her hand begins to move towards her forehead, but she manages to stop herself. 'But you see, Dr Coates, a spot requiring that much violence, there'd be nail marks, and there's none. So someone with short nails. It's not the romantic sort of thing you'd ask or allow a boyfriend to do, but a husband could do it without a second thought.' Marty takes a final drag on his cigarette, then stubs it out, half smoked, on the floor. He looks up at her after a moment. 'Right or wrong?' he says. With the Belfast brogue and the light in his eyes, it somehow comes across as vaguely charming.

Still, she's a professional, and there are standards to maintain. 'You're very good, Martin, nobody doubts that.'

'So put me back where I belong.'

'Yes,' says Coates, 'I do believe I will.'

Life, when you boil it down, comes to this: sitting in a canteen full of policemen trying to find a word that rhymes with orange, but mainly thinking about the difference between success and failure: how, on a different day, Bob Dylan would have been thrown out of his first record company for daring to sing with a voice like that. How, on a different day, if something hadn't sparked his imagination, if he hadn't suddenly hooked onto the zeitgeist, he might have turned 'Blowin' In The Wind' into a comedy song about flatulence and scored a minor but forgettable hit. Chance, and the decisions that seem small at the time but are sometimes huge and significant and historic.

Someone he used to work with comes across and says, 'Murphy, how're you doin'?'

'OK,' he says. 'Do you happen to know a word that rhymes with orange?'

And the someone laughs and walks off like he's not serious.

All these hundreds of people around him, the camaraderie, the confidence, all with one purpose in life: to do good, to help people, to save the world. Well, at least, that's how it's supposed to be, but Murphy knows different. They really want to be Travis Bickle in *Taxi Driver*, they want to go out there and cleanse the world of all the filth and degradation. But they won't, because it's against the rules, somebody might file a report, they'll sit in this canteen and talk about sport and mortgages and forget for a while the evil that's out there, and when they are forced to go out they'll do their weary best but it won't get them down because they realise they're fighting a losing battle, so why exert yourself? Do the bare minimum, get by, get by. De Niro fiddles while Rome burns.